I thought I heard something. Not in the next room or even out in the hallway, but right next to me. In the freakin' shower stall.

I turned and peered through the frosted glass of the shower door, even though I was sure there was nothing there to see. I was wrong. There was somebody in the shower.

He was just standing there in the stall, looking at me. Thanks to the frosting, I couldn't see his face. But I could tell it was a guy and not Tomi, and I was pretty sure the son of a bitch had a beard.

"Who are you," I asked, "and what the hell are you doing in my shower?" It seemed like a reasonable question.

"This place where you live," he said, as if he hadn't heard me, "is not safe. You must leave it and seek shelter elsewhere."

The guy talked funny. Very formal, very precise, and very flat. Not even a hint of emotion. It seemed to me he was tired, worn out, and had long ago given up hope that he would get any relief.

"Not safe . . . " I echoed. "Why not? What's the problem?"

"The problem is that you have an enemy, who will strike and strike soon. You must not be here when that happens."

"I'm a cop," I told him. "Or anyway, I used to be. I can handle whatever is going to happen."

"No," he said, sounding pretty sure of himself, "you cannot."

"Who are you?" I asked again, trying harder to see through the glass of the stall.

I didn't reach out and slide it aside. For some reason, that didn't seem to be an option.

I heard him sigh. "Do you not *know*?"

Copyright © 2011 by Michael Jan Friedman
Design by Aaron Rosenberg
ISBN 978-0615567013
All rights reserved. No part of this book may be used or reproduced in any manner whatsoever without written permission except in the case of brief quotations embodied in critical articles and reviews. For information contact Crazy 8 Press at the official Crazy 8 website:
www.crazy8press.com

First edition

*To Annette,
Fight the good fight!*
*Michael Jan Friedman*

# FIGHT THE GODS

## Michael Jan Friedman

CRAZY 8 PRESS

FOR FRANK FRAZETTA, WHO MADE IT HAPPEN

# ACKNOWLEDGMENTS

When I was in second grade, I read a great, little book called *Greek Myths* by Olivia E. Coolidge, thereby sealing my fate as a devoted student of things mythological. I've read many other books on mythology, but none had the same magical effect as *Greek Myths*. Mrs. Coolidge, by the way, enjoyed a prestigious career as an author and educator, lived to be 98, and had seventeen great-grandchildren at the time of her death. Good for her. I owe her big time.

A little more recently (at the age of 46), I met Wayne Baker—the father of one of my younger son's friends—who played single-wall handball. "I used to play handball when I was a teen-ager," I told him. "We should play," he said, his eyes lighting up at the prospect of running me into the ground. At first, he did just that. Then I got better.

We're still playing, mostly as doubles partners, in which role we routinely enlighten hubristic teen-agers as to their limitations. I always thank Wayne for returning me to handball, but really I can't thank him enough, and as you read the first chapter of this book you'll see why.

I'm not a cop, I've never been a cop, and at this stage in my life it's unlikely I'll ever be a cop. This made it difficult to write as if I were a former cop, like my protagonist. Sergeant Michael Beck of the U.S. Park Police made the job a heck of a lot easier. Whatever I got right about the police life is his fault. Whatever I got wrong is mine.

Some time ago, at a science fiction convention outside Baltimore, a guy named Bob Jones offered me tickets to an Orioles game. I barely knew him. I know him a lot better now, not just as an interesting person and a sweetheart of a guy, but also as a terrific writer who found his muse late in life. When I needed somebody to read *Fight The Gods* and tell me if there was a shred of hope for the darn thing, I gave it to Bob. He spent his birthday giving me comments.

I would also like to say something about my colleagues in Crazy 8 Press: Peter David, Robert Greenberger, Glenn Hauman, Aaron Rosenberg, and Howard Weinstein. The fact that you're reading this is a testament to their talents, their professionalism, and their selflessness. Make sure you look for their books as well on the Crazy 8 Press website. You won't regret having done so.

Mike Friedman
October, 2011

The man who fights the gods does not live long.
—Homer, *The Iliad*

# CHAPTER ONE

I was surprised to hear from the ghost so early in the morning.

The sun was just sneaking between the pale, square factory buildings of Long Island City, scouring them with light, as I drove to the oldest high school in the neighborhood. At that hour, even the doughnut shops weren't open yet. And yet the ghost seemed wide awake.

I had never heard from him before noon, as far back as I could recall. In that regard he was a lot like my ex-partner, Bernie O'Neill. Bernie never liked to get up early either, not if he had even the slightest choice in the matter.

*I need to speak with you*, said the ghost, as usual audible only to me.

The note of urgency in his voice was pretty hard to miss. Unfortunately, I couldn't talk with him just then. I had business to take care of, business it had taken me a lot of time and energy to set up.

*Important* business.

"Not now," I told him.

For some reason, I couldn't ever just *think* my response to him. I had to say it out loud, even if it was just sotto voce.

The high school, a stately, red-brick edifice that had been built there long before the factories, was just up ahead. I made a left at the corner and slipped into a primo parking space not far from the entrance to the school yard.

*What do you* mean *not now?* he pressed.

Ghosts can be annoyingly insistent. And the more ancient they are, the more insistent they can be. As if their advanced age gives them a legal license to prey on the sanity of the living.

"It's a bad time," I said, turning off my car and pulling the key out of the ignition.

I peered through a chain-link fence at the asphalt expanse of the yard, which sported a faded baseball diamond and a half-dozen basketball courts. But I didn't care about those at the moment. I was looking for something else.

It stood in the far corner of the yard, a sixteen-foot-high wall of precast cement tinged with the long, bloody onslaught of a particularly spectacular August sun-up. On either side of the wall was a rectangular cement apron that stretched out exactly thirty-four feet. And surrounding the whole deal was a chain link fence just like the one that hugged the rest of the school yard.

A single-wall handball court. The kind you only find in New York, like candy stores that sell the Sunday Times on Saturday night and real half-sour pickles.

At this hour on a Sunday, there was nobody around. Not the students who attended the high school, not the people who worked in the printing plant or the stained glass shop or the paint wholesaler across the street, not even a cop on the beat—which was the whole point.

The place smelled like rusted fence-iron and last night's cheap wine, smothered in air that was already too hot to breathe. The power line above me was full of crows, their feathers shining like oil slicks. They were lined up like spectators, quiet, focused, as if they knew something big was going down and didn't want to miss any of it.

Taking along my keys, the cold bottle of water on the seat beside me, and a business-sized envelope packed full of hundred-dollar bills—the last item safely tucked into a pocket of my cargo shorts—I left the car and made my way across the yard.

When I got to the court I sat down and put my back against the fence. Then I waited. I didn't have to wait long.

Junior and his boys came sauntering across the yard like they owned it, their shadows stretched out ahead of them like an advance guard. Junior was unmistakable—six-four, maybe six-five, with a long, painfully lean body. His hair was a bright red comb like a rooster's, his nose was cruelly hooked, and his eyes were so protuberant they seemed to jump out of their orbits. If he'd ever had a name besides Junior, he didn't use it anymore.

His entourage consisted of three guys, all wearing black sweatpants and muscle tees as if it were some kind of uniform. Two of them were white, though not nearly as white as Junior, with the thick necks and muscular arms associated with professional football players. The third one, a light skinned Latino, was even more massive than the others.

I knew they were packing hardware. Not that this was the worst neighborhood in New York's five boroughs, not even close. But Junior wasn't going to carry ten thousand dollars in cash without taking a few modest measures to protect it. Besides, in the game they were playing, one *always* carried hardware.

No doubt, they were a little surprised I had come alone. At five-foot-eight I wasn't exactly an imposing figure, even if I was in pretty good shape. My age probably surprised them as well. Most of Junior's challengers were in their twenties, and I was clearly a bit older than that.

But from their standpoint, ten thousand dollars was ten thousand dollars.

I had watched Junior play here and there around the city, some on West Fourth Street behind the basketball cage and some in Hunts Point. Always at odd times of day, and never for more than an hour. Someone told me he used to play Coney Island too, but he didn't do that anymore. It had gotten too *political* for him in Coney Island.

Junior ducked his head to get through the entrance to the court, already starting to strip off his tee shirt. He flung it against the fence, then pulled a blue rubber ball out of his purple satin sweatpants and began bouncing it on the cement surface.

His body was so pale and angular it might have been carved from ivory. No tattoos or body piercings, which was unusual for somebody in his position. The sound of his bouncing ball rang out like a bell, echoing.

Without a word I got up and pulled off my own tee shirt, exposing the half-dozen old scars I wore on my back and shoulders, and tossed it next to Junior's. Then I took a swig from my water bottle and put it near the fence as well.

Junior's bull-necked compadres watched me the whole time, making sure I didn't do anything *unsportsmanlike*.

"Got the money?" asked Junior, in a high, almost girlish voice, still intent on the bounce of the ball.

"Right here," I said, patting the envelope in my pocket.

One of the white guys turned me around, put my hands against the fence, and frisked me. He didn't find anything except the wad of hundreds—a fact he communicated to Junior with an upturned thumb.

"Outstanding," Junior said matter-of-factly, as if such details were beneath him.

He had an edge to him, a haughtiness, that even the inconvenient pitch of his voice couldn't dispel. I could see why people followed him, why he had become what he was.

*This is an outrage*, said the ghost, apparently not yet done with me.

He meant the way I was treating *him*, not the way Junior's bodyguard was treating *me*. "Let it go," I breathed.

Junior looked up at me, his eyes narrowing. "You say something?"

I smiled. "Just talkin' to myself."

"Yeah," said Junior, returning his attention to the ball. He tossed it into the air. "I get that a lot. But it's usually *after* they play me."

Laughter erupted from his compadres. Mocking laughter. The kind that was supposed to have me beaten a little before I started.

Junior, meanwhile, let the ball bounce lower and lower until it was only an inch or so off the ground. Then, in a long, graceful motion that belied the force behind it, he pulled back his open hand and whacked the ball in the direction of the wall. The ball struck hard and low, so low that when it came back, it didn't bounce—it rolled.

Then Junior picked up the ball and did it again. And again.

I wasn't impressed. I had played this game since before Junior pooped his first diaper, and I had seen it all. Every velocity, every angle, every spin, every attempt at misdirection. I wasn't expecting any surprises.

On the other hand, Junior was supposed to be the best. The best *ever*, a sportswriter had said a couple of years earlier in the *Daily News*, even though handball had been played in New York for more than a hundred years. And some of the people he quoted had the credentials to know what they were talking about.

About handball, at least.

Which was one of the reasons I had agreed to get up so early in this oven of an August morning to make the trip to Long Island City with ten thousand dollars in my pocket. For a long time now, Junior had only played for money. And the more his reputation as a player had grown on courts around the city, the more money he played for.

Again, the ghost tickled my mind. *This is no trivial matter.*

"It can wait," I whispered.

"You sure do a lot of talking to yourself," observed Junior.

"You think this is *doubles*?"

His entourage shared another belly laugh. It was a good line, good enough to draw most other guys into an exchange of trash talk. But that wasn't my style. *You talk, you walk*, I had heard someone say once, a long time ago. I had made it my mantra. You shoot your mouth off, you leave the court with your tail between your loser legs.

"Can I see the ball?" I asked Junior. He flipped it to me, putting a spin on it so it seemed to jump away before it angled back to me. It was the way things were done on handball courts around the city. Nothing was as simple as it looked.

Not even me.

I squeezed the ball, getting a sense of how much it would compress when it hit the wall, and therefore how fast it would come back at me. It was new, and good quality, and warm to the touch from Junior's pounding. It would be a fast game.

*My* kind of game.

But it was also Junior's kind of game, and from what I had seen of him he played it well. I hit the ball off the wall a few times, alternating between my right hand and my left. I didn't try to hit especially low or especially hard. I just wanted to get the feel of it.

Each time the ball hit the concrete, it made a resounding *thwok*. Over the years, I had grown to love that sound. It brought back flashes of other times, other games, other opponents. But none of them as tough as this one.

"Game to twenty-one," said Junior. "Volley for serve."

"My pleasure," I said.

*Suit yourself*, the ghost told me.

Which meant I wouldn't be able to get in touch with him until after he cooled off, and that could involve days or even weeks. I regretted that, especially since the ghost had gotten me out of more jams than I cared to remember. But I couldn't conduct a conversation and a handball game at the same time, could I?

Throwing the ball in a high, lazy arc at the wall, I put it in play. Then I spread my feet with my weight forward and my knees bent, and braced myself for Junior's return.

It was a rocket shot to my left, not quite low enough to be a stone-cold killer. Diving for the ball, I plunked it off the heel of my left hand, creating a little backspin. The ball kissed the wall ever so lightly and bounced maybe an inch off the ground.

Against most opponents, it would have been enough. But not against Junior. Pelting in from the backcourt, he got his left hand on the ball and swatted it to the right side of the court, where I would have a hard time reaching it—especially considering I was still getting back on my feet.

But *I* wasn't just any opponent either. Digging hard to my right, I caught up with the ball and pulled it back over my shoulder. To Junior's credit, he hadn't counted his chicken before it was hatched. He was in perfect position to take the soft bounce off the wall and shoot it low to his left, well beyond my reach.

"My serve," he said, the slightest note of disdain in his voice.

Then he went on to score the next three points, all on

closely contested volleys. It was frustrating, to say the least. Junior wasn't murdering me the way I had seen him murder most of his other opponents. In fact, the way I saw it, he was outplaying me by only the narrowest of margins.

Still, it was enough.

I had to change the tune. On Junior's next serve, I lobbed the ball high off the wall, dropping it down in the rear left-hand corner of the court.

He drifted back after it, looking completely unflustered. But when he returned the shot, his timing was off a little, and the ball hit the wall a little too high. I was able to flick it to my right, where it proved to be just out of Junior's reach.

"Lucky shot," said Junior in that crazy high voice of his.

Not really, I thought.

It was my serve for the first time, and I was determined not to waste the opportunity. As long as I could remember, I had always had the ability to turn my game up a notch. It was just a matter of concentrating a little harder.

I caught Junior by surprise. He seemed tentative, off-balance under the force of my attack. Three serves later the score was tied at three, and I had some momentum going for me.

"That's all you get," Junior told me.

Sez you, I thought.

It was a long way to twenty-one, but I was about to take control of the game. I could feel it, just like I could feel the warm touch of the sun on my back.

Then something happened. Just as I had found a higher gear, Junior seemed to find one too. Suddenly he was moving faster, hitting harder, sending me diving around the court like a dolphin at SeaWorld.

It occurred to me that he had been toying with me all along, making me think I was in the game when I wasn't. There were guys who liked to do that. But I was pretty sure Junior wasn't one of them. In the games I had watched him play, he had been all business, all lethal intent.

Somehow I hung in against him, but just barely. He started scoring points again, one after the other. A lucky break got me the serve back, but I lost it again just as fast.

"Going nowhere," said Junior, underlining the obvious.

I couldn't figure it out. The way he was playing, he wasn't just great. He was superhuman. Like one of those aliens you see in the movies. Any minute, I expected his teeth to slide out of his mouth and take a chunk out of me.

Before I knew it, the score was 6-3. Then 10-3. I was taking a beating, no way around it.

Something else was bothering me too—a pressure in my ears that had started a few minutes earlier and gotten progressively worse. It made me feel like I was on a plane going in for a long, torturous landing, and me without a stick of chewing gum.

I couldn't see any reason for it. No change in the weather, nothing. But there it was.

I worked my jaw around, but it didn't help. If anything, it got worse. As if from a great distance I could hear a ringing, a million little bells chiming in unison. Hell of a thing. Like I needed a distraction on top of everything else.

Still, I wasn't giving up. I mean, I might never have a chance to play someone like Junior again in my life.

With a dig that took some skin off my knuckles, I regained the serve. Pounding the ball with all the torque I could muster, I put Junior back on his heels and won the next couple of points. I almost added a third one as well, but my killer was just out of bounds on the wall.

That gave Junior the chance to rack up two more points of his own. The score was 12-6. I was still in striking distance but I was fading. Another run on Junior's part and he would have too big a lead for me to overcome.

He knew it, too. He didn't say it, but he had this shit-eating grin that told me he knew it.

We had been playing for an hour or more—an eternity for a game of singles. I had probably done better than Junior expected. Maybe better than anyone he had played before. At least I wanted to think so.

But if the game stayed this course, it was over. *Over.*

And that was a bitter thought. More bitter than the tang of spilled wine and fence-rust. More bitter than bile.

At the side of the court, Junior's wingmen shared a joke. They were enjoying this. I shut out their laughter, shut out *everything*, and focused on the task at hand.

With a little glance at me over his shoulder, Junior wound up for another serve. Like the last few it was a rocket, but this one had a little English on it, squeezing me so I couldn't put a decent swing on the ball. Even so, I managed to slam it hard to Junior's right, keeping it just inside the line.

He stretched for it, but missed it by a few inches. Somewhere above us, a seagull squawked.

My serve, I thought. Let me make it a great one. Let me make them *all* great ones from here on in.

It was then that I caught sight of the cars out of the corner of my eye. They were moving in slowly from both ends of the street, converging on the entrance to the schoolyard. One white, one dark blue, and both of them chock full of cops.

Crap, I thought, not now. Not *yet*.

While I was thinking it, Junior won the volley and got back the serve.

I understood why my friends in the cars couldn't have waited any longer. The game had to end prematurely—that had been the plan all along. But I had wanted to be ahead of Junior when it happened, not trailing by a half dozen points.

It galled me to think that he had dominated me that way.

And there wasn't going to be any rematch. At least, not while Junior was still in his prime. He was going away, and for a long time.

None of Junior's bodyguards seemed to catch on to what was happening. They were too busy snickering to one another, enjoying the spectacle.

But Junior himself was a different story. As he pulled his hand back to serve, he stopped cold—and lifted his head like a buck deer that had suddenly caught the scent of a predator. His eyes, filled with something uncomfortably like amusement, found me and fixed on me—but only for a fraction of a second. Then he whirled and took off, headed for the ten-foot-high section of fence to his right.

I saw what he had in mind. Beyond the fence was the street, a narrow one lined with factory buildings. But as Junior leaped high onto the fence, grasping it with his long, white fingers, a couple of cars screeched into view to block his way.

That should have been that. Junior and his entourage had been caught like fish in a barrel, exactly the way we had drawn it up.

But something happened. There was a big, white flash that blinded me for a moment. And it didn't *just* blind me—it popped my ears, relieving the pressure I had felt while the game was on.

By the time I could see again, even a little, Junior was heaving himself over the top of the ten-foot-high fence. It wouldn't have been such a big deal except the cops in the cars on the other side appeared to have been blinded too, and they hadn't recovered yet.

As I realized that, I realized also that Junior's men weren't surrendering, despite the fact that they were thoroughly surrounded. The crack of gunfire stretched across the yard as Junior's bodyguards opened fire on the cops advancing from the entrance.

Fortunately for me, they seemed to have forgotten I was there. Obviously, they hadn't put two and two together yet and realized I was part of the sting.

I could have tried to take one of them out, which would certainly have helped my brothers across the yard. But Junior was the big fish, the one we had set the bait for. If he escaped, it was all for nothing.

So, spots still dancing in front of my eyes, I started scaling the fence one fistful of chain-link after another. As I watched, Junior hit the walk on the other side and started making tracks. A few seconds later, I hit the walk myself.

He was maybe two hundred feet ahead of me. I took off after him.

I had always been fast. In my sixteen years on the force, I had run down more perps than I could count—high school track stars, running backs, point guards, it didn't much matter.

But I hadn't taken ten strides before I knew Junior was too much for me. I was going all out, all elbows and knees, and instead of closing the gap I was watching him widen it.

I kept at it, arms churning like pistons, pumping air in and out of my lungs. Sometimes, I reminded myself, even the fastest guys gave out over the long haul. But I had a bad feeling Junior wasn't going to be one of them.

Fortunately, I had an ace in the hole. Or rather, in the sky. Even as I thought of it, it swung into view between the rooftops: a sleek, black police helicopter that had been surveilling the handball game from afar, waiting for the cops on the ground to get the party started.

The chop of its blades drowned out every other sound. Its dark flank gleamed wildly, struck by spears of sunlight, its downwash sending scraps of paper and debris and dry leaves whirling in the street ahead of me.

I saw Junior glance up at the chopper as he ran. He had to know that wherever he went it would hound him, communicating his whereabouts to units on the street. Sooner or later, one of them would head him off.

But I wanted to get to him first.

Gritting my teeth, I plunged down the street in the thick summer air. Come on, I thought, make a mistake. Turn down a dead end. Twist an ankle on a pile of dog poop.

Junior didn't do any of those things. He just kept on pulling away from me, a little more with every stride. I felt my heart slam my ribs like it wanted to get out, but it didn't help. I was losing the battle, and not for the first time that day.

Suddenly, something went wrong with the helicopter. One moment it was cruising along, no problem. The next moment it was twirling like a top, desperately out of control. As I watched, horrified, it spun even faster, as if caught in the grip of an invisible force.

Then it slid to my right, past a rooftop and out of sight.

My god, I thought, thinking of the men inside the chopper.

I had barely completed the thought when I felt myself buffeted sideways, propelled by a gust of wind that came out of nowhere—a gust so strong and insistent that it felt like a giant hand. Not from the copter, I had time to think, because it wasn't there anymore.

Then I saw a metal trash can looming in front of me. For a heartbeat I fought and twisted to avoid it. Then I felt myself leave my feet and go barreling right into it.

The impact made my head swim. Forcing myself to look up, I saw that Junior was still going strong. If the wind had slowed him down, he gave no sign of it.

I tried to think: Was it the wind that had shoved aside the

chopper? Where had it come from? The morning had been so still, so devoid of anything even resembling a breeze . . .

As it was *again*, I realized.

There were a few scraps of paper still floating back to earth, but there was no longer any wind to keep them aloft. After the way I'd been thrown around, the tranquility felt positively eerie.

It was a mystery I had no time to solve—not with Junior making his getaway. Gathering my feet beneath me, I took off after him again, trying to ignore the beating I'd taken from the trash can. I was starting to appreciate how many body parts I'd managed to smash—a forehead, a knee, even a couple of ribs—as I sprinted past a cross street.

That's when I saw something on my right, and discovered what had happened to the chopper. It was one intersection over, slowly spinning around on its side like a gigantic insect who'd had one of its wings pulled off. What was left of its rotors were snapping off before my eyes, viciously hurling themselves in every direction.

It didn't look real. And yet, there it was.

Pretty soon, the chopper's fuel would catch fire. In fact, I was surprised it hadn't done so already. When it did, the cops inside would be burned to death.

Goddamn, I thought.

I hated the idea of letting Junior get away, but there were units in the area that might still take him down. No one but me was close enough to save the guys in the chopper.

By the time I got to it, it wasn't spinning so much anymore. I jumped up onto its shiny black carcass, made my way to the passenger-side door, and yanked at it. It swung open so fast I almost lost my footing, probably because the guy inside had already unlocked it. He was in a bad way, bloody and battered in places, but at least he was alive.

It was more than I could say for the pilot, whose forehead had been caved in.

As carefully as I could, I hauled the cop on the shotgun side out of the copter. There was a guy in a business suit—a good Samaritan—waiting for me on the ground. He took the injured cop's legs while I hung onto his upper body, and we shuffled him away as fast as we could.

Maybe a minute after I climbed off the copter, it blew up in a ball of fire and thick, black smoke.

I could feel the heat of the explosion on my face, like someone slapped it good and hard. Fortunately, no one was close enough to be hurt by it, though bystanders had begun to come out of the woodwork. That'll happen when a police helicopter goes down on your average city street.

An unmarked, navy-blue Impala arrived a couple of minutes later. I could see the female officer inside it peering at me from behind her dash as she called in the chopper wreck on her radio. Then she got out and ran over to where I was hunkered down beside the injured officer.

She was beautiful, one of the most beautiful women I had ever seen. Long, curly black hair, full, expressive lips, the kind of eyes that could make sapphires weep with jealousy.

Her name was Tomi Pappas. She was a detective—one of several who had spent the last six months hot on Junior's case. She was also my girlfriend.

Kneeling beside me, she put her hand on my shoulder and squeezed a little, letting me know she was glad I was still in one piece. Then she whispered into my ear, "You're an idiot, you know that?"

I knew.

But not for the reasons she thought. I had pissed off the ghost, lost a steel cage death match with a trash can, and let Junior get away scot-free.

A fiasco all around.

# CHAPTER TWO

"So you're *not* an idiot?" Tomi asked me as she drove me home through the streets of Astoria.

It was almost noon, the sun high in the sky. We had stayed with the hurt cop until an ambulance got him, and then stayed some more to help with crowd control while they removed the pilot and what was left of the chopper.

Junior's wingmen hadn't gone down without a fight. Two of the three had survived, but one of them wouldn't hang on much longer. That left only one who might be persuaded to shed light on Junior's whereabouts.

Tomi had told me that much. But beyond that, we really hadn't had a chance to talk.

"I didn't say that," I replied.

Everybody we passed on the sidewalk looked sweaty, like the world was an oven and they were half-baked pastries. Tomi too. After all, she had been working on hot asphalt all morning. But on her, sweaty looked good.

"I'm serious," she said, using her cop voice so I knew she wasn't kidding. "What were you thinking, trying to take down Junior on your own?"

I shrugged. "It wouldn't have been the first perp I took down by myself."

"When you were a *cop*," she said. "Which you're not anymore, remember? Which was why it was a really bad idea to let you talk me into this gambit in the first place."

"I didn't," I reminded her. "I talked *Gaetano* into it."

Gaetano was the captain of the 114th Precinct. He was also in charge of the task force Tomi was working with, the one that had identified Junior as an up-and-comer on the gang scene and linked him to a couple of capital crimes.

She made a sound of disgust. "Yeah. *Gaetano*."

"Hey," I said, "it worked, didn't it? We had Junior where we wanted him."

"Until he got away." She swore beneath her breath, her brow bunching over her slightly aquiline nose. "Which I still don't understand."

Tomi had been in one of the cars positioned to keep Junior from going over the fence. And no doubt they would have, if it weren't for that blinding flash.

"What happened there?" I asked her. "Everything went white for a second."

Tomi shook her head. "All I know is I couldn't see. The next thing I know you're three blocks away, making like Forrest Gump." She glanced at me. "Did you see what happened to the chopper?"

I frowned. "Yes and no. I saw the pilot lose control, but I didn't actually see it go down."

"Crazy thing," said Tomi. "I mean, there was no wind. Must

have been some kind of malfunction."

"Actually," I said, "there *was* a wind. Just for a minute."

She glanced at me again. "You mean like a squall or something? Just out of nowhere?" Her expression said she wasn't buying it.

"Sounds dumb," I said, "I know. But that's what it looked like—a wind pushing the chopper around. And I felt the same thing on the ground."

"A wind," she repeated, just to make sure we were on the same page.

"Uh huh. Slammed me into a trash can. I've got the bruises to prove it." I started to lift my shirt.

"Show me later," she said. "I don't need you getting undressed in my car."

"You didn't *used* to say that."

She chuckled despite herself. "You didn't used to be a pain in the ass."

I was pretty sure she was joking, but I asked anyway. "Is that a reference to my lack of direction?"

Tomi could have played that well-worn song again, the one in which I should never have retired so early from the force, especially without a plan in mind. But mercifully, she didn't. "Actually, it's a reference to your being a pain in the ass."

"And nothing to do with my leaving the job, right?"

I'd laid a trap for her to stomp on my ego so I could feel justified in feeling hurt. But she was too smart to fall for traps. "I understand fine, Zeno. You just didn't want to look at me twenty-four-seven anymore."

"That's crazy," I said, meaning every syllable of it. "Who wouldn't want to look at *you* twenty four-seven? I'd look at you twenty *five*-seven. I mean, you know, if there were such a thing."

"Bullshit," she said. Her eyes crinkled a little at the corners. "But *nice* bullshit."

I nodded. "Thanks."

She pulled the car over in front of a neat little brownstone with a flower box full of red impatiens. "Your stop, Cowboy."

"Want to eat out tonight?" I asked her.

She looked tired for the first time that morning. "I don't think I'm going to feel like it. Not after we get an earful from the captain."

"No problem," I said, "I'll make something." Which was the least I could do, considering I didn't have a job anymore. I leaned over to give Tomi a kiss.

"I'm on duty," she protested, but wound up kissing me back anyway. She pushed me away with a forefinger. "Maybe a nice pastitsio."

"You know, just because we're Greek—"

"The way I like it, lots of bechamel. Now get out of the freakin' car. You're making the seats smell."

"Hey," I said, putting my hands up in mock surrender, "whatever you say, officer." And I got out.

As Tomi pulled away in her blue Impala, I thought again about how fast Junior was. Olympics-level fast. It was weird.

Adrenaline might have had something to do with it. People ran faster when cops were chasing them—it was that way with everybody. And if he was fast to begin with . . .

Yeah, I thought, that's it—adrenaline.

But that didn't explain the blinding flash I saw, or the wind that knocked the chopper down, or the other wind that sent me flying into the trash can. Weird indeed.

I went up the steps, pulled out my key, and opened the front door. Then I went inside to take a shower and whip up a batch of pastitsio.

Tomi was right. Gaetano ripped her a new one, her and everybody else on the task force. They had worked on this collar for months, and had nothing to show for it but a dead pilot and a couple of punctured gang bangers who wouldn't utter a single word.

Not even "lawyer."

Junior commanded loyalty. That was for sure.

"How's the pastitsio?" I asked.

Across the table from me, Tomi shrugged. "We should have ordered out."

"What?" I said. "After I slaved over a hot stove?"

She smiled a little. "It's fine. Could have used a little more bechamel."

"I could have used the whole bottle and you'd *still* say that."

"Use the whole bottle next time, and we'll see."

One of the things I loved most about Tomi was that she didn't back down. She would have fit in perfectly on a handball court.

I pushed the pastitsio around on my plate, recalling my

game with Junior—and not for the first time. That volley when it was 10-5 and I was serving ... if I hadn't tried so hard to place that kill shot in the corner, I wouldn't have hit it out of play.

It was a big point, too. I had scored on my last two serves. I was coming back. If that killer had been in bounds, it would have made it 10-6, and Junior might have tightened up a little.

Sometimes that's all it takes—a little pressure. But I missed the shot, and that put the pressure back on me.

Suddenly, I realized Tomi was staring at me. "You're thinking about the handball game," she said, "aren't you?"

I started to protest, then stopped. What was the point in denying it?

"Of all the stuff that went down today, all the death and destruction, you're thinking about the goddamned handball game." Tomi wasn't angry. She was just incredulous.

"Of course not," I said. "What kind of jerk would be consumed by losing a handball game when a guy got killed?" Meaning the chopper pilot.

"What kind of jerk?" Tomi echoed.

We both knew what she was talking about. For as long as I could remember, winning had been an addiction with me. A *need*.

Vince Lombardi used to say, "Winning isn't everything. It's the *only* thing." That could have been my mantra. I lived for competition.

And not just on the handball court. In the pool hall, in the bowling alley, even in the bank. It killed me when somebody got on a faster line than I did.

It was a character flaw, I know. But I couldn't help it.

"That sonuvabitch was fast," I said. "Faster than anybody I ever saw." I couldn't get him out of my mind.

Tomi shook her head. "Unbelievable."

The next morning, I went to visit the injured cop at Mt. Sinai—the one in Queens, not Manhattan. His name was Arturo Wayne. He had a fractured collarbone, bruised ribs, and a cracked kneecap, but he would heal.

When I walked into his hospital room, he had no idea who I was. A minute later, he wanted to put me in his will.

"You should be a cop," he said, clasping my hand with all his might.

I told him, "I *was* a cop."

He didn't understand why I left the force so early. No one does. Most everybody waits till he has twenty years in so he can get a full pension. I was only thirty-eight.

"The problem," I explained, "was I wasn't into it anymore. My heart . . . " I shrugged. "It was somewhere else."

"Where?"

I smiled. "Good question. It's been four months now and I still don't know what I want to be when I grow up."

"You should be a teacher," said Arturo.

That was a new one. "Why do you say that?"

"You *look* like a teacher."

"Thanks," I said, though I didn't know teachers had a look.

"Think about it," he said. "If you're interested, my sister-in-law is a dean at a private school on the Island."

I promised that I'd give his suggestion some thought. Then I wished him a quick recuperation and made my way back to Astoria.

On the way home, I picked up a newspaper. The chopper crash was right there on Page One.

There wasn't much of a story to go with it—the official word was that the chopper was on a routine patrol when it ran into engine trouble. The pilot had done well just to put it down without killing any bystanders, the paper said. He was a hero.

At least the last part was true. If not for him, Arturo would never have survived.

I had made some points with Tomi by going to see Arturo.

"So I'm not such a jerk," I said, "right? Maybe?"

"*Maybe,*" she conceded over the phone. At least, that's what I thought she said. It wasn't such a good cell connection. "*Where you going now?*"

"To lunch," I said. "With Bernie, remember?"

"*Say hello,*" she told me. "*Maybe he can help you find yourself.*"

Right, I thought. But I didn't say it out loud. What I said was "Later," and then I pressed END on the face of my phone.

Bernie O'Neill had been my partner for five years. Then his arthritis got worse, he decided he couldn't take all the typing anymore, and he retired, at which point they hooked me up with Tomi. I owed Bernie big-time for that. For a lot of other things, too.

I met him at his favorite pub on the Lower East Side, a few blocks from his apartment. It was the kind of place where the beer was a little flat, the pretzels were a little stale, and they served corned beef and cabbage every day of the week—not just on St. Paddy's Day. He was already sitting at a table in the back, right under the black-and-white picture of Joe DiMaggio and Marilyn Monroe.

Small world, Bernie knew Arturo Wayne. They had met at a wedding a few years earlier.

"How come you never said anything?" I asked. "I mean, he rode shotgun in a helicopter. That's worth a mention."

"Maybe I did," said Bernie, a big, ruddy-faced guy who *still* had a full head of wavy, silver-grey hair. "Who remembers?" He smiled a sad smile. "Hell of a thing, Zee. I don't think I've ever heard of a copter crash in New York. It's crazy, like something out of a movie."

I looked at him askance. "You watch movies all of a sudden?" He never had before. Always said he fell asleep in them.

"Now that I'm retired," he said, "Mary Beth and me do lots of things I never did before. Movies is just part of it." He winked.

I held up a stop sign. "More information than I need, Bern. *Much* more."

"Well," he said, "it's amazing what a little time on your hands will do to a man." He grinned. "Oh, wait—you know that, don't you?"

"Because I'm retired too," I said sourly. "I get it."

Bernie leaned forward, grabbed me by the shoulder, and shook me a little. "Come on, Cowboy, loosen up, wouldja? It's a joke."

"To *you* it it's a joke, because you're not thirty-eight years old. No one expects you to go out and start another career."

Bernie shrugged his broad shoulders. "You'll find something. When you least expect it, probably. It'll just fall in your freakin' lap."

I nodded. "Sure." I remembered what Arturo Wayne told me in his hospital room. "Your pal the chopper jock said I looked like a teacher."

Bernie made a face. "You?"

"That's what he said. Offered me a job, even. Or actually, a connection that could *get* me a job."

My ex-partner considered me for a second. Then he said, "I don't see it. You got to be calm in a classroom. You can't be challenging the kids to a game of horse every two minutes."

How well he knew me.

"So what's going' on with Tomi?" he asked.

"What about her?"

"You been seeing her . . . what? About two years now?"

I nodded. "Almost."

"And?"

"And what? We're good."

"Just good?"

"Very good. Amazingly good."

"So?"

I leaned back in my chair. "What do you want to know? If I'm in the market for a ring?"

Bernie grinned a sly grin. "Just asking, boyo."

I studied my beer for a while. "I mean, it's not like I haven't thought about it. It's just—I don't know—she doesn't seem like she wants to make it permanent."

"So she's not ready."

I shrugged. "I don't think she'll *ever* be ready."

"I thought she was crazy about you."

"She is," I said, "as far as I can tell. But that doesn't mean she wants to get married."

He laughed. "Don't play yourself, Zee. *All* women want to get married. Even the ones who carry a gun."

I looked at him. "Yeah? Since when did you become an expert on women?"

"Hell," he said, "I been married to enough of them." The actual number was three, including his current wife, Mary Beth. "If I'm not an expert, who is?"

Then we *both* laughed.

"So," I said, "you think Tomi wants to get hitched."

"Without a doubt. And you better not wait too long. You're not getting any younger, you know."

"I'm not exactly Methuselah."

"Nah," he said, "Methuselah was only nine hundred and sixty nine."

"You *knew* that?" I asked, more than a little surprised. "Or you just came up with a random number?"

"Nine hundred and sixty nine," he repeated proudly. "You learn stuff when you're retired. And here's another thing I learned: Married men live longer than single ones. You can look it up."

Actually, I'd heard that one myself. "All right," I said, "I get it. Now drink your beer before it goes flat altogether."

I never told anyone about the ghost—not Bernie, not Tomi, nobody at all. First off, who would have believed me? Second, the ghost wasn't into conference calls. He talked to me and me alone.

I mean, if you can call that *talking*.

In my more rational moments, I had to admit the possibility that the ghost was my conscience, my better judgment, whatever you want to call it. That he wasn't *really* a supernatural spirit who had latched onto me for reasons he chose to keep to himself.

And then there were the times that I thoroughly believed he was something outside of and apart from me, something I couldn't explain. Something that didn't fit in with the logical, cause-and-effect world I lived in.

There were also moments, though not many, in which I questioned my sanity. I mean, I was too old to have an imaginary friend. A psychologist might have told me the ghost was a manifestation of my inability to cope with the demands of everyday living, or some unacknowledged trauma in my past, or who knows what.

I didn't believe that. Hell, I was the sanest person I knew. But then, crazy people *always* believe they're sane. Then they chop up a few close relatives and store the parts in their basement freezers, and the neighbors tell the news crews how quiet they were.

Fortunately, neither Bernie nor Tomi had ever questioned where I got some of my information, the kind nobody would ever put his hands on without a ghost to help him out. But then, I had a knack for taking what the ghost had given me and constructing a story about how I had acquired it.

One time, just to see what Tomi would do, I told her a little voice had tipped me off.

"Yeah, right," she said, a nasty edge to her voice. "You don't want to tell me, just say so."

Usually, the ghost was available twenty four-seven. All I had to do was think of him and he was there. But I had tried that several times since the chopper crash, and had gotten nothing even vaguely resembling a response.

So he really *was* pissed.

The longest he had ever cut me off was three days. I figured I could do without him that long, especially since I wasn't a cop anymore. With the exception of that handball game with Junior, I didn't go around risking my life very often.

But I kind of missed him.

That evening Tomi and I went out to dinner—nothing fancy, just a little Italian place on the East Side that had lots of candles and the world's best martinis. Afterward we walked up Second Avenue hand in hand, enjoying the clinging heat and humidity as it can only be experienced on a summer night in New York.

I thought about what Bernie had said about women and rings. I *wanted* to make Tomi happy—in fact, nothing would have been more satisfying to me in the whole world. Dazzled by the way her hair curled around the nape of her neck, the way her shoulder made that sexy little dimple . . . and a little tipsy from three martinis . . . I almost asked Tomi if she wanted to get married. I mean, straight out. I was *this* close.

Fortunately, I stopped myself in time. Hell, if she had really *wanted* to tie the knot, she would also have wanted a proposal that had some romance to it. And popping the question while we were waiting for a light in front of a dry cleaner didn't seem so romantic.

I mean, I could do better than "How's work? That rash still bothering you? Want to get married?"

As it happened, our love-making was great that night. Even better than usual, and that was saying something. She was so soft, so supple, I couldn't get enough of her.

Tomi fell asleep halfway through Letterman. I was right behind her.

It was early morning. I was standing in front of the bathroom mirror, dragging a razor across two days' growth. The little puffs of shaving cream and the whiskers embedded in them were falling into the sink, where they were torn apart by the current of running water.

After a while, I thought I heard something. Not in the next room or even out in the hallway, but right next to me. In the freakin' shower stall.

I turned and peered through the frosted glass of the shower door, even though I was sure there was nothing there to see. I was wrong. There was somebody in the shower.

He was just standing there in the stall, looking at me. Thanks to the frosting, I couldn't see his face. But I could tell it was a guy and not Tomi, and I was pretty sure the son of a bitch had a beard.

"Who are you," I asked, "and what the hell are you doing in my shower?" It seemed like a reasonable question.

"This place where you live," he said, as if he hadn't heard me, "is not safe. You must leave it and seek shelter elsewhere."

The guy talked funny. Very formal, very precise, and very flat. Not even a hint of emotion. It seemed to me he was tired, worn out, and had long ago given up hope that he would get any relief.

"Not safe . . ." I echoed. "Why not? What's the problem?"

"The problem is that you have an enemy, who will strike and strike soon. You must not be here when that happens."

"I'm a cop," I told him. "Or anyway, I used to be. I can handle whatever is going to happen."

"No," he said, sounding pretty sure of himself, "you cannot."

"Who are you?" I asked again, trying harder to see through the glass of the stall.

I didn't reach out and slide it aside. For some reason, that didn't seem to be an option.

I heard him sigh. "Do you not *know*?"

And then he was gone, and I was standing there alone in the bathroom, feeling a cold that started in my bones and radiated outward.

That is, until I woke up in bed.

I waited till the alarm rang to tell Tomi about my dream.

It was too weird to keep to myself. Besides, I told her everything—except about the ghost, of course.

"Stupid," I said, "I know. Probably means I need more fiber in my diet."

She didn't smile. In fact, she looked kind of grim. "Any indication of who's out to get us?"

"No," I said, pulling aside the cover and swinging my legs out of bed. "Just that he's going to strike soon."

"Did you tell him we were cops?"

"Something like that. It didn't seem to make a difference to him."

Tomi nodded, looking concerned. Which made *me* concerned. "All right," she said finally. "In that case, we need to move out. I'll call the real estate lady. You get hold of the movers."

She couldn't quite keep a straight face anymore. What really gave it away was the way she pressed her lips together.

"Very funny," I said.

Suddenly she burst out laughing, her hand darting to her mouth. "Sorry," she squeezed out, "but—"

"Great," I said. "I'm glad I amuse you."

Tomi shoved me, hard. It was something she did when she couldn't adequately express herself, either because she was too upset, or too out of it, or—at times like this one—too giddy.

On other occasions I had pretended to sprawl wildly, propelled by the power of that shove, in order to elicit a smile from her. This time, I decided she was having enough fun already. So I just sat there.

"Are you finished?" I asked.

For some reason, that made her laugh even harder. Her

eyes welled up with tears, and her face got red as if she couldn't breathe, which seemed to be more or less the case.

"Not yet," I concluded. "Guess I'll take a shower. I'll let you know if I run into anybody."

I didn't. The stall was blissfully empty.

I had an appointment that afternoon to talk with a headhunter.

This particular guy had connections in the security business. Lots of ex-cops took jobs in security. Made good money too, if they got involved with a big company or some nice, high-rent office buildings, so it made sense for me to go in that direction.

The problem was I didn't *want* a job in security. Not even a little bit. In fact, I was just seeing the guy to make Tomi happy. So I was thrilled when he called around noon and told me not to bother, because his wife had unexpectedly gone into labor.

"Your wife comes first," I said, as if he needed me to tell him that.

The last-minute reprieve left me with the day wide open. And since there was hardly a cloud in the sky, I took the subway down to the Village and played some handball. Some days I played better than others. This day I absolutely *killed*.

The competition at West Fourth Street was as good as any place in the city, and yet I was putting guys away. *Burying* them. I must have held the court for three hours.

But then, you get better by playing the best. That's what they always say. And the day before, I'd played Junior.

As I was leaving the courts, making my way through the crowd that had gathered around the basketball cage, I got a call on my cell from Tomi. She sounded frustrated.

Apparently, Junior's bodyguard—the one who was just hanging on—had expired. That left just the last of the three.

"And he's still not talking," said Tomi. Which was pretty much what we had expected, though it didn't make it any easier to swallow. "What happened with the headhunter?" she asked, no doubt hoping for some *good* news.

"He canceled," I told her. "His wife was having a baby. I told him that was no excuse, but he didn't want to hear it."

Tomi didn't laugh. "*Did you call that other guy? The football player?*"

*Shit*, I thought.

I had forgotten about the other guy—a former wideout for the Giants who owned a top-of-the-line bodyguard agency. Most of the guys who worked for him had been college athletes at least, but a friend of Tomi's at work said the guy was looking for ex-cops too.

Unfortunately, I wanted to be a bodyguard even less than I wanted to be building security.

"You didn't call him," Tomi concluded.

"I didn't call him."

"*And of course, since you had no job leads, you figured the next most productive thing was to go out and play handball.*"

"Well," I said with all the boyish charm I could muster, "when you put it that way . . ."

Silence for a moment. "*What am I going to do with you?*" Tomi said, unmasked disappointment in her voice.

"I've got some ideas," I said. I'd always believed the best

defense is a bold offense. "I hear Chinese food is an aphrodisiac."

More silence, longer than before. I waited for the verdict, knowing it could go either way.

*"Only if it comes from Wo Hing's,"* she said at last.

I smiled.

Of course, Wo Hing's was in Chinatown. It wasn't exactly on my way home—not that it mattered. "Wo Hing's it is," I assured her.

It was a small price to pay for domestic tranquility.

One thing about Wo Hing's, they cook soup a lot better than they pack it.

As usual, the white plastic bag with my takeout order was swampy with soup guts by the time I got home, which was well after six. No matter how carefully Wo Hing's sealed up the soup—even with adhesives developed for the space program—it never failed to spring a leak. A real mystery, like where one of your socks goes when you put a pair in the washing machine.

Anyway, I juggled the Chinese food to open the front door and then close it again behind me. "Tomi?" I called as I headed for the kitchen. "Got some hot and sour for you. Got some moo shoo. Nice, soft diapers, just the way you like 'em. Plenty of hoisin."

No answer. She must be in the shower, I thought.

I placed the Wo Hing's on the kitchen table and made my way down the hall. The bathroom door was open and there weren't any shower sounds coming from inside, so Tomi wasn't in the shower after all.

I kept going and poked my head in the bedroom, but she wasn't there either. That bothered me a little. Nobody was more punctual than Tomi. It was like a religion with her. Her mom and dad had been like that too before they died, as she often took the opportunity to tell me.

Frowning, I fished my phone out of my pocket and checked for messages. Only one, and that was from Bernie giving me the exact statistics about married men living longer. *"Ten years longer,"* he said, according to some studies. *"Not for nuthin',"* he added.

But nothing from Tomi.

I gave her a call. The cellular service said she was unavailable. I left her a message, put the food in the oven to keep it warm, and sat down to watch the Yankee game.

No problem, I thought. Tomi'll walk in the door any minute. But she didn't—not even after half an hour. Feeling something wasn't right, I put a call in to the precinct.

The sergeant on duty was Podabinski, who had lost an eye in a bar fight and never bothered to get a replacement. *"She left around six,"* he said. *"Maybe six fifteen."*

It was twenty-five after seven. "Did she say she was stopping anywhere?" I asked.

*"What am I,"* he said, *"her social secretary? Maybe she decided to finally dump you and get a real boyfriend."*

"Yeah," I said, "maybe. Let me know if you hear from her, all right?"

*"Sure,"* said Podabinski. *"G'night, Cowboy."*

I sat down on the couch and stared at the television for a

minute. But I wasn't really paying attention to the Yankees. I was trying to figure out what I should do about Tomi.

Maybe she's sitting in a traffic jam, I told myself. Maybe she's changing a flat. Maybe she saw somebody collapse on the street and had to stay with him till the ambulance came. Hell, that happened to me once.

Maybe this, maybe that. But as time went on, I grew more and more afraid that something worse than a flat had happened to Tomi. I could feel it in my gut.

She was a cop. She knew how to take care of herself. But bad things happened to cops too.

I didn't want to call the precinct again, but I did. This time Podabinski was more sympathetic. He must have heard the worry in my voice, and he knew I wasn't a worrier.

But he hadn't heard about any traffic jams. "Tell ya what," he said, "I'll send a couple of cars your way. How does she go home?"

I told him. He said he would see to it his guys checked every inch of the route. I thanked him and made sure my phone had plenty of charge in it. Then I sat down again and stared at the Yankee game, and waited.

But Tomi never came home.

# CHAPTER THREE

At two in the morning, I got a call from Podabinski. They hadn't found Tomi, but they had found her car. It was parked a couple of miles from the station house, its driver's-side window bashed in.

Nothing had been taken. Not the radio, which was worth some money, or Tomi's laptop, which she kept on the floor, or even her purse, which was lying right there on the passenger's seat. So robbery wasn't the motive.

I asked if there was any evidence that she had been hurt. There wasn't, thank God. No blood or anything else.

At least, not yet.

"Don't worry," said Podabinski, "we've got everybody looking for her. I mean everybody."

A couple of minutes later, I got a call from Missing Persons. They wanted to know, among other things, if Tomi had any enemies. I told them she was a cop—she made enemies every day.

But not every enemy was capable of taking an officer of the law by surprise, or prying her out of her car against her will. The Missing Persons guys reminded me of that. Did I know anybody who might have the wherewithal to do those things to Tomi?

I said I didn't.

But in my gut, I had a suspect in mind.

They gave me their number and told me to call them if anything occurred to me. I said I would do that, but I was lying. I think they knew it too.

The Missing Persons guys were notoriously thorough. After they got off the phone with me, they would be considering every angle, every possibility, so at some point the topic of Junior would come up. After all, Tomi had been part of the task force trying to apprehend him.

But there had been lots of cops involved in the sting. Even if Junior had gotten a glimpse of Tomi's face, which was a stretch, why would he have picked out her in particular? And how, in the day and a half since he got away, would he have figured out where she worked and how she got home?

Unable to answer these questions, the Missing Persons guys would try a different tack. And they would be right to do so.

But they hadn't seen the look Junior gave me just before he started scaling the chain-link fence. I mean, there's a look you give somebody when you realize he's The Man and he's done his job by closing a trap on you. The look Junior gave *me* was something else entirely.

It wasn't business, that look. It was *personal*. And as I sat there on the couch, running my fingers through my hair till my scalp hurt, I had to wonder *how* personal.

If Junior had wanted to abduct someone—punish someone—why wouldn't it have been *me*? He knew what I looked like, where I liked to hang out. It wouldn't have been so hard to find me. Not half as hard as finding a particular female cop in a city the size of New York.

But he had gone after Tomi instead. Why?

I could think of only one reason: Because he knew it would hurt me *more* for him to take *her*.

It was a leap, I admit. A *big* leap, and probably more than a little paranoid. Sure, I was the one who had set the trap for him, and in that moment when he realized he'd been played he must have hated my guts.

But how would he know that Tomi and I were together? Or where we lived? Or which precinct she worked out of, or what route she took back to the apartment?

It didn't make sense. And yet I had to make sense of it.

Bernie called me just after sun-up. Somebody at the precinct had told him about Tomi and he was sick to his stomach. Other guys called too, people who had worked with me or Tomi over the years. Annie Moskowitz in Coney Island. Dave Ramirez in Throggs Neck. Suzie Feng in the Commissioner's Office. Anything they could do, they told me, just name it.

Arturo phoned from his hospital room. After I had pulled him out of the chopper, he reminded me, Tomi had stayed there with us until help arrived. She was a good person, he said. He was sure she would be okay.

Right after Arturo hung up, I got a call from a guy named

Anderson, a professor at Brooklyn College. Something about a mutual friend. I told him I was in the middle if an emergency and couldn't talk, maybe some other time.

I needed the ghost. I must have tried to contact him fifty times, but I got no response. If he knew what had happened, I thought, he would have gotten over his tiff in a hurry. So he didn't know, and I couldn't find him in order to tell him.

As the hours wore on, I reached out to a couple of people I thought might be able to help. But mostly, I tortured myself with self-recrimination. *Why didn't you listen to the dream-guy's warning, bizarre as it was? Why didn't you keep a closer watch on her? Why didn't you take a place in Vermont or something and get Tomi off the bull's eye?*

*If there was even a chance she might have been in danger, why did you let her ignore it? Why didn't you stop her when she left the apartment?*

The answer, of course, was I'd had no choice. She was a cop. She wouldn't have run from a *credible* threat, much less one I had concocted in the nuttiest of nutty dreams.

And what *about* that dream? Was it just my subconscious boiling to the surface, picking over clues like the look Junior had given me before he bolted? What else could it be?

Then again, I talked to a ghost. I had no business making judgments about dreams or anything else.

I recalled a case, a few years back, that had ended badly . . . a woman who was abducted for reasons no one ever figured out. Her husband kept telling me the worst part was the waiting, and at the time I believed him.

But the worst part *wasn't* the waiting, at least not for me. It was the *hoping*. I would happily have waited an eternity if I knew for sure I'd see Tomi when it was over. Too bad I had no such guarantee.

I called the precinct twice, and in their kindness they talked to me for as long as I wanted to talk. Not just Podabinski, but the new captain there as well. But I knew they weren't getting anywhere. The trail was getting colder and colder.

More and more, I was convinced I wouldn't get Tomi back unless I *did* something. Maybe that was what Junior wanted, I didn't know. But I had to get my hands dirty.

At a quarter to ten, I called a guy who lived in Brooklyn. He called a guy, and that guy called another guy. I would never have gone that way if it weren't Tomi we were talking about.

But it was, so I did.

Pretty soon, I got a call back from the first guy. He gave me a location in East New York, a tire repair place. The person I wanted to see would be waiting for me in the back at a certain time that night.

I was advised to come alone, to come unarmed, and not to be late. The person who had agreed to see me didn't like being kept waiting. But I already knew that.

It made me feel better to know there were wheels in motion, even if they might not be taking me anywhere. If it were me who had been snatched and Tomi were free, she would have done everything in her power to find me. That's what I was doing—everything in my power.

The rest of the day dragged on mercilessly. I answered the

phone, but my mind wasn't on what I was saying. It was on that meeting in the tire repair place.

Finally, it got dark. I caught a train to Brooklyn that left me off maybe twelve blocks from my destination. It was a lousy neighborhood and a purple sky was leaking rain, but I didn't care. I walked the twelve blocks, studiously avoiding the stares I got from the lobbies of graffiti-covered apartment buildings.

The tire repair place was open. In fact, it never closed. On the corner, an old man dressed in a Yankee cap and a yellow rain slicker was sitting on a stool. He greeted me as I approached the place.

"You're expected," he rasped. "Lucky you."

"Lucky me," I echoed.

Inside the door, there was a big guy behind the counter. He had a sullen look and a sizable dent in the side of his skull.

"Too bad," he said, low and slow.

"What is?" I asked.

"My name's Blodgett," he told me. "As in Latik Blodgett."

It sounded familiar. I recalled a crack den in Bed-Stuy, a bust, a perp who promised he'd kill me when he got out. Big kid . . . maybe three, four years earlier . . .

"You got out pretty quick," I said.

"Latik was my *brothah*," he growled, his eyes fixed on me now. They were hard and angry. "He got himself killed in prison. And *you* the bitch that put him there."

"So if I weren't seeing Dee . . . "

"We'd have us a conversation, you and me." But I *was*

seeing Dee, so instead of "conversing" he tamped down his anger. Then he gestured for me to circumvent the counter and go through a doorway.

I went through and found myself in a garage full of tires. They were arranged in stacks six or seven high, their rubbery stench almost overpowering in the enclosed space of the garage. Three guys were waiting for me there. Two of them were muscle. The third was a light-skinned black man with startling blue eyes and a black leather baseball jacket, left open to reveal a black silk shirt. He was sitting on a short stack of tires, a cigarette burning in his long, slender fingers.

You could tell his colors by the bandana hanging out of his jeans pocket. Also, by the elaborate tattoo over his heart, though that wasn't visible at the moment.

"Mistah Five-Oh," he said, though not without a certain warmth in his voice.

"Not anymore," I said.

"Mistah *Former* Five-Oh. What can I do for you?"

When Dee Garrett had started out he was lean and hungry. His ribs could have cut glass. That hunger was what put him on the top of Brooklyn's toughest gang.

Now he was known as Dee Gangsta, and he was looking stocky, almost pudgy, a visible roll hanging over his waist band beneath his black silk shirt. But that didn't make him any less deadly.

"Long time no see, my son."

"Yeah," I said, "a long time."

He looked at his watch, one of those expensive, diamond-studded jobs. "You got five minutes. After that I got to see some people, dig?"

I got to the point. "I'm looking for information on a guy named Junior. I don't know his real name. Runs a set in Manhattan. You know him?"

Dee smiled, showing me an eighteen-karat gold tooth. It replaced the one that had gotten knocked out in his initiation a dozen years earlier. "Yeah, Slick, I know him. What's your interest in Junior?"

"My girlfriend's been kidnapped. I think he had something to do with it."

Dee's smile faded. "Don't like no one messin' witcha ol' lady. I hear ya." He took a drag of his cigarette, then dropped it on the floor and crushed it with the sole of his shoe. "Truth is *we* got beef wit' Junior too. He been takin' over the streets one by one, and not just in Manhattan. And some of those streets is *our* streets. So we responded on one occasion or another, if you catch my meanin'."

I nodded. It wasn't the first time I'd heard of rival gangs going at each other for the sake of turf.

"But despite our . . . what you might call our *best efforts*," said Dee, flashing his gold tooth, "we didn't get very far. I don't know where Junior gets his boys, but they big an' mean and well-armed, and there seem to be an endless supply of 'em."

"Anybody else try to take him down?"

"*Everybody*," said Dee. He named a couple of rival gangs. "East side, west side, pretty much everybody been up in Junior's grill. Don't matter who they are, he rocks them. You could be the baddest set this side of Watts, he put you down like a dog wit' a case of rabies."

"Sounds like he's making a lot of enemies," I said.

"A *lot* of enemies," Dee agreed. "But that don't seem to faze him. An' maybe it shouldn't. He got better security than the freakin' president. Nobody can get close enough to even *think* about puttin' a cap in his ass."

Except me, I thought. I'd been close enough to smell him, for all the good it did. "So he's into . . . what? Drugs, guns, cars . . . ?"

"Little of everything," said Dee, "and then some. Course, you already know that or you wouldn'ta been tryin' to bust him."

"You heard?"

Dee grinned. "*Everybody* heard. But Junior too smart for that. If you got close to him, it was 'cause he *let* you."

"Because he let us," I repeated.

"What I said. Sometime he do that wit' us too. He toy wit' us. Then he go out an' expand his territory some more, and we left wit' our fingers up our butt." He grunted. "Funny thing is he could be expandin' faster. A lot faster. For some reason he just bidin' his time, takin' it slow. Like he got a new kinda game nobody else played yet."

"A new kind of game?" I said. "What do you mean?"

Dee shrugged. "Somethin'. And listen up — I ain't the only one who thinks so."

Interesting, I thought. But it didn't get me any closer to finding Tomi. "Anything else I should know?"

"Ever hear of Anton Drakos?"

I thought for a moment. "Sounds familiar," I decided, though I couldn't come up with the connection.

"Cat's a billionaire. Runs a company called DrakoTech on the New York freakin' Stock Exchange. And he on the boards of half a dozen other companies just as big."

Now I remembered where I had heard of Drakos. He had given big bucks to the mayor's re-election campaign. "What's he got to do with Junior?"

"Can't say for certain," Dee told me. "But about eight months ago, I get the word Drakos lookin' for information on my son Junior, and he willin' to pay mad money for it. In fact, he want to put some of my boys on his payroll. You know, be his eyes and ears."

"You wouldn't allow that," I said. Not when it might lead to dual allegiances. Dee's boys were loyal only to Dee, or they found themselves on the wrong end of a baseball bat.

"You know me," said Dee. "But not everybody run his ship the way I do, you dig? Drakos eventually find a set willin' to be his bitches. They still workin' for him, too, twenty four-seven and then some. Wouldn't be surprised if they turn up somethin' new on ol' Junior somewhere along the way. Somethin' that might help you find your ol' lady."

I nodded. "Thanks, Dee."

"You'll return the favor some day," he told me without a hint of doubt in his voice. "Nothin' free, my son."

Then he disappeared into an office off the side of the garage. My audience with Dee Gangsta was over.

So I had sold my soul, or at least a healthy piece of it, to the devil of East New York. It was all right. I would have done it many times over to get a lead on Tomi.

After I got home, I couldn't fall asleep. I was thinking too much about Tomi, about Junior, about Anton Drakos. So I got on the computer.

When I searched Drakos' name, I came up with a shit load of references, and I mean a *shit* load. The guy had his fingers in everything. One of the newsmagazines, *Time* I think, said he was one of the fifty richest men in the world, and had been that way long before he started his tech company.

I took a shot and left a message at the *News*. Then I drifted off.

Sometime after full light, I heard my cell phone ringing. *Tomi . . . !* I thought. Sprawling across my desk, I grabbed it and answered it. But it wasn't somebody with news about Tomi.

It was Gaetano.

"So tell me, Zeno," he said, his voice thick and hot like molten iron, "*what the hell did you think you were doing?*"

He was angry, that was clear enough. But I didn't know why. Worse, I didn't know what he was talking about. Then, as the haze of sleep cleared, I figured it out.

Gaetano ran the city's gang task force. He was the one who had approved our plan to bust Junior. And he had obviously gotten wind of my soiree with Dee Gangsta.

"I had to take a shot," I said, peering at the time on my phone. It was eight-fifteen in the morning.

"You're worried sick about Tomi," said Gaetano. "We all are. But going hat in hand to a federal case like Dee Garrett? You lose your freakin' mind or something?"

I was *this* close to telling him about Anton Drakos and his interest in Junior. But instinct told me to keep it to myself. Nothing Gaetano could do about Anton Drakos anyway.

"Bill—" I started to say.

"You leave the force," he seethed, "and you forget everything you ever knew about kidnap procedures. Like Rule Number One—let the experts do their jobs."

"No offense," I said, "but the experts aren't getting anywhere. And the longer it takes—"

"The less chance we'll find her in one piece. You think I don't know that? But she's been gone, what, twenty-four hours?"

"A day and a half," I said, correcting him. "They found her car thirty hours ago."

"A day and a half, then. But being stupid ain't gonna get us any closer to her. Some bright-eyed Fed hears you had a meet-and-greet with a major gangbanger and the department won't be able to do shit for you. You and your pal Dee will be stylin' the same orange pajamas."

I nodded, as if he could see me over the phone. "Thanks for looking out for me, Bill. But I can't just sit here. It's driving me up the wall."

"You *will* *sit there,*" said Gaetano, "and you will let the freakin' professionals work the case. That's what Tomi would tell you. Am I right?"

He didn't know Tomi like I did. "I hear ya," I said.

I accidentally dropped the phone. When I picked it up

again, I saw I had ended the call.

Sighing, I put the phone down next to my computer and sank back into my chair. Maybe Bill's right, I thought. If *he* found out I saw Dee Gangsta, Junior could have found out too.

I was just working out the implications of that thought when the phone rang again. Grabbing it, I pressed the little green button and said, "Sorry, Bill. Didn't mean to cut you off."

Silence for a moment. *"Sorry to disappoint you,"* said a smooth female voice, *"but it's not Bill."*

No longer half-asleep, I recognized the caller instantly. "Hey, Sally. Thanks for getting back to me."

*"No problem,"* she said. *"What's up?"*

Sally's tone was as neutral as neutral could get. No doubt, she was doing her best to keep it that way.

She and I had had a fling about six months before I met Tomi. Though Sally was the one who had broken it off, it was clear that she still had feelings for me. Truthfully, I still had feelings for her too, though I was never going to act on them.

Especially now.

I had called Sally because she was a reporter for the *News*, and a damned good one. She had her hooks in everything from the neighborhood bodegas to the mayor's office. The gangs weren't on her radar, so she probably wouldn't have known somebody like Junior from a teardrop tattoo. But a rich guy like Drakos was right in her wheelhouse.

"You know Anton Drakos?" I asked her.

She chuckled. *"Sure. He leaked a story to me just the other day."*

Fantastic, I thought. "I need to speak with him."

"*Really. Mind telling me why?*"

"I'd rather not."

First off, I didn't want to publicize my conference with Dee Gangsta. As Bill had said, the Feds would be all too interested in the minutes of that meeting. And Dee wouldn't appreciate the publicity. Our conversation had been strictly on the down-low—that was the deal. The last thing he'd want was to see it turn up on Page Six.

"Okay," said Sally. "*Then forget it.*"

I took the high road—like I had a choice. "It's a matter of life and death, and that's not just an expression."

A pause. "*Whose life?*"

I considered lying to her, but in the end I told the truth. "My girlfriend's. She's been kidnapped, and I think Drakos can shed some light on the situation."

"*Sounds juicy.*" I could see her talons coming out.

"Maybe so," I conceded. "But I've got to be careful. I can't do anything that would put Tomi in even worse trouble."

"*Tomi. That's her name?*"

I was sure Sally already *knew* her name, but I didn't call her on it. "Yes."

"*And you love her, right? You'd do anything for her?*" There was just the slightest hint of mockery in her voice.

I didn't like where this was going. "Look . . . she's got nothing to do with what happened with you and me."

"*And I should trust you . . . why? As I recall, you started seeing me before you broke off with your previous girlfriend. And you started seeing her before you broke off with the one before her.*"

"I made some mistakes," I conceded.

"You're the prince of mistakes, Zeno. In fact, you used to creep me out on a regular basis. Sometimes I couldn't believe I was still with you. Of course, there were those other times when I loved you so much I wouldn't have cared if you were Jack the Ripper."

I *definitely* didn't like where this was going.

"And then you were gone," she said, her voice lower and more subdued, "and there was no one left to love."

"You're the one who broke it off," I said as gently as I could, "remember?"

"Only because I wanted you to fight for me," said Sally. "I needed . . . wanted to know you would do that before I let myself fall for you the rest of the way. And you failed the test, Zeno. Miserably."

I didn't know that. But then, how could I? We hadn't spoken since the break-up. "I'm sorry, Sally. Really. But for better or worse, that's in the past. And what I called about—"

"Is in the present. I get it."

She didn't say anything for a while, and I knew better than to press my case. Sally was only quiet when she was thinking about being reasonable.

"I'll make a call," she said. "I can't tell you if it'll get you a meeting with Anton Drakos, but it might. That's the best I can do."

"I appreciate it," I told her.

"I'm sure. Just promise me one thing, okay?"

"What's that?"

"If this girlfriend of yours should buy the farm despite all our good intentions . . . call me. All right?"

I was surprised Sally would ask that, being the proud,

independent woman she was. But I heard myself say I would call her if Tomi "bought the farm."

Why not? I would have promised to date Godzilla if it got me closer to getting Tomi back.

When we hung up, I felt terrible. First, I'd been reminded of the way I treated women before I met Tomi, a way I had come to regret on an almost daily basis. Second, I had given Sally a reason *not* to call Anton Drakos—because if Tomi died, I had put Sally next in line. Not so smart of me, though I didn't see that I'd had a choice.

I was still cursing myself twenty minutes later when my phone rang. It was Sally again.

*"You're in luck,"* she told me. *"Anton's got a fifteen-minute hole in his schedule Thursday afternoon."*

It was Tuesday. By Thursday, Tomi might be dead.

"I need to speak with him tomorrow morning," I said.

Sally cursed beneath her breath. *"I knew this was going to happen. You know Anton Drakos doesn't make a habit of speaking with total strangers, don't you?"*

"Life or death," I reminded her.

*"You don't know Anton Drakos. He wouldn't move up the appointment if it were* my *life hanging in the balance."*

I didn't think she was just saying that. "All right," I said. "Thank you, Sally."

*"Remember our deal,"* she said. Then she ended the call.

Of course, *she* wouldn't have waited until Thursday to see Drakos. And neither would I.

Hell, I could barely wait till the following morning.

◆◆◆

When I reached the building in midtown that houses Drakos Enterprises, I realized I'd seen it a thousand times before. So have you. It's the big, black, shiny monolith with the rich-looking silver accents that stands a little higher than the buildings around it.

I guessed that Drakos, like other incredibly rich people, was a workaholic. So I showed up at his office around dawn, when every window on the eastern side of his building was burning with gold.

His lobby too was big, black and shiny with rich-looking silver accents, something out of a science fiction movie. A guard sat in a black kiosk in the center of it.

"Do you have an appointment?" he asked me.

"I do," I told him. "I'm here to see Mr. Drakos. Name's Zeno Aristos."

The guy considered me a little more closely. Dressed in cheap khakis and a windbreaker, I was sure I didn't look like any of Drakos's usual visitors. Still, the guard turned half away from me and called upstairs.

"I see," he said after a moment. Then he turned back to me and said, "Sorry, sir. Mr. Drakos's secretary says your appointment is for tomorrow. At three fifteen."

"That's a mistake," I said, lying through my teeth. "It's got to be."

The guard shrugged. "I'd like to help you, but that's what the lady said."

"Can you ask her again?"

I was hoping that Drakos's secretary would take pity on me and squeeze me in that morning—a long shot maybe, but I was determined to play it. The guard looked at me for a moment and saw the pain in my face, which wasn't an act. Then he sighed and moved his hand toward the phone.

It rang before he could pick it up, surprising both of us. When the guard finally answered it, he looked even more surprised. He smiled at me as he hung up.

"Must be your lucky day," he said. "Mr. Drakos wants to see you after all. I'll just need to see your driver's license."

I showed it to him. He nodded, then handed it back and pointed to the bank of elevators behind him. "Go to the the last set of doors. There'll be a guy there waiting for you."

I nodded and said, "Thanks." Then I made my way to the last set of elevator doors, my heels clacking on the marble floor. Sure enough, there was a guard waiting there for me, a tall, broad-shouldered guy who could have played tight end for the Jets.

Beside the elevator there was a small, tasteful sign about the scanner inside the elevator car. If I had a weapon, I was advised to go home and come back without it.

No problem. I hadn't carried a gun since the day I left the force. To tell you the truth, they made me nervous.

"This way," said the guard, pushing the button that opened the doors. As they parted, I saw the inside of the elevator. It contained a black lacquered side table with a selection of soft drinks in both cans and bottles.

I wanted to ask if we were going to be ordering lunch, but

I thought better of it. I had gotten lucky. I sure as hell wasn't going to push it.

The guard pushed another button, this one on the inside of the compartment, and the elevator doors closed. He was silent as we made the trip to the thirty-second floor. Straight up, no stops. When we got there, the guard pushed the button again and the doors opened.

"Have a pleasant day," he told me.

"You too," I said as I left the elevator.

I looked around. It wasn't as big as the downstairs lobby, but it was a lot cozier, a lot more old-school. It looked like some Ivy League college club with its wood-paneled walls, its overstuffed leather chairs, and its big oriental rug.

A woman smiled at me from behind an unassuming cherry wood desk. She looked like somebody's favorite aunt, with her twinkling blue eyes and her generous jar of exotic jelly beans, but I wouldn't have been surprised if she owned a couple of black belts and a permit for a bazooka.

She was guarding Anton Drakos, after all.

"Good morning," she said with a hint of a British accent. "Mister Drakos is expecting you." She gestured to the door behind her. "Please go in."

On the other side of the door was another guard, this one even taller and broader than the guy who had taken me up in the elevator.

There was also a huge bird cage that hung from the ceiling by a brass chain. The bird inside, which was pure white and at least two feet tall, looked as unwelcoming as a bird can look. It made a loud clicking sound as if it were challenging my right to be there.

"It's all right," Drakos told the guard.

Without a word, the guy left the room. That left just me, Drakos, and the cranky bird.

Anton Drakos had wavy brown hair, which he wore long, and a jutting goatee to match. His eyes were set deep beneath a broad forehead, his cheekbones high, his mouth what police sketch artists call full-lipped and expressive.

His suit, a double-breasted charcoal grey number, fit him like it was made from scratch by an expensive Italian tailor. His tie, a crimson as deep as blood, was knotted flawlessly at his throat, a stark contrast to the white of his starched shirt.

His cuff links were probably worth more than my car.

I'd seen snatches of Drakos before, on television and in the newspapers, but in person he looked a lot more imposing. Not bigger, just more charismatic or something.

Of course, the floor-to-ceiling view behind him might have had something to do with that. The skyline looked different thirty-two stories up. With that kind of backdrop, I could have looked imposing too.

Drakos came out from behind his desk and held out his hand. "Good to meet you," he said. His voice was deep, cultured. The best prep schools and all that.

I said, "Same here," though there was nothing at all the same about us.

Up close, I could see that he had a couple of thin, white scars under one eye, the kind you might find on a retired hockey player. Some guys with money like to brawl a little, show people they're not soft just because they're rich. But he didn't seem like the type to do that.

More likely, he had walked into a stack of money. He had so many they were probably hard to avoid.

"You're Greek," he observed. "Aristos, let's see . . . is that from Thessaly?"

"I couldn't tell you," I said. "My family wasn't big on geneology."

"Too bad," said Drakos. "My people come from Elis, on the Peloponnesus. We've been there a long time."

I pointed to the bird, just trying to make conversation for the time being. "Is he from that area too?"

"*She*," said Drakos. "And no, she isn't. Have you ever seen a white raven before?"

So *that* was what it was. "I didn't know there was such a thing."

"They're rare. This one—I call her Hermione—comes from Vancouver Island. There's a colony of them there the Canadian authorities are trying to nurture."

But if you have enough money, I reflected, you can buy *anything*. "Interesting."

"According to our people's mythology," said Drakos, "all ravens were white at one time. Then the sun-god Apollo fell in love with a woman named Coronis. Though she became pregnant by him, he was concerned that she might be unfaithful when he was away—and he was away a lot—so he left a raven to watch over her. As it turned out, Coronis betrayed his trust with a young man named Ischys. The raven dutifully reported this to Apollo, who promptly killed Coronis and Ischys. Then he turned the raven black for being the bearer of bad news."

The raven clicked again, even more furiously, as if she were protesting Apollo's treatment of her kind. Drakos chuckled.

Then he turned back to me. "You've heard the story, perhaps?"

I shook my head no. "Sorry. We weren't big on mythology either."

"Too bad in that regard as well, then. But you didn't come here to exchange pleasantries, did you?" He looked at me expectantly, his smile just this side of polite.

"In other words," I said, staying on that side myself, "cut to the chase."

He shrugged in his expensive Italian suit. "If you don't mind. Time, after all, is money."

That expression had always given me the creeps, and generally so had the people who used it. To me, time always seemed a *lot* more valuable than money.

But I didn't argue the point. "I have it on good authority that you're surveilling a guy named Junior." I watched for his reaction, but there wasn't any. "I don't need to know why. I just need to know where I can find him."

The smile thinned a little. "I don't know anyone named Junior, Mister Aristos. But, just for curiosity's sake . . . let's assume that I do, and that I'm surveilling him as you say. What's your interest in this person?"

"Someone close to me has been kidnapped," I said, "and I think Junior's behind it."

The smile vanished the rest of the way. "I see. In that case, I wish I could help you, I truly do. I've lost people close to me as well, and I know how heartbreaking it can be. And how excruciatingly difficult to get them back."

I didn't recall seeing anything in my computer search about his "losing" someone, so the process of retrieving that person must have been a quiet one. Maybe he had paid a ransom. Maybe he had taken care of the problem in another way.

Rich guys could do those things.

But I hadn't gotten a ransom note. I didn't even know for certain it was Junior who had taken Tomi. I had nothing, and I was seriously determined to change that.

"So you know what I'm going through," I said, "and how grateful I would be for any scrap of information, anything that might lead me in the right direction."

"I can imagine," Drakos said with what seemed like heartfelt sympathy. "But I have no such information."

"Because you've never heard of Junior."

He looked at me unflinchingly. "That's correct."

Dee had told me otherwise, and I believed Dee. So what was this guy trying to hide?

"Well," I said, "if you do hear anything, give me a call." I gave him an old business card from my moonlighting-as-a-house-painter days with my cell number scrawled across the top of it.

"I most certainly will," he said, though I didn't believe him for a second. "Good luck. Really."

"Thanks," I said.

The bird clicked, no doubt happy to see me go.

Drakos pressed an intercom button and informed the woman outside the door that our meeting was over, and I allowed myself to be escorted back to the elevator. All the way down to the lobby, I second-guessed myself.

But really, what else could I have done? Threatened the sonuvabitch? Sure, but that wouldn't have gotten me anywhere. Except maybe a holding cell, and the last thing I needed was to have my hands tied when Tomi needed me most.

I couldn't just go home after that.

Bryant Park, which was behind the New York Public Library, used to be full of drug dealers. Then the mayor—always thinking of tourist business—made it a priority for the cops to clean the place up. Now it was full of little restaurant tables, and so squeaky-clean you could bring your kids there.

At that hour of the morning, there weren't any kids. Just a couple of guys in dark suits enjoying the shade and the bird songs, reading the paper over a cup of coffee before they went to work.

I didn't want to see the headlines. I was too afraid there would be a "missing cop" story among them, or God forbid something worse. I didn't even want to think about it.

But I couldn't avoid the fact that it had been two and a half days since Tomi left the precinct house. Two and a half *days*. The odds of finding her were getting longer.

I dwelled on that observation for a while, making myself crazy. Then I called Missing Persons. They had no answers for me, but they told me not to give up hope. Tomi was a cop. If anybody could make it this long, it would be her.

As the sun climbed the sky, the guys in the suits left. It got hotter, muggier. Having had so little sleep the last few nights, I didn't object when I felt myself dozing off.

Maybe it'll clear my mind, I thought. Give me a chance to see this thing from some other point of view. Eventually, I fell asleep.

I must have, because I found myself back in East New York, in the tire repair place. I was sitting on a short stack of tires. And I wasn't alone.

There was someone sitting on the next stack, half in shadow. But I could see enough of him to know it was the guy with the beard, the one who had stood in my shower stall and warned me that Tomi and I were in danger.

I still didn't know who he was or why he was showing up in my dreams, but I sure as hell wasn't going to ignore him. Not after he had all but predicted Tomi's disappearance.

"You were right to warn us," I said, even though we hadn't heeded his warning. "My girlfriend's been kidnapped. Is she all right? How do I get her back?"

He didn't give me an answer—at least not the one I was looking for. "You spoke with Anton Drakos," he said.

"Yes," I said. "What about him?"

"He told you he didn't know the one you call Junior. He was lying when he said that."

"I had a feeling," I said.

"He was also lying when he said he knew nothing about your mate's disappearance."

"I had a feeling about that too." Something occurred to me. "Did he have something to do with the kidnapping?"

"No. But he knows something about it."

It made me angry to have my suspicions confirmed. "What can I do to make him talk?"

"Nothing. You have no power over him. But when he *does* talk—and he will do so, eventually—do not trust him, or *he* will gain power over *you*."

"Then who can I go to?" I begged the bearded guy. "I can't just sit here and do nothing. I have to—"

But all of a sudden I was back in Bryant Park, the sun blinding me in one eye, the birds singing up a storm. And the bearded guy was gone.

# CHAPTER FOUR

I spent the rest of the morning haunting the courts on West Fourth Street. A few days earlier, I had been on top of the world there, unbeatable. My biggest problem had been explaining to Tomi why I hadn't seen the headhunter.

I couldn't believe how much things had changed.

Unfortunately, there was no sign of Junior—not that I had expected any—or anyone with information that could lead me to him. And after I'd asked one question too many, the guys there began to treat me less like a handball player and more like a cop. One by one, they clammed up.

Starting to feel pathetic, I took the subway home. At Forty-second street, the conductor announced there was something on the tracks. It took a half hour for the transit guys to get the train moving again.

They never said what the obstruction was, which was fine with me. I wasn't on the job anymore. I didn't want to know.

Before I got to my stop, I got a text that Tomi's car was ready. Its window had been replaced by a body shop on Ditmars, a place whose owner liked cops.

"No charge," he told me when I picked up the Impala a half hour later.

I could see in his eyes that he felt bad for me. I felt bad for me too. But most of all, I felt bad for Tomi.

When I got home, I checked my mailbox. I found the usual—credit card bills, offers of more credit cards, offers to get me off the hook if I was in too deep with credit cards.

Also, a note.

It was mixed in with the rest of the mail, though I was sure the postman hadn't delivered it, in a business-size envelope addressed simply "Zeno." When I saw the envelope, my heart started pounding. I forced myself to tear off the end of it, then slipped out the note, which was written in black ink on a piece of white copy paper.

It was done in a precise hand, the kind that could easily have been identified by forensics, and therefore not the kind I would have expected from a kidnapper. But there it was. It told me to be at a certain corner in the Bronx at two in the morning, and it underlined how important it was that I show up alone.

I didn't know the neighborhood so I called someone who might—a guy I always saw at the Hunts Point courts who ran a carnival business in the Bronx. He told me there were six or seven small factories in the area around that corner. During the day it was a busy place, people coming and going, delivery vehicles, even an old man with a sandwich truck. At night, it was the dark side of the moon.

"You want me to go with you?" the carnival guy asked, not knowing what it was about.

"No, thanks," I told him.

Like Gaetano, I had always advised people dealing with kidnappers not to try and go it on their own. I told them to lean on the professionals, the guys who dealt with scum for a living.

But *I* was one of the professionals, or had been until recently, and I knew that cops were as capable of screwing up as anybody else. Otherwise, Junior would have been behind bars already.

I couldn't afford a screw-up—not when we were talking about Tomi's life. So I didn't call the precinct. I decided to show up alone in the Bronx just as the kidnapper told me to.

Only one problem.

If the kidnapper smoked me there in the middle of the night, nobody would know about the note or what had happened, and Tomi would be as lost as she was before. So about one o'clock in the morning, as I was leaving the house, I called Bernie and told him what was going on. I finished by saying, "I'm leaving the note on the kitchen table."

He started yelling at me, trying to talk me out of doing what I was doing. Naturally. But I hung up.

Then I drove over the Triboro to the Bronx, worked my way east through the streets, and homed in on the corner identified by the kidnappers. En route, I tried to anticipate what I would find when I got there.

There had been no discussion of money in the note, so that clearly wasn't part of the equation. It left only one other motive, the one I had suspected all along. Junior (or somebody else) was trying to get to me through Tomi, trying to punish me for what I had done.

Well, I thought, let's get it over with.

I didn't think he would kill me. He could have done that any time he wanted, in a dozen different ways. But whatever he had in mind wouldn't be pleasant.

As I approached the corner mentioned in the note, I saw that the carnival guy was on the money. Mostly factories, all right. Also a couple of warehouses, and a big lot full of used cars, its metal fences topped with spirals of vicious-looking razor wire.

It was dark there, most of the streetlights out of order, the roads full of small, skittering shadows too small to be cats and too big to be cockroaches. What few trees grew on the sidewalks looked half-dead, wooden skeletons crowned with wreaths of stunted leaves. The air smelled sour and the only light came from the full moon, which looked like a fresh scrape on a kid's knee.

It was the kind of place people avoided, no matter who they were or thought they were. And yet, there I was. I parked, turned off the engine, and checked my watch.

One-fifty. I was ten minutes early.

As a cop, I'd spent hours on stakeouts waiting for something to happen. Just waiting. Somehow, those ten minutes in the Bronx went even slower. I had to force myself to breathe, too on edge to even consider turning on the radio.

There was one upside to all of this, I told myself. If we got Tomi back, she wouldn't be mad anymore about my not seeing the headhunter. How could she be?

At one-fifty eight I got out of the car, closed the door, and went to stand on the corner where the kidnappers could see me. It was windy. Some weather on its way, I thought.

Candy wrappers, crumpled napkins, and printed hand-outs skidded across the street, paused as if surprised to see me, and then skidded on. I glanced one way and the other, wondering what direction the kidnappers would come from. They hadn't been accommodating enough to let me know in advance.

There would be more than one of them, though. And they'd have guns. And they'd stick them in inconvenient places like my ears and my mouth, just to show me they meant business.

My watch beeped. It was two o'clock.

But there was no one around, and no sign that the situation would change anytime soon. The only sounds were so vague and indistinct that they seemed to come from another world. Every so often I heard what I thought was a car engine, but was more likely the wind.

Any moment now, I thought, a car's going to pull up and Junior's boys are going to pile out. Any moment.

I looked at my watch again. Four minutes after two. The kidnappers were late.

But I couldn't leave. They would know that. So, really, they didn't have to be in a hurry. They could take their time.

Eight minutes after. Ten minutes. Fifteen. Still no sign of anyone. Just those small, quick dark things hugging the curbs, looking for garbage.

Just like me.

Somewhere far away an ambulance siren wailed into the night. I felt it more than usual. Tomi . . .

At half past two, I began to wonder if I'd screwed up somehow. The note had said two o'clock, hadn't it? And this corner? I couldn't have made a mistake about something like that. Not with Tomi's life riding on my getting it right.

Two-forty. Two-fifty. Three o'clock.

At four minutes after three, I finally spotted a pair of headlights. A car was approaching. I felt my heart bang in my chest.

Be cool, I thought. Nothing stupid.

Then I saw the bubble gum machine on the car's roof, and I realized . . . it was a *patrol car*.

For a single, wild moment, I considered the possibility that Junior had gotten his hands on a cop car. But what for? He already had me where he wanted me.

The officer on the shotgun side, who looked every bit like a real cop, trained his flashlight on me. I could see he had a broad, freckled face, even with the light shining in my eyes.

"Waiting for someone?" he asked.

"I was," I said. "I don't think they're showing up."

The cops stopped the car and got out. Obviously, they weren't content with my answer.

"I need to see some identification," said the driver, a tall, darkly complected guy with a five o'clock shadow. The other guy stood back, still keeping an eye on me with his flashlight.

I opened my wallet and showed the tall guy my driver's license. He held it up to the light, read it, then nodded. "You got a friend named Bernie O'Neill?" he asked.

I would have laughed if the stakes hadn't been so high.

"What did he do, break my door down?"

"I don't know about that," said the cop with the freckles, "but we've got orders to send you home."

I nodded. "I was going anyway."

It was the truth. For whatever reason, the kidnappers had decided not to show up. It wasn't a good thing. I'd had a chance to open a line of communication, to find out why they took Tomi and what I needed to do to get her back.

And I wasn't sure I would ever get that chance again.

"You know," said Bernie, sitting at my kitchen table, "I remember now why I retired. Because I had a partner who was capable of crap like this."

He was angry. I didn't blame him. "What would *you* have done?"

"Called the cops. Let the professionals earn their paychecks." He read the note again, maybe for the hundredth time. "Or at least called your buddies for backup."

I didn't know what made him madder—that I'd gambled my life or that I hadn't gambled *his* as well. "I know," I said. "It's just that I couldn't take a chance on anyone's screwing up."

"And *you* couldn't have screwed up?" he demanded. "Seems to me you've screwed up plenty."

"But at least it would be on *me*. Tell me you get that."

"What I get," he said, "is that you're a sonuvabitch who thinks he's smarter than anybody else."

"Come on," I said, "that's—"

Bernie shot me a look, stopping me in my tracks.

"Okay," I conceded, "that was my m.o., I'll give you that. But I've changed, Bern."

And I had, ever since I started partnering with Tomi. She always seemed to be a half step ahead of me.

"So now what?" he asked. "You gonna let the cops handle it? For Tomi's sake?"

I sighed. "I don't know. I'll think about it."

"Think fast," Bernie told me. "Those guys are gonna contact you again. You got to know what you're doing."

He said the last part in a kinder voice. He knew how much Tomi meant to me.

Bernie jotted down a number on the notepad I kept in the kitchen. "That's my pal Joe the Locksmith," he told me. "He'll see to it you get a new door this afternoon."

I glanced at the one that hung askew at the entrance to my apartment. "To replace the door you broke getting in?"

"What are friends for?" said Bernie.

After he left, I played back the messages on my cell. As it turned out, the only caller was that guy Anderson who had left a message once before. Again, he mentioned a mutual friend. He sounded like an old guy, though I hadn't really noticed it before, so I made a note on a pad to call him back.

Then I went to bed. Sometime during the three hours I slept, I had another dream about the bearded guy. It was starting to be a regular thing, whenever I shut my eyes.

This time he was standing on a shelf of rock overlooking a deep valley, wearing a shapeless, grey robe. The valley was brimming over with mist, so it was hard to see the bottom of it, but something was moving down there.

It looked like an immense snake, slimy and metallic, stretching through the valley as far as the eye could see in either direction. Then the bearded guy, half-concealed by the mists himself, turned back to me, pointed a finger at the valley, and said, "Look."

Suddenly I could see that it wasn't a snake down there, but an army on the march. There were thousands of soldiers, both men and women, all of them tall and broad-shouldered and jacked like champion bodybuilders. They wore helmets and breastplates and shin guards, all made of the same dark-brown metal. An endless, unbroken procession of armored muscle, looking like it was headed for some bloody, primitive free-for-all.

I found myself pitying their enemy.

"Whose ass are they going to kick?" I asked the bearded guy.

He looked at me as if I were a child. "They are not going *to* a battle. They are coming *from* one. And much to their horror, they have lost."

Just then I got a creepy feeling about the parade of armored body-builders. I'm not sure where it came from—maybe the way they looked down as they marched, or the slow, spiritless pace at which they moved their feet. They just seemed tired of living.

"Who beat them?" I asked.

Immediately, I regretted the question. Something inside me didn't want to hear the answer.

"Don't you know?" asked the bearded guy.

Before I could answer, I woke up. I had thrown off my covers and still managed to drench my bed sheets in sweat.

As I lay there, wondering about the strange, armored warriors, my cell went off. It was Bernie's friend Joe the Locksmith. He was going to bring me a new door, he said, "at cost."

I thanked him. Then I called the precinct to see if there was any new information about Tomi. There wasn't. I hadn't expected any, but the news—or lack of it—made my throat tighten all the same.

Finally, I called Anderson. He picked up immediately. I muttered an apology for not returning his call sooner, but I'd had an emergency on my hands. He told me not to worry about it.

*"The reason I called,"* he said, *"is I've got something I want to show you."*

I waited for him to elaborate, but he didn't. "What kind of something?" I asked.

*"I'd prefer just to show it to you."*

"And this has to do with our mutual friend?"

*"Yes. Where do you live?"*

I smiled to myself. My gut was telling me not to let this go any further, but I had to admit that I was curious. Also, I had to give the old guy credit for keeping me on the hook.

"In Astoria," I told him.

*"I'm in New Hyde Park,"* he said. *"That's not far. Just over the city line."*

I knew where New Hyde Park was. I'd dated a woman who

lived there—a married woman. It was the kind of thing I didn't think twice about at the time.

"Look," said Anderson, probably thinking he was letting his fish slip the hook, "*I'm a professor at Brooklyn College. Part-time now, but still a professor. You can look me up on the website.*"

"Okay. And how will I know it's you?" I asked.

Silence. Apparently, he hadn't thought the idea through that far.

"*Couldn't you just come over?*" he asked at last. "*You won't regret it. Really.*"

"And you're not going to tell me why?"

"*I'd rather not.*" He wasn't giving in.

Against my better judgment, I said, "All right."

It wasn't so terrible. I'd be making an old guy happy. And maybe the karma, if there was such a thing, would help me get Tomi back.

In fact, there *was* a Professor Anderson on the Brooklyn College website. He taught a class on Shakespeare that met twice a week in Boylan Hall. No picture of him, though.

The address in New Hyde Park that Anderson had given me belonged to a small, well-kept Tudor in the middle of a quiet residential block. I got there about noon, parked in front, and rang the doorbell.

No answer. I rang it again. Same result.

I'd already been stood up that morning. It would have been ridiculous to get stood up a second time.

There was a small glass aperture in the front door. I peered through it into the guy's living room. It was illuminated by a couple of standing lamps posted on either side of an overstuffed couch, so I was able to see clearly that the room was empty.

But I had hardly reached that conclusion when a shadowy figure moved in the hallway beyond. As the figure emerged into the light, it became a tall, white-haired man with a stiff, shuffling gait.

He was seventy-five or eighty, I guessed, with a triangular face and watery blue eyes sunken beneath snowy brows. His skin, especially that of his nose, was shot through with thin red veins. Even though it was almost ninety degrees out, he wore corduroy pants and a green-and-yellow flannel shirt.

"I'm coming," he called, his voice muted by the closed door. But it was clearly the same voice I had heard over the phone, thin and strained with age.

I stood back from the door, so when he looked through the window he wouldn't be nose to nose with me. After all, he wasn't a young man. I didn't want him jumping out of his skin.

But when he saw me through the glass, his eyes opened wide anyway. I heard him say, "Christ Almighty, it *is* you!"

With what seemed like a lot more urgency, the guy unlocked the door and pulled it open. Then he stuck out his hand.

"Bob Anderson," he said, smiling genially.

I grasped his hand, which still had enough strength for a firm grip. "Zeno Aristos."

He shook his head and muttered, "I can't believe it." Then he stepped aside and said, "Please, come in."

I did as he asked.

Despite the air conditioning, his place had a mustiness born of windows that hadn't been opened for a long time and fabrics that had absorbed too much DNA over the years. Anderson directed me to a generous armchair with floral-print upholstery. I sat down.

He sat too, on the couch, which stood opposite the chair. He couldn't seem to stop staring at me.

"It's really amazing to see you," said Anderson.

I smiled politely. "You told me over the phone that you had something to show me. Something to do with our mutual friend."

He nodded, frowning deeply. "I'm afraid I lied."

At first, I thought I had heard him wrong—until I saw the shame in his eyes. "You lied?"

"About the friend," said the professor. "I was afraid you wouldn't return my call. I'm sorry. Really."

I didn't like being lied to. Did anyone? "What's this about?"

"If you give me a second," he said, jerking a thumb over his shoulder, "I can show you."

I had half a mind to walk out. But, hell, I had already gone to the trouble of driving out there. "Sure," I said, "go ahead."

"Thanks," he said. Then he disappeared into the hallway.

When he came back he was holding a black and white photograph, eight and a half-by-eleven size. He offered it to me, then took a step back as if I might hit him when I saw what was in the photo.

I studied it. It showed me a couple of guys in white fencing uniforms, swords in hand, in what looked like a gymnasium.

They were smiling for the photographer. One seemed to be Anderson at the age of twenty-five or so. He was thinner and even taller in those days, with thick blond hair and a broad smile.

But the guy with him was the one who really got my attention. Because as far as I could tell, he was . . .

*Me.*

There was no doubt about it, no room for interpretation. I looked up at the old guy, wondering why he had edited my face onto someone else's body. I mean, it was a damned good job—I looked like I was really there. But of course, that was impossible.

The people in the picture had to have posed for it fifty years earlier.

"What *is* this?" I asked, caught between being curious and being more than a little annoyed.

Mind you, I was still miffed at having been deceived. Now, it seemed, the deception was deepening.

The professor smiled a sad smile. "It's me," he said, "back when I was in graduate school at NYU. And you, of course. Me and you."

I looked into those watery blue eyes, wondering what Anderson's game was. He didn't strike me as being senile, though I was certainly no expert in that area. No, I decided, he had an angle. I just couldn't figure out what it was.

"I saw you on the internet," he said, "on my friend's website. She's a history professor. Likes to go around town and take pictures of bizarre events. She got one at the helicopter crash."

"And I was in it."

"Right."

"But how did you know who I was? Or how to find me?"

"My friend doesn't just take pictures—she researches them. Apparently, one of the police officers on the scene referred to you as Aristos. She has a friend in the department who was able to take the last name and give her the rest of it."

"And my number's listed," I said, "so the rest was easy." So much for working undercover.

"When I saw you in that picture . . ." Anderson shook his head. "I know it seems impossible, to me no less than to you. But there it is."

I looked at the photo again. "You're saying we went to graduate school together. Maybe half a century ago."

"Either that," he said, "or you're a dead ringer for my friend Nikolas. And I mean a *dead* ringer."

It was more than a passing resemblance, all right. But how could somebody back then look so much like *me*?

"And you didn't doctor the photo?" I asked.

He shook his head. "Scout's honor."

I was still convinced he was working a con of some kind. Then I noticed there was someone else in the background, standing behind us in the gym. And as unlikely as it seemed, *he* looked familiar too.

I pointed to the figure in the background. "Who's that?"

The professor took the photo from me and peered at it. "That's . . . um, Alex. Yeah, Alex. His last name was . . ." He scrunched up his face in an effort to remember. "Dade? Kade?"

Suddenly, his eyes lit up and he lifted a professorial forefinger. "Drake! Alexander Drake!"

"Who was he?" I asked.

Anderson shrugged. "Another grad student. He was a year behind us, maybe two. I didn't know him too well. Don't think you did either."

I heard a clock ticking somewhere, though I didn't see one in the room. "Do you have a magnifying glass?"

The professor said he did. He left the picture in my hands, went into the back of the house again, and made sounds that suggested he was fumbling around in a drawer. Then he came out with what I had asked for.

I used the glass to magnify the image of Alexander Drake. It didn't help much. The background of the photo just wasn't as sharp as the foreground, magnified or otherwise.

But from what I could see, Drake looked a lot like Anton Drakos.

"What is it?" asked Anderson.

I told him, and watched his brow wrinkle. "You know who Drakos is?"

He said he did. "I've got some stock in Drakos Tech. But I've never paid much attention to what Drakos himself looks like, so I can't say if that fellow in the picture resembles him."

But *I* could. After all, I had seen the bastard just the day before.

My head was starting to hurt pretty good. It seemed unlikely that the professor would know of my meeting with Drakos—especially since he had begun calling before Dee Gangsta ever mentioned Drakos's name to me.

So why were Drakos and I in that picture together?

"It's real," said Anderson. "I know it seems nuts, but it's real. That fellow in the fencing den was my best friend, and he looked just like you."

"What happened to him?" I asked.

The professor shook his head. "We drifted apart about the time we turned thirty-five or so. He took a job in California and that was the last I saw of him." He smiled apologetically. "Until now."

It occurred to me that it would have been harder to doctor several pictures than to doctor just one. And if Anderson had been so close with the guy . . .

"You have any other pictures of your friend?" I asked.

The professor thought for a moment, then nodded. "It might take me a minute to find them, though. You want some soda? I've got ginger ale, seltzer . . . "

I shook my head. "No, thanks. I'm good."

For a third time, Anderson disappeared. He stayed out of sight for a good five minutes. Finally I heard a cry of triumph, and he came out with another photo in his hand.

This time, there were five people in the picture—Anderson, me, a couple of guys I didn't recognize, and a girl. We were standing around a headstone in what looked like a graveyard, though the background was even harder to make out than it was in the other photo.

Each of us had a live flashlight in hand. Each of us was smiling, though the smiles had edges to them. And each of us was dressed pretty nicely, as if we had just come from a party.

"We were looking for ghosts," Anderson explained. "Not really, of course. We'd had a couple of drinks and we were just having fun. And I had the hots for the girl, so I was trying to spook her a bit in the hope she would jump into my arms."

I tried to read the name on the headstone, which was illuminated by a couple of the flashlight beams. It looked like *John Theodorou*. I couldn't make out the dates.

"Where was this?" I asked the professor.

"A town in New Jersey," he said, "name of Iraklion. Maybe twenty miles from the George Washington Bridge."

There was something about the name "Iraklion" that struck a chord. As if I had been there before. Maybe more than once.

That's stupid, I thought, frowning at the graveyard photo. It can't be me in this picture. It's *impossible*. Yet the more I stared at the headstone and the people around it, the less impossible it seemed.

"I need to see this place for myself," I said.

"I understand," said Anderson. "Sure." And then, "Mind if I tag along?"

"To New Jersey?" I asked.

"Well . . . yeah."

My first impulse was to say no. The last thing I needed was a sidekick, much less an elderly one. Then I figured, What the hell. Maybe Anderson would shed some light on the mystery of how I could have been alive fifty years ago.

If he hadn't been lying about the whole thing from the start.

# CHAPTER FIVE

Iraklion was about thirty-five miles from New Hyde Park. Anderson made some sandwiches with what he had in the fridge and we headed out.

Neither the Expressway nor the approach to the Holland Tunnel was as crowded as I had expected. When we came out on the Jersey side of the tunnel, the professor insisted that we pull into one of the gas stations that lined the street and fuel up.

"A gallon is thirty cents cheaper in Jersey," he pointed out.

He was right, of course. And I was down to an eighth of a tank. It wouldn't have done Tomi any good for us to run out of gas on 78W.

Halfway to Iraklion, Anderson broke out a chicken salad on whole wheat. "You want one?" he asked.

I said I wasn't hungry.

"I used to eat two meals a day," he said. "Breakfast and dinner. That was it. Now I have to graze all day or my stomach acts up on me."

I nodded just to be polite. But really, I had more on my mind than the old guy's eating habits.

"My wife was a great cook," he added. "Her meatloaf was to die for. I mean it." He made a soft clucking sound. "She passed a couple of years ago. Breast cancer."

I glanced at him. "Sorry to hear it."

"Women on Long Island have one of the highest rates of breast cancer in the world. They say it's from all the pesticides we use. Our lawns, our golf courses . . . they're nice and green. And our women are dying."

More than ever, I needed to find Tomi. "It's a shame," I said.

Anderson pointed to the GPS device suctioned onto my windshield. "You like this thing?"

I shrugged. "It helps me avoid arguments."

He smiled. "How so?"

"When we get lost, my girlfriend insists I ask for directions. I don't *like* asking for directions."

Anderson chuckled. "Who does?" Finished with the sandwich, he took out a paper napkin and wiped his mouth. "What's she like, your girlfriend?"

For all I knew, she too had been in the picture of the helicopter crash. But I didn't say so. "She's great." I was careful to use the present tense because I couldn't stand the thought of the alternative.

"A good woman is hard to find," said the professor. Then he fell silent for a while. Almost all the way to Iraklion, in fact.

The cemetery was just a mile or so off the highway. It didn't look any different than it had in the photograph. Some stones, some grass, some shrubs. But then, graveyards don't change much, do they? They just get more crowded.

The property stretched from a gravel parking lot all the way up a gentle, green slope. At the far end, there was a line of trees. And everywhere between, there were headstones.

We couldn't drive between them. There was no road, and even if there had been there wasn't a car narrow enough. So I turned the engine off.

"The stone in the picture," I said, thinking it was as good a starting place as any. "Where would we find it?"

"I'll show you," said Anderson.

As we got out of the car, I noticed that the temperature had dropped. There was a cool breeze coming from behind us. Turning, I saw clouds starting to pile up on the horizon, some light and some dark.

"Looks like a storm," said Anderson.

I nodded. It happened a lot in the summer time.

"Follow me," said the professor.

The stone in the picture was farther back by the trees. Anderson headed right for it. Apparently time hadn't dimmed his memory, at least not when it came to this.

As I pursued my guide, making my way among the dead people, I got an idea. *Ghost?* I thought hopefully.

It was worth a try, wasn't it? I was in a cemetery, and ghosts—if all those horror movies had it right—liked to hang around such places. Hell, if Anderson's photo was on the level, maybe this was where I had hooked up with the ghost in the first place. Maybe I had met him in some past life and he had rejoined me in this one.

And never told me about the other one? Yeah, that made

lots of sense. Even horror movies had to be believable on *some* level.

Anyway, the ghost didn't respond. He still wasn't talking to me. Hell, as far as I knew, he would never talk to me again.

"It's over here," said Anderson.

He pointed, and I followed the gesture to a headstone. I knelt in front of it, shaded my eyes against the light, and checked it out. Sure enough, the name *John Theodorou* was etched into its surface.

The same name I had seen in the professor's photo. So the stone, at least, was real. In the distance, thunder grumbled a little.

Anderson looked back at the clouds and frowned. "We may regret not having brought umbrellas with us."

I stood up and scanned the stones around us. If they had something to say, some secret they might have shared, they kept it to themselves. And I didn't know where to look for it.

So I walked around a little and read the names on the other stones. Hell, we had come all that way. Why *wouldn't* I walk around?

It wasn't until after I was standing at the limits of the graveyard, close to the woods, that I realized there were stones among the trees as well. They seemed smaller and more crudely made, but they were definitely headstones.

"Ever see these?" I asked Anderson, approaching them to get a better look.

"I have," he told me, following me up the slope. "So have you. We used to talk about them."

"And what did we say?" I asked, knowing all the while how absurd it sounded.

"That they were probably the remnants of an older cemetery, parts of which may have been plowed under to make this one."

"Doesn't seem right," I observed, looking for poison ivy as I made my way into the woods.

They were cool, dark, a relief after the heat of the day. Sweet-smelling, too. Maybe a little too sweet for my taste.

Unlike the stones we had left in the sunlight, these were worn down and, in some cases, tilted a little to one side or the other. The names on them were hard to make out. I caught a number on one that looked like 1789, but it could as easily have been 1889.

As I was trying to figure out which it was, I heard some more thunder. It was a little louder and a little closer than before, but it wasn't so close that we had to worry about it. We would be in the car long before the rain came, if it came at all.

"You see the ones up there?" asked the professor, who had followed me into the woods.

"Where?" I asked, scanning the spaces between the trees until I found them.

As it turned out, there were many more old headstones than the few I had already inspected. Dozens of them, stretching way back deep into the woods.

I walked that way and Anderson followed, though he moved more slowly and a lot more cautiously. The last thing he would want to do was trip on a root and crack an ankle. At his age, an injury like that would take a long time to heal.

Tomi had said again and again that I'd make a terrible old person because I didn't have the sense to know my limitations. I never disagreed with her. Discretion wasn't my strong point.

And just then I cared even less what happened to me. All I wanted was to see her again.

"Careful," said the professor, as if he had been channeling Tomi. He pointed to the ground in front of me.

I looked down and saw something bright among the shadows, shivering in and out of existence. Then I realized what the bright thing was: a slice of sunlight reflected in water.

And not just a *little* water. Peering through the woods to my right and left, I saw that I was standing in front of a creek. Or maybe a river.

Having grown up in the city, I had never really understood the difference between the two. I figured a river was bigger, but where were you supposed to draw the line? How big did a creek have to get before it wasn't just a creek anymore?

Anyway, the water was moving. I could hear it gurgling.

"I know," said Anderson. "I was surprised too the first time I saw it. I mean, you don't normally find a graveyard straddling a river."

Peering into the forest, I could see there *were* graves on the other side. "I guess not."

He chuckled. "Y'know, you said the same thing, pretty much, the first time we were here. But you got comfortable with the idea soon enough."

I glanced at him. "What do you mean?"

"You used to come down to this part of the cemetery and

vanish for a while. The rest of us would decide to leave and we'd call you, and you wouldn't answer. Finally, we'd go looking for you. Around here is where we would always find you."

More thunder, a bit louder than before. The professor didn't seem to like the sound of it. "If it's all right with you, I'll wait in the car."

"Be my guest," I said.

I turned back to the river and the headstones beyond it. There was something about them that made me want to get a closer look at them, something stronger than mere curiosity. As if they were going to help me in some way.

What the hell, I thought.

I rolled up my jeans to the knees and waded into the water. It wasn't deep at all, maybe a foot at most, but it was colder than I thought. You wouldn't think it would be that cold in the middle of the summer, but it was.

Off to my left, something moved—something big and dark. Thinking it was an animal, I whirled in that direction. But there was nothing there.

Funny, I thought. I could have sworn I had seen something, if only in the corner of my eye.

I moved on. The water made cooing noises as it slid by me, freezing my skin. Then I reached the other side and took a step up onto solid ground.

That was when the mist closed in.

I didn't get it. It was cool in the woods, but not so cool that I should have been surrounded by water vapor all of a sudden.

And I don't mean a *little* water vapor, the kind you get when there's a sudden downpour on hot summer asphalt and the water starts to lift in little white twists. Not like that at all.

I'm talking thick, heavy blankets of mist, so thick and heavy you can barely see through them.

I looked back to see if the mists had settled over the river, because when I was wading through the water I hadn't seen even a hint of them. But it was no longer possible to see the river. Like everything else, it was obscured by the mists.

"Professor Anderson?" I called, thinking he might not have reached the car yet.

No answer. No sound at all, in fact, except for that of my own breathing.

"This is ridiculous," I muttered to myself.

Then I saw someone standing there in the mist. This time, I was sure of it.

"Someone there?" I asked. It was a stupid thing to say, but really, what else *could* I have said?

"I am here," came the response.

It sent shivers up my spine. First off, normal people use contractions. Second, normal people don't hang out in cemeteries.

"You all right?" I asked.

"The question," said the man in the mist, taking a step toward me, "is whether *you* are all right."

Now I was *really* creeped out.

I was getting ready to hit the guy if he came any closer. Then I noticed that he had a beard, and something clicked in my head, and I realized that I had heard his voice before—

In my dreams.

"You," I said. The guy in my shower stall. And in Dee Gangsta's tire store. The one who had warned me that Tomi was in danger.

It was impossible. Unless . . . this was a dream as well.

It would have explained a lot. The way the mists had surrounded me . . . stuff like that doesn't happen in real life.

But if it *was* a dream, when had it started? When I went to see Anderson? When I drove out to Jersey? Exactly *when* had I fallen asleep?

And if I was dreaming . . . how could I be aware of it? Didn't that violate the rules of dreams, even weird dreams like the ones I'd been having for the last few days?

"Do you know me?" asked the bearded guy.

I nodded. "You're the one who warned me about my girlfriend, and told me not to trust Anton Drakos."

"Yes," he confirmed. "I said those things."

"I still need your help," I told him. "I—"

"You wish to know by whom she was abducted," he said even before I could get the question out. "You will have your answer before long. But first, I must show you something."

When he turned away from me, I became afraid that I would lose him. So as soon as he moved, I moved too.

"Where are we going?" I asked, unable to see anything but him in the mist.

"Not far," he said, leading the way.

I stayed with him. After a while, it occurred to me that the ground was rising beneath my feet. We were going up, if only a little at a time. Maybe ten minutes went by.

"Not far?" I asked.

"Not far at all," he said without a hint of irony in his voice.

But another ten minutes went by, or maybe it was twenty, before he stopped walking. I moved up until I was right next to him, but if there was something in front of us I couldn't see it.

"There," said the bearded guy, and pointed down.

I followed his gesture and realized that we were standing on a shelf of rock overlooking a valley. Because of the mist, it was hard to see too far down. But there was something dark and sinuous that looked like it might be sliding along the bottom.

Suddenly, I got the feeling that I had been in this place before. Then I realized . . . it was just that morning, in the dream I'd had after I came home empty-handed from the Bronx.

I turned to the bearded guy and I could see, now that I was looking for it, that he was wearing a robe. As far as I could tell, it was grey.

Great, I thought, now I'm re-running my dreams like old TV shows. How crazy does *that* make me?

But it didn't *feel* like a dream. It felt real, as real as anything I had ever felt in my life.

"Look," said the bearded guy, the same way he had said it in my dream. I looked down into the valley again, and I could see the dark and sinuous thing was an army. The same one I had seen before, made up of those bodybuilders in dark-brown armor.

This time, I didn't ask whose ass they were going to kick. I already knew that someone had kicked *their* ass.

"They are the Bronze Men," said the bearded guy. "Made by Zeus in ages past."

I turned to him. "Zeus . . . ?"

Suddenly, I felt a hand clamp down on my arm and pull at me—pull *hard*. Caught off-balance, I pitched sideways. But I didn't fall because the grip around my arm held me up.

Even through the mist, I could see the bearded guy's eyes open wide with something like horror. He screamed a desperate, high-pitched scream: "Noooo!"

"Come on!" someone urged me in a smooth, deep voice. "While you still can!" The pulling became more insistent. "Come on, damn it! Do you want to stay here *forever*?"

I dug my heels in and tried to jerk my arm loose. And I would have, if I hadn't felt the fiery insult of a knife burying itself in my back.

"God*damn!*" I groaned between clenched teeth, writhing in the grip of the stiff, unyielding metal. I tried to reach around and grab the handle of the knife, but that only made it hurt more.

"He's mine!" I heard the bearded guy shriek.

Then I heard a *crack*, like a miniature thunderbolt, and the shrieking was over. I gathered that the newcomer, whoever he was, had put the bearded guy in dreamland.

A different face loomed up at me out of the mist. Red hair, red chin stubble, movie-star good looks. Something in his eyes made me want to trust him and not trust him at the same time.

"Stand still," he said. "I'll get the knife out."

"Then do it," I grunted.

I couldn't wait. It was like having a soldering iron stuck between my shoulder blades.

A moment later, I felt it go out of me. The fire was still there, but at least I could breathe again.

"You all right?" asked my new pal.

I nodded. "I've felt worse." Which was true. I'd had my share of stab wounds in my time as a cop. This wasn't even in the top five.

"Then let's go," he said.

I looked at him. "And who are *you*?"

He looked disappointed. Just the way a movie star would look if he wasn't recognized by his fans.

"Listen," he said, sidestepping my question, "you can't get out of here on your own. Let me give you a hand, all right?"

He wasn't kidding. There was no way I could retrace my steps in all this mist. And I'd need a doctor before too long.

"All right," I said, tabling the question of who he was for the time being. "Take me back in the direction of the river."

"Can you walk?" he asked.

"I'll be fine," I told him.

He nodded, then started walking. For all I knew he was leading me in exactly the opposite direction from the one I'd come. But as he had pointed out, I didn't have a whole lot of options.

Like the bearded guy, he stayed quiet as we walked. He seemed to be looking out for something. I wondered what.

Finally, after what seemed like a very long time, the movie-star guy stopped and looked back at me. "We're here."

I looked around. "Where?"

He made a motion with his hand. "If you walk straight ahead, you'll find it. But I have to ask . . . do you really not know me?"

I studied his face. "Should I?"

He smiled a little half-smile. "You used to call me Ithaka."

"*I* did?"

"Absolutely."

I knew a town upstate by that name. And an island back in the old country. But not this guy.

"Sorry," I told him, "but it doesn't ring a bell."

He looked even more disappointed than before. But that didn't stop him. "We were friends," he said. "*Close* friends. We did everything together."

It was the second time that day that someone had claimed to be my friend. I didn't remember this guy any better than I did Anderson.

"Thanks," I said. "Take care of yourself."

I was *really* hoping that I was in a dream. My wound was starting to throb like a sonuvabitch.

"Wait." Ithaka grabbed me by the arm—though more gently than before. He looked around, as if to see if anyone was watching. "You were going to *help* me."

I didn't know what he was talking about. "Help you to . . . ?"

"Help me get *out* of here," he said, a wild flash of anger in his voice. Immediately, he seemed to regret it. "Sorry," he said, letting go of my arm. "It's just that . . . you're out there and I'm in here, and . . . " He looked away, his lips pressed together.

"If you want to leave," I said, "just do what I'm doing. That is, if it's really the river up there."

"It is," he said. "But I can't leave the way you can." He made a sound of exasperation. "Don't you know that?"

Now I was really lost. Was the guy insane? Or was he caught up in some kind of nonsensical dream logic that would seem like gibberish when I woke up?

"Look," I said, "I'd help you if I could, but I don't even know where I am."

Again, he looked around. Then he turned back to me and said, with what seemed like the deepest suffering in his eyes, "You told me that the last time, too. But the more you came back, the more you remembered."

The last time? The more I came back? "I've got to go," I said.

Then I turned and walked in the direction of the river, or at least what Ithaka had *said* was the direction of the river. After about twenty paces, I was beginning to doubt it. Then I felt the cold of the water lapping at my bare feet. As I moved forward, it got deeper, until it was almost to the bottom of my rolled-up jeans.

And just like that, the mist fell away. I was back in the real world of trees and rocks and little white piles of petrified bird crap.

Unfortunately, the hole in my back was still there. I could feel it every time I breathed, a deep, insistent ache that demanded a healthy dose of morphine.

I wondered what Anderson would say when he saw it. Did

he still drive at his age? I hoped so. And I hoped there was a hospital with a good emergency room nearby.

"Anderson?" I called out, though not so loudly that it would excite the knife wound.

I didn't get an answer.

Just the hiss of falling drops through the leaves. It had finally begun to rain.

"Anderson?" I called again, a little louder. The pain made me wince.

As I waded across the river, I recalled something the bearded guy had said about the bodybuilders: that they were "made by Zeus in ages past." At the time, I'd thought that a little odd.

The only Zeus I knew was the Greek god. The one with the thunderbolts. Had he meant *that* Zeus?

In spite of everything, I had to laugh a little. Whether he was in a dream or not, the bearded guy was definitely nuts.

When I got to the other side of the river, I stepped up onto dry land again. "Anderson?" I ventured.

This time, the professor's response was instantaneous. But it wasn't the kind I was hoping for.

It was a cry for help, thin and strained with anxiety. "Nikolas . . . !"

My first thought was that he had gotten himself in trouble—turned an ankle maybe, or cracked a bone on a rock. Or—even worse—the excitement had taken its toll on his heart.

Then I saw movement through the trees. Three guys—no, four—approaching through the woods. Something told me they weren't the Chamber of Commerce.

"I'm a cop!" I called out, despite the shoot of pain it cost me.

It wasn't quite true anymore, but it was never a bad idea to invoke the badge. If these guys were cops themselves, they would give me the benefit of the doubt. And if they were punks, they might think twice before taking me on.

As it turned out, they didn't respond to my announcement at all. They just kept coming, slowly and deliberately, without a word of explanation, and as they came they began to fan out. If I didn't do something, they would surround me.

I didn't like the odds, and I liked them even less if these boys were packing. I couldn't even try to make a break for it—not with Anderson their prisoner.

It occurred to me to go back across the river—to regroup under cover of the mist, try to figure out who these guys were. But even if that were advisable, it was already too late—too late, in fact, to do anything but fight, because suddenly the bastards were bearing down on me.

I barely had time to be impressed with how fast they were before the first one was on top of me. I managed to juke at the last moment and spare myself the worst part of his attack, but the jolt he gave me as he went by was still enough to set off a bomb in my back.

By the time the second guy got to me, I had picked up a stick and was swinging it as best I could. But he swatted it aside and sent me flying into a tree trunk. The pain doubled me over like a fist, leaving me helpless when he hit me over the back of the head.

The world turned red and very quiet. The next thing I knew

I was being dragged to my feet, surrounded by my attackers. There were four of them, all of them dressed in dark clothing. But they weren't wearing masks.

That was unusual. Kidnappers were typically pretty touchy about being identified.

And they *had* to be kidnappers—the same ones who got Tomi, I figured, or somebody else who was working for Junior. Otherwise why would they have followed me to Jersey and gone after me like this?

"Come with us," one of them said.

*Like I've got a choice.* "Where are we going?" I asked, putting aside the searing pain in my back.

"Somewhere safe."

It was a strange response under the circumstances. "What about my girlfriend?" I asked. "Is *she* safe?"

"I don't know," he told me.

That was an even stranger response. "I don't get it. You said in your note—"

"We didn't *send* you any note," he said, "but we know who did. Believe me, you don't want to deal with them. If we don't get out of here—and I mean now—none of us will be of any help to your girlfriend."

I studied his face, a big, squarish one with a broad nose beneath big black curls, as if that would help me figure out who he was or why he'd want to help me. It got me nowhere.

I had two choices. I could go with the guy as he asked, or I could try to get away. My choice was to try to get away, knife wound and all.

I didn't get very far before one of them took me down from behind. I had time to think that we were all screwed—me, Anderson, and Tomi especially—before something quick and hard put me down for the count.

# CHAPTER SIX

I woke up with my head hurting and my knife wound hurting worse.

The first thing I noticed was the linen bandage wrapped around my chest and back. Whoever had put it there hadn't used adhesive strips, which was a good thing because I hated the way they took my chest hair with them when they peeled off.

The second thing I noticed was that I was lying on a wood-frame cot, my bare feet caught in a shaft of warm sunlight. It came through a wide rectangle of a window with a piece of blue sky wedged into it, set in what looked like an old plaster wall. The other three walls had no windows, just dark, wrought-iron braziers.

No electrical appliances that I could see. In fact, no electrical outlets.

Quaint, I thought.

There was a heavy saltiness in the air that reminded me of the seashore. Was that where the guys in black had taken me? More importantly, was that where they had taken Tomi? They had denied knowing anything about her, but I didn't know if I should believe that.

I hoped they had left Anderson alone. He was an old man, after all. But my instincts told me they would have taken him too. Otherwise he would have gone to the police, and that could have posed a problem for them.

On the other hand, they had already kidnapped a New York City cop without losing any skin off their noses. If they could get away with that, they could get away with anything.

I swiveled ninety degrees on the cot, sat up, and put my feet on the smooth, mortared stones of the floor. My shoes were still on the bank of the river back in New Jersey. My shirt, which would have been punctured and thoroughly bloodstained, was absent as well.

Just as well, I thought. With my wound, I probably couldn't have pulled it on.

The room's only door, a tall, wooden affair, stood between two braziers. I got up, padded across the floor, and tugged on the door's twisted iron handle. It wouldn't budge—not that the fact surprised me.

Of course, I could have tried to bust the door down, but it looked too sturdy for that. I knocked on it and felt how solid the wood was. *Yep, definitely too sturdy.*

Looking for options, I turned to the window. Unfortunately, it was too small for me to slip through. But when I shoved the cot across the floor and stood on top of it, I was able to at least get a peek at what was outside.

First of all, there was the sky. The little sample that I had seen through my window didn't do it justice. It was a shade of blue so bright, so intense, that it made my eyes hurt just to look at it.

But it wasn't just the sky that jumped out at me. It was *everything*. The small, squarish buildings painted in pastel colors that all but covered the promontory beneath me. The cascades of green trees and gray boulders that poured into the spaces between the buildings. The dark blue sea that crawled around the edges of the land, moving slowly and rhythmically like a living thing.

And of course, the brassy afternoon sun.

They were all unbelievably clear, unbelievably defined, as if everything I had ever seen to that moment had been filtered through a scratched and dirty lens, and all of a sudden it was all thrown into sharp, clear focus.

Sliding my head as far as it would go to my left and then to my right, I got a better idea of the size of the place. I saw that it wasn't just one headland pushing out into the sea but a whole bunch of them. In fact, they raced side by side for miles and miles in either direction, each one covered with hundreds of pastel-colored villas.

There were also some big, open buildings with gabled roofs supported by white stone columns. Like little Parthenons, I thought, though I wasn't exactly an expert on classical architecture.

The streets in my part of town were deserted, but farther away, down by the beach, I could see plenty of people. Men, women, children, older folks, pretty much everybody you'd expect. None of them was wearing much in the way of clothing, but why would they? It was a vacation climate if I'd ever seen one.

The place reminded me a little of the Amalfi Coast in the south of Italy, but bigger and more mountainous. Each hillside started as much as a thousand feet above sea level before it began its long, dizzying plunge to the water.

Beautiful, I thought. Just beautiful.

If there was a resort like it anywhere on Earth, I had never heard of it. And with all those satellites they send into orbit looking down on us all the time, how could anyone keep a place like this a secret?

It was a good question, one I might need to answer before I could find Tomi and get the hell out of there. Or get the hell out of there and *then* find Tomi, depending on whether I decided to believe the guys who took me down in Jersey.

Either way, I wasn't going to get it done sitting in my "hotel" room.

I got down off the cot and looked around. If neither the door nor the window were going to be of any help to me, I had to find a different way. Not the walls or the floor—they looked too solid. But ceilings weren't usually built that strong.

I looked up at the rough, white surface above me. It was worth a shot. All I needed was a tool. I considered the idea of dismantling the cot, but without it I wouldn't be able to reach the ceiling.

That left the braziers.

Would they come loose? There was one way to find out. Getting a grip on one of them, I propped my foot against the wall beneath it and yanked as hard as I could. My knife wound cried out in protest, forcing a groan from me.

Worse, the brazier didn't budge. I pulled on it again, even harder than before. This time I felt a little give, and saw signs of cracking in the wall around it.

But it cost me in the raw, open hole-in-my-flesh department. A wave of cold sweat washed over me. I had to stop and take a couple of deep breaths before I could even stand up straight again.

Still, I had made progress.

Each time I tugged on the brazier, the pain kicked my ass. But I didn't stop. I couldn't. Finally, after maybe thirty tries, the damned thing wrenched loose in a shower of plaster fragments.

The next step was to drag the cot over to the section of wall by the door, get back up on top of it, and slam the sharp part of the brazier into the surface above me. Right away I saw results as pieces of ceiling came raining down on me.

Again, it hurt. *A lot.* But not as much as the thought of never seeing Tomi again.

After five or six hard, productive shots, I uncovered the wooden slats behind the material that made up the ceiling. Above them was an empty space and then the terra cotta tiles of the roof. All I had to do was break a couple of slats, pull myself up there, and crack through the tiles. Then I would be up on the roof and home free.

Easier said than done, of course. My knife wound was going to make it nearly impossible for me to haul myself up there. But first, the slats . . .

I was hammering away at the first one when I heard the creak of a hinge. It took me by surprise. Whirling, I saw the door start to swing open.

Knowing I had to react quickly, I jumped off the cot, brazier still in hand, and met the guy behind the door just as he poked his head past it.

I didn't know if he had heard the banging or was just coming in to check on me. Either way, I wasn't going to let all my hard work go for nothing.

Before he could throw up a hand, I cracked him over the head with the brazier. A second blow wasn't necessary. He fell like a sack of potatoes and lay sprawled in the doorway, out for the count.

The guy was dressed funny—and I mean *funny*—in a breastplate and a little skirt, as if he had just come from the set of a gladiator movie. He even had a short, kind of vicious-looking spear laying next to him. I wondered why—who wouldn't have? But I had no time to figure it out.

Shading my eyes and stepping over Gladiator Boy, I saw there was no one else around. *So much for having to climb out through the roof.*

The street outside led down to the water in zigs and zags. It occurred to me that I'd make better time going that way than up the hill. But when I was done, I would be down by the water rather than up by a major road.

Which way would be the better escape route? I didn't have a clue.

And which way would take me to Tomi, if she was even in

the neighborhood? Again, no idea.

I called on the ghost, thinking he was the only one who might be able to help me. But if he heard me, he still wasn't taking my calls.

I tried to assess the situation. Eventually, my kidnappers would check on the guy I'd knocked out and realize I'd escaped. If Tomi was in the neighborhood, these guys would contact their home boys and tell them to watch her extra carefully, which would make it even harder for me to break her out.

But what if Tomi wasn't anywhere nearby? What if she was still back in Astoria, tied up in somebody's basement?

I was still her only means of getting out of her situation alive. It would be terrible if I hung around this place, thinking I was helping her when I wasn't, and got caught again for nothing.

Come on, I told myself, holding the palm of my hand to my forehead. *Think.*

That's when I realized what I should have realized before—that if Tomi was somewhere in the vicinity, my best chance of finding her was lying in my prison's open doorway. If I hadn't killed the guy, if I could wake him up and get him to talk . . .

I needed to pull him back inside, close the door, and make it look like I was still a prisoner. And I needed to do it before someone noticed a guy with a bloody bandage and bare feet running around the place.

Then it was too late, because a voice started yelling in a language I didn't understand.

Whirling, I looked down toward the water and saw a knot of five or six men rushing up the hill at me. But they too looked like something out of a gladiator movie, all breastplates and skirts and sandals. If I wasn't fighting for my life, it might even have been funny.

I looked for guns in their hands but there weren't any. Instead, they had the same kind of spear the first guy had been carrying. *Spears!* What kind of place was this?

Again, one of the spear guys yelled something at me. It didn't sound like "Have a nice day."

Quickly, I considered my options. The street I was on crossed another one just up the hill. I went that way. When I reached the intersection I turned left, just to get out of sight.

For a time I was running by myself, the only sounds those of my breathing and the slap of my feet on the cobblestones. Then the spear guys turned the corner behind me and made some sounds of their own, the deep-throated kind that echoed from one pastel-colored building to another.

I was sure I could outrun them, barefoot as I was. After all, they were wearing armor. But I was afraid that their cries would bring other people interested in stopping me.

It was a fear that quickly turned into a reality. As I approached a cross-street, another handful of spear-guys turned the corner and boiled up in front of me. Glancing back, I saw that the first bunch was still in pursuit.

I felt like a perp, the kind I had chased down dozens of alleys in my time as a cop. But now I was on the other end of the hunt.

Seeing I had nowhere to go, they took their time closing in on me.

Clearly, I was outnumbered. And they were armed, which I wasn't. But I had a feeling that if they caught me they would kill me, which might end any chance of anyone's finding Tomi—and I didn't like that outcome or anything about it.

So I fought.

For a moment I had an advantage in that the spear guys didn't seem to have expected a struggle. Before they knew it I had gotten in among them, where they couldn't use their weapons, and smashed a couple of noses. Blood spurted. There were cries of pain and confusion, all of which helped my cause.

I had a shot, I told myself. I could get away.

It was right about then that the tide turned. Little by little, I got the snot beat out of me. At some point, I found myself with my cheek pressed to the warm surface of a cobblestone.

Somebody snarled an order, and somebody else dragged me to my feet. But I hadn't quite given up on getting away, so somebody had to hit me a few more times.

Maybe a whole lot more, I don't know. After a while, I lost count.

"He's awake," someone said.

If they were talking about me, they were right. I felt like crap, but I was conscious. Otherwise, I couldn't have heard them talking, right?

But where was I? Sitting in a chair somewhere, by the feel of it . Somewhere bright—too bright for me to open my eyes. So I didn't.

"You can let go of him," someone said.

It wasn't the first guy. This voice was closer and a lot deeper. What's more, I had heard it before. Where? *Back in Jersey. The guy with the curly black hair.*

Despite the brightness, I opened my eyes and confirmed it. He was the guy, all right. Except he wasn't wearing the Black Ops outfit he'd been rocking when he and his pals grabbed me in the woods.

He was wearing a toga. So were the other dozen or so people in the room, a couple of whom looked like they were there to make sure I behaved myself.

Togas. Breast plates. Spears. I'm in ancient Rome, I thought, making myself chuckle. *Ancient freakin' Rome.*

Either that or a really big frat party.

"Is something funny?" asked Curly, bending down to look me in the eye. Judging by his expression—or more accurately, his *lack* of expression—he didn't think it was funny at all.

"Not a thing, I told him, "unless you find it unusual for people to be wearing bed sheets out in public."

"He's referring to our robes," said someone behind Curly—a tall, blond guy sitting on the other side of the room. He, at least, seemed amused.

"Yes," Curly said with the same stone-faced lack of enthusiasm, "I know."

"I told you he wouldn't be of any use to us," said Blondie.

"I disagreed then and I disagree now," said Curly, still facing me though he was addressing the other guy.

"He doesn't trust us," Blondie observed, "and nothing we do is going to change that."

"I'd like a chance to prove you wrong," said Curly.

Blondie sighed. "All right. Go ahead."

"Momentarily," said Curly. His eyes narrowed. "First there's something I need to do."

I was waiting to hear what it was when he slugged me square in the mouth, sending me and my chair flying backwards. The next thing I knew I was on all fours, my overturned chair sitting beside me, a thick red goo dripping from my nose and mouth onto the tile floor.

My back was on fire. I felt like I had gotten stabbed a second time.

"Ajax!" said Blondie, on his feet now. "He's our guest!"

Were they doing the good cop, bad cop thing? I was too beat up to think straight.

Two big guys picked me up and put me back in my chair. Curly watched them, his arms folded across his chest.

Wait . . . what had Blondie called him? *Ajax*. Wasn't that a laundry detergent?

"What was that for?" I muttered, wiping blood from my mouth with the back of my hand.

"The man you hit with the brazier," said Ajax, his voice full of emotion, "was my aunt's boy, my cousin. You came within a hair's breadth of killing him."

"My apologies," I told him, trying to speak distinctly enough to be understood. "But if you don't want him hurt, you should find him another line of work."

"Is this how you prove me wrong?" asked Blondie, directing his question to Ajax.

"No," said Ajax. He took a breath, then slowly let it out. "Tell me," he said to me, his voice considerably calmer, "Do you know who you are?"

It was an odd question. "The Easter Bunny," I said. "Now I've got one for you: What did you do with my girlfriend?"

He scowled. "We're not the ones who took your woman. I told you that."

"Just before you knocked me out."

"You tried to run. We couldn't afford to waste time chasing you."

"Sorry to be a bother," I told him.

"Ajax . . ." said Blondie, leaning back in his chair.

Ajax jerked a thumb over his shoulder. "Sasterion and my other colleagues think you're too stubborn to be of any help to us."

*Sasterion?* I liked "Blondie" better.

"Help is a two-way street," I said, smelling an opportunity. "Maybe if *you* were to help *me*—"

"I've *been* helping you," Ajax spat. "Otherwise, you would've died in the—" He swore under his breath, whirled to face his pal Sasterion, and threw his hands up.

"The Bronx," said Sasterion.

Ajax turned back to me. "In the *Bronx* the other night. You have no idea what would have happened to you if we had not intervened."

"So that was why no one showed up? Because you stopped them?"

"Because we stopped them," Ajax confirmed.

"And why would you do that?" I wondered out loud.

"Because we have a mutual interest. Your enemy is our enemy."

Now we were getting somewhere. "And who *is* that enemy?"

"You know that all too well," said Ajax. "You encountered him in Long Island City. You tried to capture him and failed."

"You mean . . . Junior." Which was exactly what I'd thought.

"That is what he calls himself. But he is much more than what he appears."

"How much more?" I asked.

"That," said Ajax, "we have yet to determine."

It sounded like double talk but I played along. "So what do you want me to do, exactly?"

Again, he glanced at Sasterion. "My colleagues and I have yet to agree on that. But first, we must know if you are willing."

I wiped some more blood from my mouth. "When you ask so nicely, how can I refuse?"

It was an easy thing to say, and my buddy Ajax knew it. But at least I hadn't dismissed the possibility out of hand.

It was raining lightly as Ajax and a couple of his enforcers walked me down a winding street between ranks of pastel-colored houses.

I looked up at the sky. It was still that same impossible blue all around us except for a single dark-bellied cloud blotting out the sun.

"So it *does* rain here," I noted.

Ajax nodded. "Occasionally."

"And where, exactly, are we?"

"On Polyphemos Street."

"We're in Greece?" I asked, since Polyphemos sounded Greek to me.

"No."

"Then where?"

Ajax eyed me. "Nowhere you have ever been before, I assure you."

"But you're not going to give me any details?"

"All in good time," he told me.

Maybe halfway down to the water, we came to a plain, white building the size of two houses put together. Ajax led the way inside.

It was cool in there, a good ten or fifteen degrees cooler than the air outside, and surprisingly dark. At a gesture from Ajax, his enforcers moved around the place and lit the braziers hanging on all four walls.

No electricity here either, I remarked inwardly. In fact, no electricity anywhere, as far as I could tell.

As the place filled with a flickering, golden light, I noticed a series of stone slabs suspended from the walls at regular intervals. There were ten of them, the face of each one carved into a relief sculpture.

"They were rendered," said Ajax, "by a fellow named Neleos. This place was built to house his work."

"Very nice," I said. "And what am I supposed to do here?"

"I don't know. Meditate."

"Meditate," I repeated.

"There are worse ways to spend one's time than to meditate on the works of Neleos."

"So you knocked me out, dragged me here—wherever *here* is—and locked me up just to give me the chance to meditate? Damned thoughtful. Remind me to send you a fruit basket sometime."

"That would be nice," said Ajax.

And he left me standing there.

His strong-arm guys left too, but I could see them stop just outside the doorway. No doubt, Ajax wanted them there in case I decided to skip meditation class.

There has to be more to this, I told myself. Did Ajax expect something to happen if I meditated? What, exactly? And just what kind of meditation did he expect me to do?

I had tried the transcendental kind a long time ago, when I was a rookie cop and I walked a beat all day in Spanish Harlem. Sometimes it had calmed me a little, sometimes it hadn't. Sometimes it just made me fall asleep, which wasn't a bad thing either.

Would Ajax be okay with me falling asleep there on the floor? Something told me otherwise.

I looked around at the friezes. "The works of Neleos," I said out loud, hearing the echo. "Well, if that's all there is to do around here . . . "

I approached the first slab, which was hanging next to the door. It showed what looked like a sword battle in ancient times—maybe Greek, maybe Roman. I was certainly no expert. What I saw was a handful of guys in breast plates, capes, and plumed helmets on one side fighting a handful of guys in breast plates, capes, and plumed helmets on the other side.

It reminded me of the line play in a professional football game. Bone smashing bone.

Unfortunately, I hadn't been a football fan since my team took residence in Jersey. I moved on.

The next slab sported an image of a king with a crown of leaves on his head. He was seated on a throne and, as in the other freeze, dressed like someone in ancient times. Something about him, maybe the lack of a beard, made me think he was too young to sit where he was sitting.

As before, I moved on.

The third frieze was a study of a foot race. Everybody in it was naked and barefoot. Obviously, I thought, this was in the days before sponsors.

The fourth slab was more interesting to me than the others. On the left side as I faced it, it showed a guy and a gal standing in a chariot, both of them wearing breast plates and plumed helmets. The gal was the one driving the thing, managing the horses, while the guy looked like he had just thrown something.

On the other side, I could see what he had thrown: a spear. It was sticking out of another guy's belly. But the guy with the spear in his gut was huge, almost twice as big as the couple in the chariot, and he was floating a few feet above the ground.

A god, I thought.

He had to be. Who else floated in these ancient stories? And who else was so much bigger than life? I'd seen the movies. I wasn't born yesterday.

But in all those movies, I had never seen a woman driving a chariot. It made me wonder about her. Who was she?

I ran my finger over the raised contours of her face. She was nice enough looking, but not what you would call pretty. Too businesslike to be pretty, I thought.

I made a mental note to ask Sasterion about her, doubting that Curly—or rather, Ajax—would have the patience for such things. Then I moved to the next slab over.

It had a warrior trying to fight an enemy with his foot pinned to the ground by an arrow. The wound looked painful. In the next frieze, another warrior was picking up a stone—actually, more of a boulder—while his buds looked on.

Good for you, I thought. All those hours at the gym paid off.

Slab number seven was the first one that showed me something even vaguely familiar. It was a picture of a guy, fully armed and armored, dropping out of the old Trojan Horse. His shield, which had a picture of a wild boar's head on it, was held in front of him as if he expected trouble.

Huh, I thought. Where had I seen that shield before?

I looked back at the previous frieze and saw that the guy picking up the stone had a shield at his feet. It was propped against a rock or something so its insignia could be seen. And that shield too had a boar's head on it.

In fact, when I reversed direction and checked out slab after slab, I noticed that every one of them had a shield somewhere with that boar's head on it. Even the frieze of the young king on his throne had a shield leaning against his leg.

Next I went forward again, past the slab depicting the Trojan Horse scene to the one after it. It showed me a warrior driving his sword into an old man. Not so nice. But there was the shield again.

Likewise in the next frieze, which featured a couple of guys pulling some horses by their reins, and the one after that, which showed a lady in a helmet offering a guy a small statue, and the last one, which showed a guy in armor being stopped by a woman in front of an open gate.

The shield with the boar's head was prominent in all of them.

Obviously, it meant something.

But what? That the figures in the friezes were all from the same family? Or maybe, taking the observation a step further, that they were all the same guy?

If so, who was he? The ancestor of some mucky-muck there in town? And did he have something to do with my meditations, or had Ajax just figured he would put me somewhere quiet?

Would one of my guards know? Probably. But if they knew, would they tell me?

Moving to the doorway, I poked my head out. Immediately, two of Ajax's guys converged on me.

"You're supposed to remain inside," one of them said in pretty decent English.

"I know," I told him, "but I had a question. That artwork in there . . . who's it supposed to be about?"

The guards exchanged glances. Then the one I had addressed said, "It doesn't matter. Just go back inside."

I frowned. "So you know, but you're not saying."

The guy just stared at me. Seeing I wasn't going to get anywhere with him, I turned to the other one. But it was pretty obvious that he wasn't going to say anything either.

"Fine," I said, and went back inside as I'd been instructed.

Since there was nothing else to do, I went to look at the friezes again. After a while, something *else* occurred to me. The woman in the chariot and the woman offering a guy the statue looked very much alike.

Of course, it could have been just a stylistic thing. I'd seen comic books in which all pretty girls were drawn the same way, the only way to tell them apart being the color of their hair. Maybe that was how Neleos rolled as well.

For the hell of it, I assumed that it *wasn't* a stylistic thing—that the two female figures represented the same woman. Then what? Who was she? And what difference did it make to Ajax or me or anyone else?

I was still wondering when I heard someone cry out. In *pain*, I thought. Moving to the entrance, I stuck my head out again—just in time to see one of Ajax's men slam into the outside of the building and go limp.

*What the hell . . . ?*

I caught a glimpse of a guy with a gun. Before he could fire at me too, my reflexes took over and I pulled back inside.

My mind racing, I tried to figure out what was going on. I had to figure it out quickly, too, because whoever was out there was either a really huge Neleos fan or was coming straight after *me*.

I would have loved for it to be Bernie at the head of an NYPD task force, but I had a feeling it was someone else. Someone like Junior and his boys.

Ajax told he had saved me from Junior and his peeps that night in the Bronx. Maybe that was true. Maybe Junior, frustrated in the Bronx, had decided to come get me *here* instead.

But why would he do that? Was I that big a threat? I didn't know half as much about him as Ajax seemed to know.

Then I felt a chill crawl up my spine. Was this part of some bigger assault, one designed to take out not just yours truly but also Ajax and his people into the bargain?

I heard someone bellow something from right outside the door, and realized question-and-answer time was over. A heartbeat later the barrel of an assault gun come nosing its way past the doorframe.

I waited until the guy attached to it began to slide into sight as well, and then I grabbed the barrel with one hand and drove my fist into his jaw with the other. The pain in my back? Don't ask.

As I'd hoped, the blow loosened the guy's teeth enough for me to get sole possession of his weapon. I was going to use the stock to knock him senseless, but I saw he was unconscious already. Obviously I'd hit him harder than I thought.

By the time a second guy came charging in, I had the first guy's gun tucked into the hollow of my shoulder. At such close range, I didn't have to aim. I just fired.

With a grunt, the guy went down. But the recoil felt funny—different somehow.

I had barely registered the fact when something hit me hard in the left shoulder, spinning me around. Before I could fire back, somebody was on top of me. No—more than *one* somebody. A whole wave of them, wrenching the gun out of my grasp and wrestling me to the floor.

I kicked and punched and bit as best I could, but it didn't make any difference. I was dragged to my feet, my left arm numb from the shoulder down.

My assailants, I saw, weren't Junior's boys at all. For one thing, they were wearing sand-and-cream colored camo gear. For another, they were shooting rubber pellets—which was why my shoulder wasn't bleeding, much less shredded, as it would have been by a bullet at that range.

"Let him go," someone said.

I had heard the voice before, I thought.

My assailants released me, and I saw the one who had given them the order. He looked as comfortable in Neleos' house as if he owned the place. But then, he owned so *many* places . . .

"Drakos," I said.

He inclined his head. "At your service."

He had left the expensive threads behind in favor of the camo suit worn by his hired hands. But even *that* looked as if it had been custom-tailored.

"You don't look well," he observed.

"What are you doing here?" I asked.

"Isn't it obvious? I've come to get you."

"Of course," I said. "And just why would you want to do that?"

Before he could tell me, one of his men put a hand on Drakos's shoulder. "We should go, sir," he said, with just a hint of urgency.

"Go where?" I asked.

Drakos smiled at me. "Home. Where else?"

# CHAPTER SEVEN

It's a funny feeling waking up on your couch in the middle of the day. It's even funnier when you can't remember having gone to sleep.

And when one of the richest men in the world greets you with a chipped Yankees mug full of wake-up coffee . . . well, now you're in a whole different stratosphere of *funny*.

"I didn't see anything but decaf," said Drakos, who had exchanged his camo outfit for a navy blue polo shirt and khaki slacks, "and I thought you'd prefer the caffeine, so I took the liberty of picking up some *real* coffee."

I swung my legs around, sat up, and accepted the cup from him. "*You* did that?"

"Actually," said Drakos, "it was one of my men."

"Right," I said. "Of course." *That's what I do when I want something—I have one of my men pick it up.*

"It was," he added, "the least I could do."

"Thanks." I took a sip. It was good—*damned* good. "Where did you get this?" I asked.

"A restaurant on the Upper East Side."

"You went all the way to Manhattan for coffee?"

"The place specializes in exotic blends," Drakos said, as if that were a reasonable explanation. He told me the name of the restaurant but it didn't sound familiar.

"Now," I said, "if it were me, I would've just gone to the coffee shop around the corner. Obviously, we travel in different circles."

He smiled. "Perhaps."

I took another sip of coffee, then asked him, "How did I wind up on the couch?"

"It was necessary to put you out before I brought you back to New York."

"Why was that?"

"The way from here to there isn't commonly known. I like to keep it that way."

"*They* seem to know it," I said, referring to Curly—or rather, Ajax— and his men.

"And," said Drakos, "*they* like to keep it that way, too."

*How cozy.* "So . . . you chloroformed me or something?"

"Chloroform is rather crude. We used a more effective, less toxic substance."

"People keep doing that to me," I said. "Knocking me out, I mean. For the record . . . don't do it again."

"I hope I don't have to," he replied amiably.

"Then you . . . what? Carried me in here?"

"Discreetly, yes."

I looked around, but there didn't seem to be anyone else in the apartment. "Where are your men now?"

"Except for the one you shot in the midsection, who is now

receiving medical attention, they're waiting in the car."

I got up and looked out the window, half-expecting to see a stretch limo parked outside. Instead, I saw a shiny black Hummer.

"Slumming?" I asked.

"I thought it best," he said, "not to attract too much attention."

"You would have been better off with a Volkswagen."

Drakos nodded. "I see you haven't lost your sense of humor."

"How would you know—?" I started to ask. Then I remembered Anderson's photo. "That's right. You and I knew each other about . . . I don't know . . . fifty years ago?"

I waited to see his reaction. He just said, "Longer than that."

"Really? Then why don't I look it?"

"Why doesn't either *one* of us look it?" said Drakos.

"I asked you first."

"So you did. But I choose to withhold that information. All I can tell you is that you were on board with the idea when I presented it to you. I didn't extend your lifespan without your consent."

I looked at him. *Extend your lifespan.* As if he were talking about changing dental plans.

"Your next question," said Drakos, "is why I would *want* to extend your lifespan."

"That's right," I said.

"The answer is that you used to work for me."

Had I heard him wrong? "I worked for *you*?"

"It was some time ago," Drakos noted matter-of-factly,

"before you ever considered joining the police force. You were my chief of security, I guess you'd say."

I stared at him, trying to imagine myself as his bodyguard. I couldn't.

"That," he continued, "was why the people who abducted you decided to do so—because at one time you knew a lot about me and my operations. It was also one of the reasons I went after you. I didn't want what was buried in your brain to fall into the wrong hands."

"All right," I said. "Let's say I worked for you before The Beatles broke their first guitar strings. Why don't I remember any of it?"

Drakos's expression hardened. "Because I don't want you to. And don't bother asking me *why* I don't want you to. People in my employ enjoy a great many luxuries in life, but knowledge of my personal affairs isn't one of them."

"How long I've been alive," I said, "is *my* personal affair."

He shook his head. "Not anymore, it isn't."

I could have argued the point. Instead I got to the *real* question. "What about my girlfriend—Tomi?"

Drakos's eyebrows came together over the bridge of his nose. "I'm working on that."

"The guys who kidnapped me back in the—what's the name of that place, anyway?"

"The Isles."

"They said that Junior took her. You know who Junior is, don't you?"

He had denied it before, but he didn't deny it this time. "I do. And yes, he seems to be the one who has your girlfriend. But I'll get her back for you. It's just a matter of time."

I wanted to believe him. I also wanted to be rid of my damned knife wound. Then I realized . . . it hadn't hurt me in a while. I moved my shoulder around experimentally.

If there was still a wound there, I couldn't feel it. Come to think of it, my face didn't hurt either. I felt it. No cuts, no swelling, no bruises.

But how?

"My wound . . . " I said.

"You're welcome," said Drakos.

"You did that?"

"It's not as impressive a feat as you may think. You just need the right . . . technologies."

What the hell kind of world had I gotten myself into? Drakos had "extended" my lifetime, apparently without blinking, and closed a wound that should have taken weeks to heal. Clearly I was out of my league.

And I was beginning to wonder if I should trust *anybody*.

After all, Ajax claimed to be on my side, but his people had knocked me over the head and put me in what amounted to a jail cell. And Drakos, for all his talk about helping me, had lied to my face up in his office.

I remembered what the bearded guy in my dreams had said about Drakos: "When he *does* talk, don't trust him or he'll gain power over you." Or something to that effect.

Sure, the bearded guy had turned out to be a lunatic. But he had also been right about Tomi being in danger, and I had a feeling he was right about Drakos as well.

Something else occurred to me. "Any idea what happened to Anderson—the old guy who came with me to New Jersey?"

"He's fine," said Drakos. "My people found him at the cemetery and brought him back to his house. On the way, they made an adjustment to his memory. He no longer recalls your visit with him or your trip to Iraklion."

Was there anything this guy couldn't do? "You tampered with his *memory*?"

"Just short-term. As I said, he's fine."

It was better than I had expected, I had to admit. Besides, it was too late to do anything about it now.

Drakos got to his feet. "For the time being, you should be safe here. Junior doesn't seem to like attention, and the Isles people won't bother you now that they know I'm involved."

"That's comforting," I said, "but how am I supposed to sit here while Junior's got Tomi?"

"You *have* to," said Drakos. "I know you find that difficult to accept. But if you attempt to get involved, you'll only jeopardize your girlfriend's retrieval. Tell me you understand that."

"I hear you," I said.

"Your hearing," said Drakos, "has never been an issue. Your ability to comply, on the other hand . . . " His voice trailed off meaningfully.

"Get her back," I told him, "and we won't have to worry about my complying."

"As I said," he replied, "it's only a matter of time." He reached into the pocket of his slacks, took out a business card, and handed it to me.

"What's this?" I asked.

"My private number. Call whenever you want."

Now Drakos was offering me *his* number. It was an interesting turnaround.

"And you'll answer?" I asked.

"If I can."

I put the card down on my end table. "Thanks."

"You're welcome," said Drakos.

"By the way," I asked, as he went into the kitchen to place his cup in the sink, "any idea what they expected from that little art museum they put me in?"

As he emerged from the kitchen, Drakos was shaking his head. "None. Do you?"

"Not a clue," I said truthfully.

He remained silent for a second, apparently pondering the art museum question. Then he shrugged and said, "Don't forget, leave your girlfriend's situation to me."

And he left.

I went to the window and watched Drakos get into the black Hummer. As soon as he closed his door, it pulled away from the curb and disappeared down the street.

And I was alone in my apartment. As alone as I had been before I went to see Anderson.

God help me, it felt like I had never left.

I couldn't just do *nothing*.

Even if Drakos had told me the truth when he said my getting involved would mess things up, it wasn't my nature to sit around and wait for others to take care of my business.

He seemed to know it too, which gave his story about having been my employer some credence. Not a lot, but *some*.

Unfortunately, I had no way of nailing that story down one way or the other. I couldn't just call the Internal Revenue Service and ask if I'd been employed back in the eighties, just before my boss unnaturally extended my lifespan.

However, I *could* check what Drakos had said about Anderson. He'd assured me that the professor was safe, that he had tweaked the old guy's memory and put him back where he belonged. As long as my butt was stapled to the couch, I could at least verify Drakos's report.

It took me a while to find the phone number, but I got a response after the first ring: "Hello?"

"Professor Anderson?" I said.

"*Yes?*" It's his voice, I thought.

"This is Zeno Aristos. I'm returning your call."

"*Right,*" he said, a note of rising excitement in his tone, "*thanks very much for getting back to me. You see, I—*"

"I can't really talk right now," I said. "Things are kind of hectic. I just didn't want you to think I was ignoring you."

"*I appreciate that.*" He was disappointed, though. "*If there's a better time . . . ?*"

"I'm sure there will be," I said. "I'll give you a call when I can clear a little space in my schedule."

"*Great,*" Anderson said, making the best of it. "*That's great. No hurry. Just let me know, all right?*"

I assured him that I would do that, though I was lying through my teeth. It seemed he was clear of any trouble. I wanted him to stay that way.

"Goodbye," I said.

"*Goodbye,*" said the professor.

I hung up and put my cell phone down on the end table next to the couch. Then I looked around. *No more Anderson to take care of.* What was I supposed to do next?

Go wash up, I thought. *After all, Drakos might call and tell you he needs your help with Tomi. In a hurry, maybe.* If that happened, I had to look halfway decent, didn't I? Decent enough to leave the apartment without scaring people?

That got me moving in the direction of the bathroom. Once inside, I glanced at the shower stall—just to see if there might be a bearded guy standing behind the curtain. As much as I wanted him to be there, he wasn't.

I considered myself in the mirror. No question about it, I looked like crap. No visible signs of having gotten stabbed, knocked out, or beaten up, but like crap all the same.

How was I supposed to look? I was no closer to finding Tomi than I had been the day she disappeared. I'd been a cop for almost twenty years. I should have been able to get at least a lead on her, but I'd failed completely.

Shaving my face wasn't going to change any of that. But if Tomi were there, she would have insisted on my doing so anyway. She hated stubble—said it made her face itch. So, for her, I threw on some shaving cream and dragged a razor across it.

I really should have changed the cartridge. The blades were dull and I was scraping the hell out of my skin. But that was all right. I *wanted* to punish myself a little.

It was only after I had shaved one side of my face from the sideburn down to the chin that I noticed something: I was *glowing*. I had to look hard to see it, but once I did there was no mistaking it: I had an aura. A *green* aura, even though it was only visible where I had exposed my skin with the razor.

I looked around for the source of it. It had to be a reflection, right? A bounce of light off something green and shiny? But I couldn't find either the light or the reflective surface.

Curious, I pulled my razor down the cheek that still had the shaving cream on it. As I shaved away the fluffy, white foam, I saw the aura emerge there too.

That's crazy, I thought.

But then, I had been told not once but *twice* in the last couple of days that I hadn't aged in half a century. I'd had dreams that warned me about danger in the waking world. And for years I'd been talking to a ghost.

Who was *I* to say what was crazy?

I finished shaving and got a look at myself. A *good* look. And the harder I looked, the more I realized that the aura wasn't just where I had shaved.

It was *everywhere*. In my ears, under my hair, even over my eyeballs—though it didn't seem to impair my vision. It was thin, barely noticeable in most places, but it was *there*.

I laughed. I couldn't help it. It was just too weird to look at *without* laughing.

And then I got another surprise—because when I laughed, the aura *jumped*. Big time. Instead of a thin green film it became a burst of green light, an all-over flare that rose maybe six inches off my skin and then receded again.

I shook my head. *Not happening.* I closed my eyes, insisted on it. *Not happening.* But when I opened my eyes again, the aura was still around.

Or was it just my tortured imagination? After everything I had been through, it wouldn't be a shock if I'd started seeing things. There had to be a way to find out . . .

And then it came to me. I walked into the bedroom, opened the top drawer in the dresser, and took out the digital camera we had bought forty-percent off on Forty-second Street. Then I pointed it at myself and took a picture.

The flash blinded me, so it was a minute or so before I could look at the digital photo. As far as I could tell, there was no aura around me. I laughed and took another picture, closing my eyes this time. When I opened them and checked out the picture, no aura again.

Just to be certain, I walked back into the bathroom and took some pictures there as well—laughing, not laughing, of me directly, of me reflected in the mirror. None of them showed any sign of the green aura.

So the camera couldn't see it. What about another person? I put on some clothes and went outside. Then I knocked on our neighbor's door.

Mrs. Shabazz was a nice lady—unlike Mr. Shabazz, who had left her for a waitress six months earlier. After I had knocked a few times too many, she came to the door and said, with some concern in her voice, "Yes, Zeno?"

I looked at her. "Do you see anything different about me, Mrs. Shabazz? About my skin?"

Her brow furrowed as she scrutinized me. "I don't know," she said. "Are you sunburned?"

She didn't see it either. So more than likely, it was just me. I thanked Mrs. Shabazz, though I didn't make it clear for *what*, and went back to my apartment.

What the hell was going on?

I went to the window and looked outside. There was a whole city out there full of people leading normal lives, working jobs and coming home and eating dinner and watching reality shows on television, who had never seen the things I'd seen lately or heard the things I'd heard, and had no idea how fragile their world was.

I envied them.

Just then, my phone rang. I was about to answer it when I noticed something across the street.

A guy wearing jeans and a white tee shirt. Kind of tall, shaved head. Leaning against a street lamp. Drinking soda from an orange can.

Nothing really unusual about him. The kind of person you saw on the streets every day. Unless, of course, you took into account the fact that *he* was glowing too.

I forced myself to move away from the window, to sit down on the couch. Then I got up and looked out the window again. The guy was still glowing.

The same way I was. The same way *nobody else* was. Just him and me.

I didn't get it. Why us and no one else? What was different about us? And hell, did the guy *know* he was glowing?

I was tempted to go outside and ask him. You know, just walk up to him and say, "You're glowing green. Any idea why?" But before I even considered something like that, I wanted to observe him for a while.

I didn't stand by the window the whole time. I moved around the room as if I were tidying up, and only glanced his way every so often. But I saw enough to realize something interesting...

*He wasn't going anywhere.* Everybody else came and went the way people do, but the glowing guy was pretty much a fixture next to that street lamp.

Why would he stay there so long? Wasn't there something he had to do at some point that would pull him away even for a little while? There was only one answer. The bastard was watching me.

But who was he working for? Not the police. That was for sure. No self-respecting cop would ever hang out in plain view as long as this guy had.

Drakos, then? Certainly possible. He had withheld a lot of information—maybe he didn't trust me. Or maybe he just wanted to make sure I followed his advice about Tomi.

But Drakos's men were professionals too. If they were watching me, they wouldn't have made it so obvious.

Could the guy have been one of Curly's people? They couldn't have been happy about losing me. Maybe they were looking for a chance to get me back.

Maybe—but I didn't think so. Drakos had their number. Knowing he was in the game would have forced them to be circumspect—maybe even more so than before—and leaving a guy out there all day was definitely *not* circumspect.

That left one last angle—that the guy was working for Junior. Of course, Junior could have had me any time he wanted me, and he knew it. All he had to do was tell me Tomi's life depended on it.

So maybe it wasn't *me* he was watching. Maybe he was there to see who came by to *visit*. The more I thought about it, the more likely it seemed—that Junior wanted to keep tabs on who I was associating with.

But why was the guy *glowing*? Why was *I* glowing? I was no closer to answering those questions than I had been before.

Over the next couple of hours, I treated the glowing guy like a science experiment. I manipulated the variables and saw how he responded.

I went to the pizzeria across the street and picked up a hero. He followed me there and back. I went to the cleaners to drop off a couple of shirts that weren't actually dirty enough to warrant cleaning. Again, he followed me there and back.

Clearly, his job was to stick with me, to go where I went and see who I saw. I wondered how long he had been watching me before I noticed his aura. Since Tomi was taken? Since the handball game with Junior? Maybe even before that?

But not the whole time, right? He had to eat, sleep, go to the bathroom. Eventually, someone else had to take over for him.

At three in the morning, that's exactly what happened. Like at Buckingham Palace, a changing of the guard. Except it was just one guy leaving and another guy showing up, which wouldn't have represented much of a tourist attraction.

Unless, of course, those tourists could see what I saw out my living room window—that the guy who took over was glowing too. Now there were three of us, which made it even weirder.

What did we have in common? Was I one of them in some way?

There was only one place I could think of to go for an answer. I picked up the card Drakos had given me and called the number on it.

I would have been happy to take the subway to Drakos's building, but he insisted on sending a car for me. It wasn't the Hummer, though. It was a black Volkswagen.

At least he'd been listening.

Of course, the guy with the aura couldn't follow me into the car. No doubt, that was a source of some frustration to him.

Unlike the last time I visited Drakos in his building, the guard in the lobby ushered me right in. I didn't even have to show him my driver's license.

"Looks like you're coming up in the world," he said, smiling.

"Looks like it," I said.

The elevator was waiting for me the same way as before. There was a different guard holding the door open, but he was just as big as the first one—maybe bigger.

When I got out on the thirty-second floor, the woman with

the jelly beans and the British accent was there to greet me. But this time she mentioned my name, and there was no guard waiting for me in Drakos's office when I walked in.

I found him standing next to the oversized bird cage, wearing another expensive-looking suit. He and the white raven turned to me at the same time.

"Zeno," said Drakos, apparently pleased to see me. The raven clicked, as inhospitable as ever.

I was about to tell Drakos about the auras. I was about to ask him if he knew what they meant, why I could see them, and if I would ever *stop* seeing them.

I was about to ask him all of that—until I realized that *Drakos was sporting an aura too.*

"You've come about your girlfriend," he said. "Good. I was just about to call you."

An *aura*, I thought. Around *Drakos* . . . ?

"Call me . . . ?" I echoed, trying to regain my equilibrium.

"Don't worry," he said, "it's good news. She's alive. And she's well, all things considered."

I weighed the words, one by one. A couple of minutes earlier, I might have put more faith in such information. And I still desperately *wanted* to.

But the guy with the beard had told me not to trust Drakos. And Drakos had lied to me once before. And now there was a freaking *aura* around him, the kind I had seen only around guys clearly surveilling me.

Were they Drakos's guys? I hadn't given the idea much credence before, but now I was forced to.

"Where is she?" I asked. After all, Drakos would expect me to.

He looked apologetic. "*That* my contacts don't know yet. But we'll find her. It may take a while, but we'll find her."

"Every minute they've got her . . . " I said, because he would expect me to say that too.

"I understand. And I assure you, we're working with a heightened sense of urgency. She won't remain a captive a moment longer than is absolutely necessary."

I nodded. "Thank you."

"It's the least I can do for you."

I could have asked Drakos about his aura and ended the suspense right there. *So that green glow I see around you . . . what's up with that?* But something told me it would be a mistake.

Drakos's eyes narrowed. "What is it?"

I shook my head. "Nothing."

"Please," he said, "go ahead. Whatever is on your mind, you can trust me with it."

I didn't, but I had to think of something or he wouldn't stop asking. "All right," I said, settling for a question I had asked before, "I keep coming back to that place—the building where you found me. I still can't figure out why they put me there."

Drakos nodded. "It's a tough one. Since we got back I've discussed the matter with my security personnel, the ones who are most familiar with the Isles people, and they don't have any insights either."

I looked as perplexed as I could. "I just wish I knew."

The raven clicked impatiently. It seemed to be saying, *The sooner you're out of here, the better.*

For once, I agreed with her.

"I need to get some air," I said. "I think I'll walk a bit."

"No need of the car?" Drakos asked. He indicated the window behind him with a gesture. Rain drops were starting to streak the glass. "I can have it meet you somewhere."

"Thanks, but no."

He looked me in the eye for a moment, as if trying to read my mind. Then he said, "Suit yourself. Just let me know if you change your mind."

"I will," I assured him.

"And try to get some sleep, for godsakes. You look like you've been up all night."

All of a sudden, he was my mother. "I'll sleep better when Tomi's back home."

Drakos put his hand on my shoulder and ushered me out. "Remember," he said, "it's only a matter of time."

"I'll remember," I said.

And I left, with even more to think about than before.

# CHAPTER EIGHT

As I emerged from Drakos's lobby, I wasn't paying much attention to anything around me—not even the rain that had started to fall in earnest. I was too bowled over by the idea that Drakos had an aura too.

It opened up all kinds of possibilities, only some of which I could wrap my head around.

For instance, that the guys watching my apartment were Drakos's people after all. *He* had an aura, *they* had auras. It made sense—especially if I had been one of his employees as well, once upon a time.

So why wasn't I completely sold on that notion?

Because I still couldn't imagine a top-shelf security force being so unprofessional. Drakos wouldn't have tolerated it.

If only I knew what the auras were about. Maybe I *had* known, back in the day when I was working for Drakos. But that, like everything else about my past, was out of reach now.

I remembered an article I'd read once about factory workers back in the fifties—young women, mostly—who painted little green dabs of radium on the hands of alarm clocks. The clocks were really popular because people could use them to tell time in the dark without spending money on electricity.

At the time, no one thought that radium was bad for you, so these workers would use their lips and tongues to make points on the ends of their paint brushes. Needless to say, a lot of them died.

But before that happened, did they glow? Did they have little green auras?

A stupid question, I know. But the auras had to come from *somewhere*.

The other question was why *I* was the only one who saw them. What was that about? And why did I begin to see them only *after* I'd come back from the Isles?

Had Ajax and his people done something to me there while I was unconscious? Had they drugged me? Was all this aura stuff some kind of psychedelic hallucination?

I didn't think so. I felt fine. And why drug me anyway? What could they have accomplished by messing me up?

I needed answers, not more questions, and to that point there was only one guy who had given me any. I had to see the bearded guy again, talk to him, even if it meant getting stabbed a second time.

Right then, as I stood in the rain outside Drakos's building, I made a decision. I wasn't going back to Astoria, where it would be hard to make a move without some glowing guy knowing about it. I was going straight to the cemetery in Iraklion.

No sooner had the thought crossed my mind than I caught something out of the corner of my eye. Something to my right. I turned as if looking for a taxi—and saw a guy with an aura standing in front of the newsstand on the corner, sheltered from the rain by the stand's overhang.

It wasn't the guy I had left standing across the street from my apartment. It was the *other* guy—the *first* one I had noticed wearing an aura.

Trying not to let on that I'd seen anything unusual, I crossed the street and checked out the display window of a department store. Like Drakos's office window, it was streaked with raindrops. But I wasn't really interested in the display. I was studying the reflection in the glass.

Aura Boy had remained by the newsstand on the other side of the street. He was pretending to read a paper, but I doubted that he was any more interested in the news than I was in the department store.

Was he Drakos's man? It would have explained why he'd been out there waiting for me.

If he were working for someone else, how would he have known where to find me? Unless, I thought, the car gave it away. Or were the aura guys watching a whole bunch of places, Drakos's building being just one of them?

It didn't matter. Whoever he was, I was going to lose him. Otherwise, I wouldn't be able to get back to the bearded guy and ask him what I had to ask.

Was I crazy to think I could find him? After all, the magic mist might not be there anymore. Maybe it was like *Brigadoon*, and I could only reach the bearded guy's place every hundred years.

But Anderson had said I used to disappear into the deep

woods part of the cemetery all the time, back when he and I were fresh-faced college guys at NYU. I had to think it was more than the creek drawing me back time and time again.

Now I was going back one more time, to see what I could see. I was glad I had decided to wear my running shoes to Drakos's office. It looked like I would need them before the day was over.

Just as I thought that, I heard a voice in my head. It said one word: *Zeno . . . ?*

"Ghost!" I said, loud enough to attract some stares. "Boy, am I glad to hear from *you*."

He said something in response but it was garbled. Like a bad phone connection.

"I didn't catch that," I said, beneath my breath this time.

He said it again, or at least I thought he did. Unfortunately, it was no more intelligible the second time.

To avoid attracting any more attention, I held my phone up to my ear and pretended to talk into it. "Listen," I said, "I don't know if you can hear me, but someone's taken Tomi."

*. . . know that,* the ghost said, his voice suddenly coming through more clearly again.

*Progress.* "It's Junior, right? The guy I played handball with the day you were trying to talk to me?"

*Why . . . think it's him?*

I recalled the look Junior gave me that day on the court. "I think he's got it in for me, I'm not entirely sure why. And since Tomi is my girlfriend . . . " I let the ghost fill in the rest.

*No,* he said. *Not . . .*

Frustrated, I swore to myself. "Not *Junior*, you mean?"

*Not Junior*, he said with unexpected clarity.

I felt as if somebody had pulled the rug out from under me. No—make that the whole floor. Curly had told me it was Junior who abducted Tomi. Drakos had confirmed that it was Junior who abducted Tomi.

And now the ghost was telling me they were full of crap.

Or maybe just misinformed. That was a possibility too.

Or maybe it was the *ghost* who was misinformed. But in the past, he'd always been right on the money. If I was going to bet on someone's being right, it would have to be *him*.

"Then who *did* take her?" I asked.

*Don't . . . tell you.*

I tried to patch the words together. "You don't know or you would tell me?" I suggested.

One word: *Right*.

I felt my heart sink in my chest. Before, I had at least *thought* I knew who abducted Tomi. Now I was back to Square One.

And when you're on Square One, you have to start with who you can trust. I already knew that Drakos was capable of lying to me. Ajax, I wasn't so sure about.

But there was that one guy, besides the ghost, whose information had been consistently reliable. "I've been having dreams," I said. "There's a guy in them, a guy with a beard. He tells me things."

*. . . trust him*, said the ghost.

"Was that *trust him* or *don't trust him*?"

No answer. Not even static.

"You still there?" I asked.

Nothing. The ghost was gone again.

On one hand, he'd answered my biggest question, even if it wasn't the answer I'd wanted. On the other hand, I could have used some more help when it came to my informants. Without it, I could only pursue the plan I'd *been* pursuing, and hope for the best.

First and foremost, I had to get away from Aura Boy. Fortunately, I had an idea about how to make that happen.

The nearest subway station was on Forty-second Street between Fifth and Sixth, alongside Bryant Park. Making that my destination, I started walking south along Sixth.

There were lots of other people doing the same thing, fighting the wind behind their umbrellas. Most of them were moving faster than I was. It was lunchtime, after all, rain or no rain. In New York, people didn't screw around when it came to lunchtime.

Traffic, on the other hand, was moving at a crawl, and the rain alone couldn't have been the cause. Maybe there was an accident somewhere, or some construction. Whatever the reason, even the taxis were making like box turtles.

Somewhere behind me, Aura Boy was matching my pace, maintaining whatever he thought was a discreet distance. I was tempted to look back, to see how close he might be. But I resisted the impulse.

I mean, my only advantage was that he didn't know I knew about him. As soon as he saw me looking at him, that advantage would go away. He would call for backup and it would be a whole lot harder for me to bolt.

So I kept my eyes trained straight ahead. It wasn't as easy as it sounds. As a cop, I'd been trained to dissect a crowd as if it were a frog back in high school biology, picking out the lunatics before they did something everybody would regret.

But this time I let the lunatics slide.

Pretty soon I crossed Forty-fifth, which was already starting to puddle up. Then Forty-fourth. At Forty-third, I stopped for a red light with all the other rain-flecked pedestrians.

That meant the guy with the aura had to stop as well. I allowed myself a glance at the window of an electronics shop, thinking I might see his reflection. No such luck.

When the light changed, I moved on.

At Forty-second, I made a left and walked half a block. Next to Bryant Park, I found the green globes that marked the subway station.

Swinging around between them, I descended the steel-reinforced stairs. The draft of air that hit me in the face carried a metallic smell with some questionable accents, but nothing I couldn't handle.

Down in the station, it was all people smells and muted lights and echoes. There was a static-torn voice on the loudspeaker trying to say something about a change in the train schedule, but I couldn't make it out and I was sure no one else could either. What else was new?

As I pulled out my wallet and extracted my yellow-and-blue Metro Card, I wondered if Aura Boy had one too. It was a funny thought—me getting away because he didn't have a card to get into the subway. But I wasn't counting on it.

Picking a turnstile, I slid the card into the appropriate slot. Impatient as I was, I still had to wait until I saw the readout that said the stile had subtracted the fare from the card. Only then was I able to get through.

Before I could get to the platform, I had to negotiate a corridor with murals on either side. On occasion, I had lingered there to read the words and absorb the pictures, as if I was in an art museum. But not this time.

This time, I headed right for the platform.

Actually, the Forty-second Street stop had *two* platforms—the southbound, which I was on, and the northbound. Each platform gave you access to two tracks—a local that ran alongside the tunnel wall and an express that ran through the middle of the station. The two expresses were almost close enough for a guy on the southbound side to reach through an open window and high-five a guy on the northbound side.

Not that anyone would want to do that. Even in New York. Subway cars ran as fast as autos in some places. A high-five at that speed could take your arm off at the shoulder.

What I *had* seen people do was try to run across the tracks. This was inadvisable for two reasons. The first was that a train might be coming. The second was that each track had an electrified third rail, which was where the trains got their power. One brush against that baby and it would take days to get the stench of burned flesh out of the station.

Of course, there were plastic sheaths laid on top of the third rails, but the sheaths didn't cover everything. So it wasn't smart for a train-track runner to depend on them. Or on rubber soles, for that matter, even if you happened to be wearing running shoes the way I was. A little splash of standing water and neither sheaths nor soles were going to keep you on the right side of extra-crispy.

But the rails weren't the only obstacle for the train-track runner. There was also the barrier the Transity Authority had erected *between* the rails, a little Berlin Wall cutting the station in half. The funny thing was that the barrier had a series of short, narrow archways cut out of it, which gave you access to the other side in an emergency.

So if you really wanted to, you could still bolt across the tracks.

You just had to be a little more nimble than before.

Anyway, now that I was on the platform, I could get a sense of where my pursuer was without giving anything away. First I glanced at my watch, as if I were wondering where the train was already. Then I leaned out over the yellow-rubber safety strip and craned my neck to peer along the tracks.

Sure enough, Aura Boy was right there on the platform with me, not more than a hundred feet away. He was hard to miss—for me, at least. No one else had anything even resembling a green glow around him.

I frowned, because we New Yorkers do that when we don't see the train coming, then glanced the other way down the tracks—in the direction of the northbound line. In fact, it was the northbound train I was really interested in.

So why was I on the southbound side? As I mentioned,

I needed to shake my pursuer. And if my timing was right, I would do just that.

If it was wrong . . . well, I'd be a pretty good bet to make the five o'clock news.

"Excuse me?" someone said.

I turned and saw a couple of gray-haired nuns standing beside me on the safety strip. One was about seventy, I figured. The other one looked old enough to be her mother.

"Can I help you?" I asked, though my mind was on what I had to do next.

"We were wondering," said the younger one in a Southern accent, "if this is the right train for St. Patrick's. I'm afraid we've gotten ourselves lost."

"Actually," I said, "you want to be on the other side. Northbound."

The nun sighed. "We were just *on* the other side, and we were told we needed to be on *this* side."

Normally, I would have escorted the sisters to the right platform and seen them onto the train. In fact, I got the feeling that was what they were angling for. But I had the aura guy right where I wanted him, and if I waited that might change.

Fishing in my pocket, I pulled out a twenty. Then I pressed it into the younger nun's hand. "Tell you what," I said, "forget the subway and take a taxi, okay? Just do me a favor and pray for me."

Just as I said that, I caught sight of a light in the northbound tunnel. I couldn't see the rest of the train yet, just the light.

The nun looked pleased to go along with my request. "Of

course we will. Any particular reason?"

"I'm going straight to Hell," I told her.

Her face scrunched up with concern. "I beg your pardon?"

There was no time to explain. The northbound train was getting closer. As I watched, it began to separate itself from the darkness of the tunnel.

"My son . . . ?" said the nun.

I'd often heard the saying that timing was everything. It had never felt so true as at that moment.

As the train slowed down to pull into the northbound side of the station, I dropped off the southbound platform onto the tracks. For a moment, people were too astounded to say anything. Then they began to yell at me, to scream.

By that time I was on the move, hoping to get to the platform on the other side before the train had a chance to slam into me.

The key was for me to make it unscathed over the two third rails. Unfortunately, they were too close together for me to hurdle one of them and then the other. It was both or nothing.

And the barrier, even with its cutouts, raised the level of difficulty a notch. Because I would have to duck to make it through an opening, and it's damned hard to execute a decent long jump while you're ducking to avoid getting hit in the head.

On top of that, I didn't have the luxury of five or six strides to build momentum. It was two steps into rat-infested puddles, leap for all I was worth, and then lots of positive thinking.

As I left the ground, tucking my knees up into my gut as far as they would go, I had my doubts about whether I had enough juice to get the job done. And just before I landed, I could have sworn I felt one of my heels brush the farther rail.

But I must have cleared it because I wasn't Kentucky Fried Zeno. I was still breathing, still a burden on friends and family, and still chugging for the far platform.

Of course, I had the oncoming train to worry about. And it was close—*real* close—looming just to my right, its twin headlights glaring at me like a couple of big, angry eyes.

Shouting a curse, I took two more ragged steps, coiled, and leaped for the platform. Come on, I thought, get *up*!

I landed on my toes, clearing the edge of the platform by inches. That was the good news. The bad news was that I didn't have my balance. As the train rumbled by behind me, brakes screeching, I found myself falling back into it.

That is, until someone reached out and grabbed me by the neckline of my shirt. I found myself looking into the face of the biggest black guy I had ever met—seven feet tall if he was an inch, with huge shoulders, and hands the size of small children.

"Thanks," I said.

"No problem," he told me, releasing my shirt.

"Not for you," I said. "But for me, it could have been a *huge* problem."

By then, the train doors were opening. I peeked through the window on the other side of the car and saw Aura Boy making his way across the tracks, obviously desperate to stay on my trail. Unfortunately for him, I had other ideas.

The stairs that led up to the street were farther down the platform, just past the turnstiles. Without another thought, I bolted for them.

I didn't wait to see how long it took my pursuer to get around the subway train, or how he proceeded afterward. I didn't even know if he cleared the third rails.

I just powered through a turnstile, ate up the steps two at a time, and spilled out onto Forty-second Street again. The same street, the same rain, except now I was a little farther down the block.

As it happened, I still had every intention of taking the subway uptown. Just not the Sixth Avenue line.

Knowing the aura guy would eventually figure out where I'd gone, I left the sidewalk for the street—and began to weave my way through the traffic, which had done me the timely favor of stopping for a red light.

I was like a point guard picking my way through the lane. Two cars forward, one to the left. Two more cars forward, another to the left. Drivers glared at me from behind the arcs of their windshield wipers, wishing they could get out and move the way I was moving.

As a bonus, there were plenty of nice, tall trucks in the mix. Even if Aura Boy got lucky and came out of the subway where I had, it would hard for him to find me with all those trucks in the way.

When the light changed, the taxis leaned on their horns and the cars started to inch forward. Like a crazy man I moved with them, as if I believed *I* was a car too.

Believe me, it wasn't the strangest thing people would see that day. After all, this was New York.

Not surprisingly, I got honked a lot. It wasn't personal. It was just that everybody around me thought I was trying to get myself killed and screw up their insurance premiums.

Finally I saw an opening in the traffic going in the opposite direction, and scooted to the other side of the street. I was still hidden by the trucks, but just to be sure I shot a look back over my shoulder in the direction of the subway station.

No auras anywhere. Inwardly, I cheered.

But I wasn't taking anything for granted. I made my way east at a brisk jog, which was as fast as I could move on the wet sidewalks without knocking somebody over. The light was with me as I crossed Fifth Avenue, and then again when I crossed Madison.

Grand Central Terminal rose up on my left, a bunch of rain-slicked Greek-god types clustered around its clock. I was almost where I needed to be—and still no Aura Boy in sight.

As I passed Vanderbilt, I saw that a shiny red bus had pulled to the curb in front of Grand Central's main entrance and was letting out a flood of tourists, so I swung back out into the street and did an end-run around them. Then I popped into the next door in line, which led me down an escalator to the Lexington IRT subway line.

Usually, people just stand there on the escalator and wait for it to do its thing. I roared down the metal steps like my life depended on it.

Or like Tomi's did.

I was tempted to hop the turnstile and get down the stairs to the subway tracks as quickly as I could. But that would only draw the attention of the station manager, who would call the cops, and I didn't have time to deal with that.

So I took out my Metro Card as I had before, slipped it into the slot, and watched the system deduct another fare. Then I pushed the bar, entered the station, and went downstairs to wait for my train.

Lucky for me, it was pulling in just as I got there. I slipped inside, willed the doors to close until they actually did so, and then took out my cell phone.

Unfortunately, I was living in the Stone Age when it came to personal technology, as Tomi so often reminded me, so my phone didn't have an internet connection.

But I could call somebody who did. Punching in the number, I waited for Bernie to pick up.

Come on, I thought. You're retired. You've *got* to be home.

A moment later, I heard a click. A *good* one.

"Zeno?" said Bern. "*How are ya?*"

"Do me a favor," I said, dispensing with the pleasantries.

"*Sure, boyo. What?*"

"You near a computer?"

"*Not too far.*"

"Look up car rental places. In the vicinity of Lex and Eighty-sixth."

Eighty-sixth was five stops away. I figured that would give Bernie enough time to find something. It would also put a quick couple of miles between me and Aura Boy.

"Car rental?" Bernie echoed. "*Something happen to your—*"

"Never mind. Just get me a rental place."

A second went by but it felt like a lot longer. "*Zeno, tell me you didn't get another meet-me-if-you-want-to-see-Tomi-again note."*

"I didn't, all right?"

*"Then what's this about? Why do you need a rental car all of a sudden?"*

"I just do."

The train slowed to a stop at Fifty-first Street and the doors opened. Nobody with an aura got in. I made sure of that.

*"Hell,"* said Bernie, *"I could lend you my car. I'll gas it up for you and everything."*

"I don't want your car," I told him. "I want to rent one."

The conductor announced the next stop. The doors slid closed again.

*"This is crazy, Zee."*

"For the love of *God*," I said a little too loud, drawing concerned looks from the other people in my car, "tell me where I can rent a goddamned *car*."

People who were getting off at Fifty-ninth Street started to get up from their orange seats. I turned my back to them and spoke more quietly into the phone.

*"Please,* Bern. I'm begging you. I'm on my knees."

He cursed a few times, liberally mixing in the word "Greek" and the word "stubborn." But in the end, he did what I asked.

Fortunately for me, Bernie always left his computer running. On the other hand, he wasn't exactly the fastest mouse in the West.

Fifty-ninth Street came and went. "Bern . . . ?"

*"I'm looking, Cowboy. Keep your shirt on."*

No problem, I thought.

As we approached Sixty-eighth Street, Bernie cursed a blue streak. *"The damned thing just froze on me."*

"It *can't* freeze," I pleaded. "Not now."

"Wait," he said. "Okay, it's working again. Yeah, right there. I got one for you. It's—"

I couldn't hear the rest. Of course, it was only recently that the city had started wiring the subways for cell phones. There were still some dead spots.

Patience, I told myself.

The doors opened again, closed again. Sixty-eighth Street became a fond memory.

Suddenly, Bernie's voice came back even louder than before. *"Did you get that?"*

"No," I had to tell him. "You faded out for a minute. Give it to me again, okay?"

"Sure. It's Five Boros Car Rental. Sixty-seven Eighty-fourth street, between Lex and Third. I just hope to Heaven you know what you're doing."

I hope so too, I thought. I repeated the address so I wouldn't forget it: "Sixty-seven Eighty-fourth Street. Sixty-seven Eighty-fourth Street . . ."

We began to slow down for Seventy-seventh Street. As we stopped, I scanned the faces of the people waiting on the platform. Still no auras.

*"Anything else?"* Bernie asked.

"That'll do it, Bern. You're a pal."

*"Great. So I'll be the first guy to speak at your funeral."*

"Don't say that," I told him, as the doors opened. "I'll call you when I can." And I ended the connection.

A couple of minutes later, the subway doors opened again—this time at Eighty-sixth street. I popped out of the car and went up the stairs two at a time. When I reached street level, I took a second or two to look around.

There were no auras there either. The skies were darker, the rain was heavier, and the fight for taxicabs was at a fever pitch. But no auras.

I ran down Lex in the direction of Eighty-fourth, cutting a sometimes tortuous path among my fellow New Yorkers. No one thought anything of it, either. The way the rain was coming down, I wasn't the only one making like a running back at the Super Bowl.

I remembered being in that neighborhood just a few days earlier, wondering if I should take Bernie's advice and propose to Tomi. I wanted that night back. I wanted another chance.

At the intersection of Lex and Eighty-fifth, I came within a couple of inches of getting hit by a taxi. Naturally, the driver had made it a lot closer than it had to be. *That* would teach me to try to juke an oncoming cab.

At Eighty-fourth Street, I hung a right. Five Boros Car Rental was in the middle of the block.

It had seen better days. The formica on the eggplant-purple counter was chipped in places, exposing the pressed wood underneath. There was a faint smell of stale cigarette smoke in the air. And the plastic sign on the back wall was missing the letter "r" in the word "Boros."

Five Boos, I thought. It didn't exactly inspire confidence.

The strawberry blonde at the counter looked like she had just gotten out of college. "How can I help you today?" she asked me.

"A car," I said.

"Full size?" she asked.

I nodded. "Sure."

Then I looked back through the window at the people rushing past us in the rain. Lots of umbrellas, but no one with any kind of glow around him. I was grateful.

"How many days?" asked the blonde.

"A week." That would give me some leeway, if I needed it, before they started to wonder where the car was. After all, I might be gone a while.

"Will you be traveling out of state?"

"Yes," I said. *Way* out of state. "And I'll take all the insurance, whatever you've got." Normally I was more discerning, but I figured it would be faster that way.

The woman had a couple more questions for me. I answered them, and gave her my credit card and my driver's license. Then I signed the rental agreement and initialed "here, here, and here."

Next to the storefront, there was a ramp that led down into the bowels of wherever Five Boros kept their cars. I waited in the shadows just inside the opening, hoping to stay dry as well as unseen.

Well, maybe not dry, exactly. Just not any wetter than I was already.

When the car surged out of the depths, I saw it was a Charger.

Red. Powerful-looking. The kind of vehicle I wouldn't have minded driving when I was a kid.

But not now.

I should have asked for something less conspicuous, I thought. Something silver, something gray. *Dumb, dumb, dumb.*

But switching to another car at that point would take time. So I took the keys from the kid who'd brought up the Charger, gave him a few bucks, and got behind the wheel. Sparing a glance in either direction through the rapid sweep of windshield wipers, I made sure one more time that none of the auras were around. Then I swung the car out of the driveway and headed east on Eighty-fourth Street.

At Third Avenue, I made a right and kept going till I was well past Central Park South and all the tourists. Further down, there were no horse-drawn carriages, no cycle rickshaws to slow up traffic—just the rain. On Fifty-first street, I plowed through a puddle and went west.

A left just before the river put me on Twelfth Avenue, which fed into Eleventh and then West Street and took me down to the Holland Tunnel. The tunnel was clear until about the halfway point. Then traffic slowed to almost a standstill.

Great, I thought.

I kept looking in my rear view mirror, though I wasn't sure what I expected to see. Even if the auras were coming after me, even if they somehow knew where I had gone, they would be stuck two or ten or thirty car lengths behind me. If I couldn't move, they couldn't move either.

Then I got a crazy thought: *Unless they went into the tunnel on foot.*

No way, I told myself. Not in front of everybody in the tunnel. The auras liked to stay in the background, right?

Still, I couldn't stop checking out the rear view, expecting a swarm of glowing guys to come bounding after me like overgrown green frogs.

I almost jumped when I heard the voice in my head again.

*. . . me, Zeno?*

The ghost was back, and I was glad to hear from him. After our last hiatus had gone on for days, I wasn't sure how long this one would be.

Since I wasn't on the street anymore, I didn't have to pretend to be speaking into my phone. I could talk to the ghost without anybody thinking I'd gone around the bend.

"I read you," I said.

*. . . difficult to get hold of you,* he said, still plagued by the static problem.

"You've got me now," I assured him.

He said a bunch of words. "Bearded" was the only one I could identify with any certainty.

"That's right," I said, "I was talking about the bearded man. The one in my dreams. Actually, the last time I saw him was *outside* my dreams."

*You . . . Hell,* said the ghost.

People used that word in trivial ways all the time. But I had a feeling this was different. Though I hadn't really confronted the possibility, the place where I met the bearded guy face to face . . . it was a lot *like* Hell. Not with a lower case H, but with a capital. Or at least what I always thought Hell would be.

"Hell," I repeated, just to make sure.

*Yes. He . . . keep you there.*

"I know," I said. "He actually stabbed me when somebody tried to take me away from him. But, still, he seemed to know what he was talking about."

*Avoid . . .* said the ghost, with what sounded like a fair amount of urgency.

"I would," I replied, "except he's been my only dependable source of information. If I've got to take my chances with him, so be it."

*. . . careful.*

"Don't worry," I said, "I will be."

*. . . again . . . I can.*

"What?" I asked.

But he was no longer on the line.

I shook my head. *Damn.*

It was another few minutes before I came out on the other side of the tunnel. It wasn't raining half as hard as when I went in—go figure—but traffic still didn't let up for a while. In fact, it only started to break after I got past that lineup of gas stations in Jersey City.

At that point, Iraklion was only twenty miles of open road away. I took one last look in the rear view, saw absolutely nothing, and followed the big green sign for 78W.

A minute later I passed the Statue of Liberty on my left, her torch poking defiantly at the dark underbelly of the rain clouds. I thought about that poem on her base and the line about huddled masses yearning to breathe free. By then, I was beginning to entertain a hope that I could start breathing free myself.

I mean, I wasn't at the cemetery yet, but I was starting to see that I'd been a little paranoid back there in the tunnel. The whole aura thing had made me jumpier than I'd wanted to admit. But for the time being, I'd left it behind.

Another minute and I was sailing over the Newark Bay Bridge, which had always seemed to me to be long enough to be three bridges . . . until I found out it actually *was* three bridges. The bay water under all of them looked dark and angry in the rain, but it was just water. It wasn't glowing green or anything.

I had to slow down with the traffic when I got to the exits for Newark Airport. You're right near the runways there, so it's not all that unusual for a big old jet to come roaring over the highway, scaring the bejeezus out of you.

I thought about where people might be going on such a plane. It occurred to me that wherever it was, it wasn't a hundredth as crazy as the place *I* was going.

The ghost had been pretty explicit about it: It was Hell.

But looking back, I didn't think he meant the *real* Hell—the one I had heard about as a kid in Greek church—where God sat in judgement on his throne and sinners roasted in eternal flames. After all, I hadn't seen anyone even vaguely resembling God in that place, and I hadn't seen anybody roasting. Just a shitload of mist.

On the other hand, no one seemed especially happy there.

The bearded guy was pretty grim, not to mention pretty nuts. The armored guys down in the valley looked like they had given up hope of things ever getting better. And Ithaka, despite his Hollywood smile, wanted desperately to find an exit ramp.

So maybe it *was* Hell, and the Church had just gotten the details wrong. No divine presence, no hideous torments, just a lot of water vapor and long faces.

By the time I got to weighing that possibility, I had left the airport far behind. I just wasn't familiar enough with 78W to know how *far* behind, or how much driving I still had ahead of me.

Out of curiosity, I turned on the GPS device in the car and tapped in the number of my exit. I had less than ten miles to go, it told me. It also told me that the road surface might be slippery.

I had to laugh. *If that's my worst problem, I'll—*

Then I saw the auras, and I stopped laughing. There were two of them, maybe a football field behind me in the front seat of a light blue El Dorado.

*No way!* I thought, my heart pounding in my chest. *How did they—?*

Then I answered my own question: *They guessed I'd be going back to Iraklion, and the quickest way to get there was through the Holland Tunnel. So if they had to deploy their guys* somewhere, *the tunnel would have been as good a place as any.*

Maybe they had men at *all* the Hudson River crossings. I didn't know, and at the moment, I didn't care.

My only focus was the El Dorado.

The car was maybe ten years old, but I wasn't about to underestimate it. It probably still had plenty of muscle under the hood.

At the moment, it wasn't using any of it to catch up to me. It was just hanging back, doing the same speed as the rest of the traffic. As far as the guys in the El Dorado knew, they weren't doing anything to attract my attention.

Of course, they didn't know that they were glowing like two fair-sized chunks of Kryptonite.

Strange, I thought. I couldn't have said whether these guys were short or tall, bearded or clean-shaven, Polish or Puerto Rican. But their auras? Those I could see a mile away.

Unfortunately, seeing the guys wasn't the same as being able to do something about them. I couldn't let them follow me all the way to Iraklion—that much was clear. But how was I supposed to stop them?

I didn't dare pull off the highway, not in Jersey. Hell, *I'd* get lost before I lost *them*. I probably couldn't outrace them either, though it looked like at some point I might have to try.

Just not yet.

As long as the El Dorado wasn't making a move, I didn't have to make one either. I had time to burn, time to think of something.

But all I could think about was how complacent I'd been. How *stupid*. I should have known somebody would find me. After all, between Junior, Drakos, and Curly, there were boatloads of people looking.

Just as I thought that, I caught a break. Out of nowhere, a

silver Range Rover went barreling sideways into the El Dorado, sending it skidding toward the shoulder and the metal divider beyond it.

At first, I thought it was an accident—that the Rover was just changing lanes without looking. But when the El Dorado swerved back on course, the Rover smashed into it a second time.

I didn't know who was in the second car. Maybe a guy who thought the El Dorado had cut him off a mile back. Maybe something even crazier.

It was Jersey. Stuff happened.

Anyway, it wasn't up to me to figure it out. Taking advantage of the diversion, I finally gunned the engine. Let a cop come after me, I thought, watching the needle on my speedometer swing toward a hundred. I'll take my chances.

I had barely started putting some distance between me and the other guys when I saw the Range Rover begin to speed up too.

I cursed to myself. So it wasn't just a matter of getting back at the El Dorado. The guys in the Rover were coming after me too—and, more than likely, had been all along.

I didn't see any auras around them, but that didn't rule anything out. They could still have been Junior's boys, or Drakos's, or Curly's, or maybe some other party I had yet to identify.

Obviously, it was open season on Zeno Aristos. You didn't need a hunting permit to join the fun.

Not that I was going to let that stop me.

About fifty yards up ahead, there was a knot of cars all doing sixty in the rain, effectively blocking the roadway. If I'd been patient, they would probably have cleared the left lane for me.

Eventually.

But I didn't have the luxury of being patient. Dragging the Charger onto the left-side shoulder, I roared past the laggards. The Range Rover did the same thing. What's more, it began to gain on me. I hadn't read enough car magazines to know how likely that was, but it didn't matter. It was happening.

And more to the point, it was happening to *me*.

Come on, I thought. *Do something*.

I was looking around for options when the El Dorado climbed back into my rear view. Weaving back and forth, cutting off one driver after another, it clawed its way even with the Rover. Then I saw a gun pop out of the sedan and fire a round or two at the SUV.

I can't say it was a complete surprise when the guys in the Rover fired back. Or when the two cars slammed into each other again with a screech of tortured metal, the Rover trying to drive the El Dorado off the road.

Behind them, drivers were slamming on their brakes. Up ahead of me, cars were pulling over to the right. All of them were trying to give the combatants as wide a berth as possible.

All except me, of course. I was speeding up, hoping to make some headway while my pals in the bumper cars kept each other busy.

Finally, the Rover proved too much for the El Dorado, plowing it into the divider until it spun out of control, flipped over, and went skidding on its side. A bad thing, and not just for the guys inside the El Dorado—because without the other car to worry about, the Rover could focus on me again.

As before, it started to gain on the Charger. I could see it looming larger and larger in my rear view, blowing past everybody in the legal lanes. There was no way I was going to outrun it, I told myself.

No freakin' way . . .

# CHAPTER NINE

It was at that moment, as I was watching the Rover bear down on me like a giant, metallic pit bull, that I heard a long, shrill siren. I didn't have to be an expert on police procedures to know a Jersey State Police unit had joined the party.

A moment later I saw the unit itself, an unmarked black Torino. Lit up like a pinball machine, it was coming up on the right-side shoulder, moving as fast as the Rover.

I was impressed.

It couldn't have been more than a couple of minutes since the Rover and the El Dorado had started going at it. The trooper must have been sitting by the side of the road, concealed behind a bridge or something, when he got the call.

It could have been a chopper that had caught sight of the tussle between the Rover and the El Dorado, but it didn't have to be. People had cell phones. At the first sign of something bad going down, they would have rung nine-one-one.

Like the transit commercials always said, "If you see something, say something." More than likely, someone had said something.

The trooper didn't seem too concerned about the El Dorado

in his rear view, despite the fact that someone could have been expiring in it at that very moment. So another unit was probably right on his heels—a unit that would attend to the accident, leaving him to concentrate all his energies on running down the jerks still drag racing on the highway.

Me being one of them.

And if he caught me, it wasn't going to do any good to tell the guy I was a cop. First of all, this wasn't New York City. Second, I was driving like a NASCAR wannabe. Third, I was a *former* cop.

So he'd book my ass like anyone else. I couldn't let that happen.

"Sorry, pal," I told the trooper, and dug my foot that last little bit into the gas pedal.

At the same time, the trooper slid from his side of the highway to mine, deftly avoiding the cars in the lanes between. Of course, the Rover—being directly behind me—was in a position to get to me first.

Or to be *gotten* first, depending on how you looked at it.

It would have been nice if the trooper could have convinced the Rover to pull over and then allowed me to escape unhindered, but I knew that wasn't going to happen. Maybe in my dreams, but not there on a wet, dreary stretch of 78W.

The trooper had a few options. One was to nudge the Rover's rear wheels and send it into a fishtail, except that maneuver wasn't recommended with sport utility vehicles or cars moving at a high rate of speed. So, really, that wasn't an option at all.

If he'd had other troopers riding with him, they could have

boxed in the Rover and slowed it down gradually. But the guy in my rear view was all by himself.

That left him with two choices—to shoot the Rover's tires out, which would have presented a danger to the people in the other cars, or to follow the Rover until he got some help. Me? I would have just followed.

As New Jersey roared past me at more than a hundred miles an hour, I watched to see what the trooper would do. As far as I could tell he was staying in the game, nothing more.

Good choice, I thought.

The guys in the Rover, on the other hand, weren't content to just pace me. They wanted to catch me. And as they closed the gap between us to almost nothing, they were on the verge of accomplishing that objective.

Then what? I asked myself. Were they going to shoot at me the way they had shot at the El Dorado? Or try to run me into the divider?

Whatever they'd had in mind originally, the appearance of the trooper had to have complicated it. If they tried to light me up, he'd have to do his best to stop them. And if he couldn't stop them, he'd still be a witness to the bloodbath.

In one way, I was intrigued to see what move the Rover boys would make next. But in another way, a much more *selfish* way, I was determined not to let them make that move.

What I needed was a break in the legitimate traffic lanes—and all of a sudden, as if some New Jersey wet-highway genie had granted my wish, I got one. In fact, it couldn't have been a better opening if I had picked up each and every car on 78W and put it down exactly where I wanted it.

Knowing the situation wouldn't stay that way, I yanked the wheel hard to the right and pulled the Charger back through the crowd. By the time the opening closed I was on the opposite shoulder, putting the pedal to the metal again.

Getting my bearings, I saw that the Rover was still riding the shoulder on the left side with the Torino right behind him. It was a beautiful thing.

I glanced at the GPS screen. A little more than three minutes until I reached my exit. And the trooper would almost certainly go after the SUV in front of him rather than the Charger across the way.

I was starting to feel good about my chances of making Iraklion when I heard the last thing I wanted to hear—the wailing of another siren. Cursing out loud, I checked my mirrors and saw the flash of a spinning blue beacon light somewhere back in traffic.

No, I realized, not just one light—*two* of them.

And as I watched, my jaw clenching, I saw the cars swing out onto the shoulder. *My* shoulder.

That's great, I thought. *Really great. Now we have a whole damned chase scene.* It was a pity someone didn't have a movie camera.

The newcomers could have helped out with the Rover. That would have been the friendly thing to do. But for whatever reason, they appeared to have pegged me as the more serious threat to public safety.

Or maybe just the guy more likely to escape. Who knew? In

any case, I had an even bigger problem than before.

I looked up ahead for the exit. No indication of it. At least not yet.

Had there been a sign? I was too busy scoping out my pursuit to know for sure.

Suddenly, I heard a mishmash in my head that might have been a sentence somewhere along the line. I couldn't figure out the words, but I knew where they were coming from.

The ghost was back.

Three times in one day. He was making up for lost time.

Unfortunately, I couldn't drive at a hundred miles an hour and decipher his advice at the same time. "I can't talk now," I said.

*Crap.* Wasn't that the same thing I had told him on the handball court? And how had *that* gone?

*. . . your friend . . .* said the ghost, *. . . watch out . . . him too . . .*

His words weren't any easier to make out than before. "I didn't hear you," I told him. "And even if I did, I still can't talk."

The ghost didn't say anything back. Was that because he understood my situation, I wondered, or because he had gone silent again? Or—a third possibility—because he just couldn't get through whatever barriers to communication existed between us?

I didn't know. And at the moment, I had other things on my mind.

For instance, the sign that told me I was a mile from my exit. It came up pretty fast at the speed I was going, but I was still able to read it.

So I hadn't passed it before.

That was good. I didn't think the troopers closing in behind me would give me a chance to get off the highway and get on again in the opposite direction.

By then, the Rover was nowhere in sight. I didn't know what had happened to it, but with luck I would never see it again.

As the lead trooper loomed larger in my rain-dappled rear view, I knew I had two things working in my favor. The first was that there were innocent people around. The troopers probably wouldn't discharge their weapons for fear of hitting an innocent bystander.

The other thing was that Iraklion was just ahead. If I could hang on for another minute or two, I had a shot at doing what I came to do.

"Pull over or I'll shoot out your tires," the lead trooper blared over his loudspeaker.

He was bluffing. At least, I thought he was.

Anyway, I wasn't stopping. There were a few tense seconds when I waited to see what the trooper would do next. As it turned out, he did nothing.

Then again, why should he? He probably had help up ahead in the form of a few black-and-whites. But it was help he would never get a chance to use if I reached my exit first.

As I came around a long bend in the road, the ramp showed up on the right. Fortunately it wasn't one of those hairpin deals, so even in the rain I would be able to negotiate it without slowing down too much.

On the other hand, the troopers wouldn't have to slow down either. If anything, with the kind of suspensions they had, they would be able to take the ramp faster than I could.

I took the exit with my tires screeching like the souls of the damned. I didn't dare look in the rear view to see how the troopers were faring, or I'd have wound up in the woods somewhere. I just followed the ramp and came out of it flooring my gas pedal.

The road ahead of me was a straight shot. I knew where the sign for the cemetery would be—less than a mile away, on the right. That mile went by in no time. As I caught sight of the blue and white sign, I breathed a sigh of relief.

Almost there, I thought.

I didn't slow down until I was nearly on top of the entrance to the parking lot. Then I hit the brakes hard, yanked on the wheel, and fishtailed into the lot in a cloud of flying gravel.

The last time I had seen the place, the sky was just beginning to fill with rain clouds. This time, it was pouring already.

As soon as I could, I threw open the driver's-side door and jumped out. It cost me some fabric—and some skin—as I hit the gravel and rolled.

The car slid past me, still moving, and crashed through the white wooden fence that marked the perimeter of the lot. At the same time the cops on my trail came tearing in from the road, lights flashing and sirens wailing.

By then I was on my feet again, sprinting in the direction of the gravestones. I was sure the troopers wouldn't chase me on foot if they could help it—not in all that rain. But if they fired at me, they ran the risk of hitting the stones. That wouldn't have looked good in the papers the next day.

Besides, where was I going to go? Into the woods? With back-up on its way, and they *had* to have called for back-up, there was no realistic chance of my escaping.

Or so they must have thought.

Going as hard as I could, I cut through the cemetery and headed for the tree line. Then I *did* hear shots, though I was pretty sure they were aimed at the sky and not at me.

Once I was among the trees, I felt safer. Not that a well-placed bullet couldn't still have taken me down, but it was darker there, and I knew the river wasn't far away.

The troopers yelled after me, advising me to stop. I respectfully ignored their advice. But the I deeper I went into the woods, the more I began to wonder if Iraklion had somehow double-crossed me.

Where was the river? I was sure I should have hit it already. Had it moved? And if it had, would that have been the *craziest* thing that had happened to me in the last few days?

I was beginning to panic when the ground suddenly fell away beneath my foot and I went pitching forward into something cold and wet. The river, I thought gratefully—until a bullet went whizzing by my shoulder.

Seriously hating the idea of getting reeled in so close to my objective, I got up and started running again, keeping my knees high to clear the water as much as possible. The troopers squeezed off another couple of shots, tearing off some bark from the trees ahead of me.

But as the water got deeper, there was just no way to move quickly. And the troopers, who still had both feet on solid ground, would be swiftly closing the gap. Not at all a good combination.

I kept expecting to feel a bullet plow into me from behind. I was still expecting it as the water mercifully started to get shallower again, and shallower still, and I felt my feet hit dear old terra firma.

Suddenly the rain stopped, and the river behind me vanished in the grasp of a thick, cloying mist. I was back in Hell, which—considering what I was leaving behind—was a lot better than being in Jersey.

I looked around for the bearded guy. The last time I was there, he had been waiting for me as if he knew I would show up. If he was waiting this time, I couldn't tell.

But I heard something—a murmuring I didn't remember from my last visit. I looked around, trying to locate the source of it. It took me a moment to realize that it was coming not from just one place, but *from all over*.

Then I saw the faces. They were pale and expressionless, and none of them looked familiar. They seemed to fade away into the mist, then come back again a little closer and a little clearer.

"I'm looking for someone," I said. Unfortunately I didn't know his name. All I could say was, "He has a beard."

It didn't turn out to be a conversation starter. The faces were still getting closer, crowding around me. If they were saying something, in answer to my question or otherwise, I couldn't make it out.

I didn't usually mind being the center of attention, but this was ridiculous. I decided to move.

It occurred to me that the crowd might try to stop me, but it didn't. It just moved along with me as if I were the most popular guy in Hell. And maybe I was.

But I couldn't find the one guy I was looking for.

"Go away!" someone cried out clearly and unexpectedly.

I recognized the voice. It was the redheaded guy, the one who had wanted me to help him get out of Hell. *Ithaka*.

"Shoo!" he said, shouldering his way through the crowd, growing more distinct the closer he got to me. "Get lost, all of you!"

His efforts had an effect. The faces began receding into the mist. Before long they had dispersed altogether, leaving just the two of us standing there.

Ithaka shrugged. "Sorry. Word travels quickly around here."

"What do they want?" I asked.

"What does anyone here want? To be somewhere else." And though he didn't mention it again, he was no exception. "It's good to see you."

I cut to the chase. "I need to find the bearded guy. The one who went nuts on us the last time I saw him."

Ithaka tilted his head. "Are you sure? I mean, you *did* get stabbed in the back."

"Still," I said.

Ithaka sighed. "I hope you know what you're doing. Come on, it's this way."

I let him lead me through the mists. Interestingly, none of the faces showed up again. Had Ithaka scared them off? I guessed he had, though I didn't quite understand what dead people had to be scared of.

I didn't know much about him, I thought as I followed him, so I didn't know what he was capable of. Maybe I didn't want to know. And with luck, I wouldn't have to.

"Here we are," he said abruptly.

At first, I didn't see anyone standing there in the mists. Then I realized that someone was hunkered down in front of us. Ready for anything, I moved closer.

As I'd hoped, it was the bearded guy.

He was sitting with his back against a withered, lifeless husk of a tree, his arms wrapped around his knees. He looked pale, worn out, as if he had been through a tremendous ordeal.

"Slowly and quietly," Ithaka said in my ear. "It's easily startled."

"*It?*" I asked. "Why not *him?*"

The redheaded guy looked at me. "*You* are a him. *That* is an it."

I still didn't get it. "What makes him an it?"

"You really don't know?"

I turned to the bearded guy again and studied him more closely. His features seemed a little more sunken than when I had seen him last, a little more skull-like.

"He looks like he hasn't been eating enough," I noted.

Ithaka laughed. Then he must have seen my expression because he held up a hand by way of apology. "Sorry, that was insensitive of me. But the truth is it's *never* eaten. *Ever.*"

I was tired of the games. "Why not?"

"Because shades don't eat."

"Shades?" I repeated. "What's a shade?"

"A shade," Ithaka said patiently, "is what's left after someone dies. At least in most cases."

I considered the information. "You mean like a ghost?"

"More or less. But this," he said, pointing to the bearded guy, "is a different kind of shade. A lesser kind. Because the person it was is still walking the earth."

Now I was *really* lost. "So he's the ghost of someone who's still alive?"

"That's one way to put it."

Suddenly, the shade seemed to notice us. His eyes came alive like tiny fish, the kind that inhabit tide-pools and flit away from even a shadow.

What was it he had said the last time I was there among the mists, when he thought Ithaka was taking me away?

"*He's mine!*"

If Drakos could be believed, I had lived longer than a normal lifetime. How much longer, he wouldn't say. But if you were trying to be poetic, you might say I had outlived my natural death.

I stared at the shade, at his eyes and nose and mouth. They looked familiar, at least a little bit. If he didn't have a beard, if he had a little more flesh on his bones . . .

Talk about creepy.

"It's *me*," I asked Ithaka, "isn't it? I'm the one who's still alive, and this is my ghost."

He didn't say anything in response. He just smiled. But that was confirmation enough.

I recalled something else. Ithaka had asked me, either just before or just after I was stabbed, "Do you want to stay here *forever*?"

Did that mean my shade, if that was what he was, had some kind of power over me? Some kind of bond he could use to keep me with him if I wasn't careful?

I asked Ithaka if that was true also.

"Absolutely. It's lonely, you see, even lonelier than before now that you've come to visit it again. And the longer you linger here, the easier it is for it to make you stay."

All the more reason for me to get what I came for and leave. I moved closer to the bearded guy and knelt in front of him. "I need your help," I said. "I want to understand what's going on."

He stared at me for a moment. Then, in a hollowed-out voice, he said, "Ask."

"The armored ones," I said, "the people who were filing through the valley after they lost their battle . . . you said they were the Bronze Men, and that they were made by Zeus."

The bearded guy nodded. "In his desire to achieve perfection, he created a race of bronze warriors. But after a while he saw how cruel they were, how unrelentingly violent, and banished them from the earth. In the thousands of years that have passed since their exile, the Bronze Men have waged war upon war and honed their skills on the battlefield. But they were still not strong enough to stand against the invaders."

"The invaders . . . " I echoed.

"Yes. The invaders cut them down the way a scythe cuts the wheat of the plain. And as the Bronze Men fell, watering the ground with their blood, they appeared in this precinct of Hades."

I didn't ask how that worked. I had too many more pressing questions.

One thing was clear: The Bronze Men were big and strong, and if my shade was right, all they had ever thought about was making war. And yet, these invaders had beaten the crap out of them.

"Who *are* the invaders?" I asked.

"A new race," said my shade, "never seen before on your world or any other. A mighty race. You should know—you engaged in sport with one of them."

"I don't think so," I said, certain that I would have remembered such a thing. Then I realized what he was talking about.

The other day. The handball game. *Junior.*

The way he had gone up that fence . . . at the time, I had been more than a little amazed. I had never seen anyone so quick, so agile. Or so fast. Now I knew why.

He wasn't human. "So Junior, the guy I played handball with . . . he's one of these invaders."

It put a whole new spin on things.

Then the spin began to accelerate. "He's not just one of them," said my shade. "He's their leader."

You know those carnival rides where the floor tilts under your feet? I felt like I was on that ride.

Because if Junior was as powerful and inhuman a being as my shade was suggesting, he had to have sussed out that action back in Long Island City. He had to have known what was going down.

Yet he had walked into our trap anyway. Why?

I put that question to my shade. "Hubris," he said. "A desire to prove himself equal to any challenge."

I had been accused of that myself—but never when the stakes were so high. "So he put himself and his people at risk... just to play handball with me?"

My shade nodded again. "Yes."

"Why would he do that?" I wondered out loud. "I'm good, but there are guys who are better."

My shade didn't say anything. Growing impatient, I looked to Ithaka for help. He just shrugged.

Suddenly, my shade released his knees and leaned forward, reaching out for me with one hand. "There is someone else you need to be leery of," he said, his voice wracked with anxiety, "one so powerful she can only be an Olympian."

"An Olympian?" I asked, pretty sure that my shade wasn't talking about an Alpine skiier.

Ithaka looked as if the ground had split in front of him. "A god," he explained soberly. "Or in this case, since our friend here has mentioned a 'she,' it would have to be a goddess."

I'd swallowed some strange things since I set out to play handball with Junior—a guy who came to me in my dreams, a picture I'd taken fifty years ago, the sight of people glowing like fireflies. Even a place where I could talk with ghosts.

But... a goddess?

"She's angry," said my shade, his eyes shrunken with fear as he looked at me, "And dangerous. Very dangerous. But to get your mate back, you will have to stand before her."

Before a *goddess*. It seemed crazy.

"Where is she?" I asked. I meant Tomi, but I could have just as easily been talking about the goddess.

My shade shivered a little, as if he'd been caught in the grip of a sudden chill. "On Olympos."

Now *that* name I knew.

My friend had opened a restaurant a few years back, a place with all the greek specialties, and he had named it Olympos. I remembered him telling me that that was where the gods lived, so it was all right to charge a little more for souvlaki.

Now it had a different meaning for me. It was the place where I would find Tomi. And I was going, angry goddess or not.

"Ask him *which* goddess," said Ithaka.

"Does it matter?" I asked.

Then I realized it might. Like anyone else, different goddesses might have different agendas.

I turned to my shade. "Do you know *which* goddess?"

For a moment, he looked like he might tell me. But in the end, he didn't. He just shut his eyes, as if he needed to rest.

"I don't think you'll get any more from him," said Ithaka. "We should go."

"Hang on," I told him. Then I leaned closer to my shade, keeping my eyes on his hands in case he was thinking about ventilating me again, and asked, "Is there anything I can do for you?"

After all, he was *me*—or at least, someone very much *like* me—and it was my fault he was so lonely. So if I could improve his lot in that place a little, I wanted to do so.

He didn't open his eyes. He just said, "You can die."

There wasn't any anger or resentment behind the words. It

was just the answer to my question.

But I didn't have any intention of dying. At least not for a while. "Well," I said, "if anything else comes to you, let me know—all right?"

No response. Apparently, my shade too thought the conversation was over.

As I got up to leave him, I felt the way a parent must feel when he leaves his child in school for the first time. That is, the way I *imagined* a parent would feel, never having been one myself.

At least, as far as I knew. As I was learning, there was a lot more to me than met the eye.

"Come on," said Ithaka.

"Where are we going?" I asked.

"Somewhere a safe distance from here. That shade of yours may seem tame now, but you've seen what he's capable of."

I nodded.

As I followed Ithaka through the mists, I thought out loud. "It still doesn't make sense. What's so special about me that Junior would take a chance on getting caught by the police?"

To that point, Ithaka hadn't given me any indication that he knew who Junior was. But he gave me one then—he looked away from me.

"You *know*," I concluded, "don't you?"

No answer.

"*Don't* you?" I insisted.

I had a feeling that I was pushing open a door, and that behind it, coiled in the dark like a nest of snakes, lay all the answers—even the ones to questions I didn't know enough to ask.

Ithaka frowned. "Yes. But I don't think I should tell you."

"Why not?" I asked.

"You told me not to."

*What? "I* told you not to?"

He nodded. "More than once."

"When?"

"At a time when you knew who you were. I can't say exactly when it was from your point of view. Time passes differently here—it's hard to equate it to the passage of time in your world."

"And I told you not to tell me anything about *myself*?" It seemed unlikely.

Ithaka's frown deepened. "You said there might come a time when you returned and wanted to know certain things. You forbade me to tell you about them." He bit his lip. "In my desire to help you, I may have said too much already."

"I'm telling you now," I said, "you can forget whatever I said before."

His eyes flashed. "Do you think I *want* to anger you? You're my only hope of escape from this place. If I deny you now, it's because you made me swear to do so—and because there will come a time when you hold me accountable for that vow."

I wanted to kill him—except as far as I could tell, he was a ghost already. Besides, he was only trying to help me, or so he claimed.

"It's all right," I said. "Never mind."

Ithaka looked grateful. "I'm glad you understand."

I *didn't* understand. I didn't *want* to understand. I wanted to know what everyone else knew.

The ghost, my shade, Curly, Drakos, Junior . . . all of them seemed privy to information about me that I myself couldn't access. I had the feeling that I was playing a game of Blind Man's Bluff, and that I was the poor sap wearing the blindfold.

"So," said Ithaka, "what's our next stop?"

"There isn't any," I said.

"You're going home, then?"

I hadn't thought things out that far. But I definitely couldn't go back to Astoria. It would be a step in the wrong direction, and a big one.

Besides, I knew now where Tomi was. "To Olympos," I said.

Ithaka looked at me as if I were a child, and not a very bright one. "You really don't remember *anything*, do you?"

I held my hands out in an appeal for help. "Why? What did I say?"

"You can't get to Olympos from *here*. At least, not directly."

"All right. Then where *can* I get to?"

He told me. "That will at least put you in the vicinity."

I considered the option. I might not find a rousing welcome in the place Ithaka had suggested, but it seemed I had little choice in the matter.

"That'll work," I said. "Can you show me the way?"

"Of course. What are friends for?"

He led me through the mists again. But we hadn't gotten far before I heard the murmuring.

Ithaka seemed to hear it too. "We'd better move," he said.

"They'll be harder to drive away this time."

I didn't ask why that would be. I just followed him as he picked up his pace.

The murmuring got louder anyway. And closer. After a while I began to see the faces looming at me out of the mists, crowding me and receding and then crowding me again. At first there were just a few of them, but they seemed to multiply with every step I took.

"How much farther?" I asked my guide.

"Just a little," he said, denying me anything more specific.

He had said time was different in Hell. Maybe it was the same with distances.

As I thought that, I felt a hand alight on my arm. I brushed it off. But a moment later I felt one on my other arm, and two more on my back.

"Get out of here!" Ithaka barked at the faces.

It didn't help. They kept closing in on us.

And they didn't want to just touch me, it seemed. They wanted to pierce me, crawl inside me, *be* me.

I pushed them away over and over again, occasionally earning a respite for myself. But I couldn't keep them all away at once. I kept hearing them mutter the word "Die," or something that sounded like it.

Would the ghosts benefit from my death the way my shade would? Would my death make them complete in some way? I didn't see how, but I was hardly an expert on the subject.

Suddenly, I realized that I had lost sight of Ithaka. I called his name, but got no answer. For all I knew, he had been overcome by the other ghosts, swept under by the sheer weight and number of them.

And where did that leave me? I couldn't stay there in Hell. Not while Tomi needed me.

But I didn't know my way around the place. All I could see were the faces and the mists. I could walk for hours, days, maybe even years and never get any closer to finding an exit.

Not that I would be allowed to wander for so long. My shade would see to that. Then I would be like the rest of them, hungry for the company of the living, longing to leave though there was no chance of escape.

Abruptly, I felt a grip on my forearm that was much stronger than the rest. *Ithaka?* I thought hopefully. His face slid toward me out of the mists, his eyes wide with what looked like fear.

"This way!" he cried.

I didn't need to be told twice. Gripping his wrist even as he gripped mine, I let him pull me along. Hands clutched at me but couldn't find purchase. As long as we kept moving, I thought, we'd be all right.

Of course, it was at that moment that Ithaka decided to stop in his tracks. He looked back at me, pain in his eyes, and said, "Don't forget about me!"

Then he whipped me past him, planted his hand in the small of my back as I went by, and *pushed*.

# CHAPTER TEN

Propelled by Ithaka, I felt the ground fall away under my feet. All of a sudden, I was in the water.

But it wasn't a shallow river—not this time.

I found myself plunging to a depth that was definitely deep enough to drown in, a region that was wild enough to toss me around like a load of laundry on spin cycle. Fortunately, I could make out the sun as a bright spot high above me, so I wasn't too far from a mouthful of air.

Kicking hard, I launched myself upward. A moment later, I broke the surface and looked around with eyes full of stinging salt water. It took a moment for them to clear enough for me to see anything.

Then I saw that I was rocking in the waves just off a horseshoe-shaped beach. The sea around me was a startling, foam-laced expanse of blue—so blue, in fact, that it looked like toilet bowl cleaner. It reminded me of the sea I had seen from the prison Curly put me in, except for one important difference: this time I was *in* it.

Fortunately, the current seemed to be nudging me toward the beach. That was a good thing. The only problem I could see was what I *couldn't* see—the possibility of rocks jutting up just under the surface.

I tried to look out for them, but all the foam made them difficult to spot. All I could do was keep my knees up and my feet tucked underneath me. That way, I would hit the rocks with the soles of my shoes if I hit them at all.

Sure enough, I felt a jolt as my heel made contact with something hard, unyielding, and unseen. But to my relief, that only happened once. And in less time than I would have guessed, I was washed into the shallows just off the beach.

Fighting the push and pull of the surf, I trudged the rest of the way onto the sand. Then I looked back at the seemingly endless expanse of water behind me. I was grateful that I'd gotten through it without anything ugly happening.

Okay, I thought. *So where am I?*

It was definitely *not* the place Ithaka had described to me. Had he made a mistake? Or misled me on purpose?

I cursed, and not softly. Every misstep, every blind alley was making it harder for me to get to Tomi.

On the other hand, whining wasn't going to get me anywhere. Wherever I was, I needed to scout the place out. Only then could I figure out how to remedy the situation.

From where I was standing, the land rose at a pretty steep angle into a jumble of big grey rocks and hardy-looking trees, all of them bent under the influence of the sea winds. Whether the slope stopped at that point or leveled off a bit and kept going up again, it was difficult to tell.

But there was no other land around. At least none that I could see.

Then again, thanks to the headlands on either side of the beach, I could look out in only one direction. For all I knew, I was standing on the end of a peninsula. If I climbed the slope, I would have a better idea of where I was and what I could do about it.

It turned out not to be an easy ascent. The friendliest-looking parts of the incline were a few long, narrow stretches of grey rock. But I soon discovered that they were covered with a layer of tiny pebbles that made it hard to get any traction. I found myself sliding back time and again, managing to keep my feet underneath me but making very little progress.

Eventually, I took to a disorderly cascade of rocks and trees instead, pulling myself from one formation to the next. It was harder work by far but at least it got me some place.

The sun blazed overhead, blinding me when I looked up at it. I could feel it burning my skin, unhindered by even a hint of a cloud, but the breeze kept me from overheating.

Finally, after what had to have been an hour or more of wrestling with the landscape, I reached what seemed to be one of the higher points on the island. But the trees grew too close there for me to get a good view of anything. I wouldn't be able to see what was on the other side until I reached the far slope.

I hadn't been hiking among the timbers for long when I came to a clearing. But the place wasn't really *clear* because it was filled with a bunch of tall, narrow monuments, each of them about my height. Inspecting the closest of them, I saw that it had been chiseled with some skill from a hunk of red-veined marble.

On its top sat a marble creature with the head and body of a lion, the wings of an eagle, and the tail of a snake. Below it, a frieze showed an old man sitting in a chair, a bunch of small children gathered at his feet. The frieze was painted with red, black, and blue pigment.

It wasn't the work of that guy who carved the friezes Curly had shown me. *What was his name? Neleos.* Anyway, I remembered his style, and this was different.

At the base of the monument there was an inscription. I couldn't read it but it looked to me like ancient Greek, the kind of writing I had seen in history museums.

I looked past that particular monument and tried to estimate how many more of them were in the clearing. Hundreds, it seemed to me. And I caught glimpses of even more of them in the woods beyond.

It was a cemetery—of course. It wasn't an accident, then, that I had walked through a graveyard the first time I entered Hell—through a graveyard and across a little river.

This time, too, I had crossed a body of water to reach a place where people buried their dead. The only question was . . . where were the people who had done all this burying? Were they still nearby, or had they left this region a long time ago?

I kept on walking.

The farther I went, the more monuments I saw. As far as I could tell, no two were the same. They were topped with galloping centaurs or men with fishtails leaping out of the water or goat-boys playing pipes as they kicked up their hooves. The friezes, I guessed, showed men and women doing whatever they had done in life—treating the sick or wrestling or standing at the bow of a boat—and some of them used green pigment instead of blue, or orange instead of red.

Finally, the clearing gave way to dense woods and the monuments grew further apart. After a while, it was hard to find any of them. At the same time, ever so gradually, the land began to slope downward under my feet.

More than likely, I was past the highest point on the island. It'll be all downhill from here, I thought.

Just then, I caught a glimpse of something through the narrow gaps between the trees—a mosaic of pastel colors gleaming in the afternoon sun. I had seen those colors before . . .

On the slopes of Ajax's island.

So Ithaka hadn't steered me wrong after all. He had sent me where he said he would send me, more or less. Now it was up to me to take the last few steps.

And take them I did. With each one, the angle of the ground underfoot got a little steeper, the woods thinned out a little more, and the sweep of pastel-colored houses in the distance got a little easier to see.

Finally, the grass gave way to stretches of grey stone, just like the ones on the other side of the cemetery. And like the ones on the other side they were covered with a layer of tiny pebbles, making the going pretty treacherous.

In the end I found one of those tree-bearing rock beds I'd negotiated on the way up, and used it to make my way down. Little by little, the vista opened up before me, and I could see that I wasn't on a peninsula after all. I was on an island.

As a matter of fact, it was one of *many* islands. Ajax's was by far the closest, but there were others beyond it—maybe four or five altogether, all of them covered with pastel-colored houses, so it was hard to say exactly where one island left off and the next one began.

So far so good, I thought.

*Then I noticed the boats.*

There were a couple dozen of them, maybe more, anchored all along the shore of Ajax's island. Long, lean sailing vessels, with hulls made of mahogany or some other dark red wood. And they didn't look friendly, if the black sails furled under their masts were any indication.

I thought back to when I was imprisoned in the room with the cot, and looking out to sea. I didn't recall seeing any ships at all off the coast of the island, much less so *many* of them.

As I studied them, I noticed another thing—a wisp of something thin and dark coming up from among the pastel-colored houses. It was hard to see because the winds were tearing it apart once it got to a certain height, but it looked like a plume of smoke.

Then I realized that it wasn't the only one. There were other, smaller wisps coming from other places—from other *fires*, I thought, correcting myself.

What the hell was going on?

I didn't think it was a coincidence that so many blazes were going at once, or that the ships with the black sails happened to be there to witness them. Unless I was way off base, Ajax's island was under attack.

I didn't know for sure who the assailant was, but I could guess. Not Drakos. After all, he had used rubber bullets when he came to free me from Ajax's people.

That left either Junior or somebody I hadn't heard of. My gut told me it was Junior.

It seemed absurd in a way, because I still thought of him as a gang banger, and gang bangers didn't typically lead invasions of tropical islands. But he had destroyed the armies of the Bronze Men, which made him a little more than your average gang banger, so maybe the idea wasn't so absurd after all.

In any case, *someone* was unloading on Ajax's people. Someone was wreaking havoc and starting fires, and probably spilling people's blood while he was at it.

I remembered the glimpses I'd caught of kids and old folks on Ajax's island. They were like my neighbors back in Astoria. If Junior took over the island, would he spare their lives? Or he would he kill them too?

I didn't know the answer, but I had a suspicion I wouldn't like it.

Maybe Ajax had the clout to turn the invaders back, and I was worried about nothing. Maybe he did it every day of the week—I couldn't say. What I *could* say was that my plan to get Tomi back was suddenly on life support.

*After all I've gone through to get here.* Everything had fallen into place. I was going to get Tomi back. I was so *close*.

Overwhelmed by the fear that I would fail her, that I would

never see her again, an animal rage erupted from inside me. I bellowed into the wind long and loud, until my throat hurt.

The wind didn't seem to give a damn.

Calm, I thought. *Be calm, Zeno. Go over the facts.*

I'd come back to find a way to Olympos, where Tomi was supposedly being held by a goddess. I'd hoped I could talk Ajax into taking me there, or at least pointing me in the right direction.

But how could I ask for his help if I couldn't reach him? So, invaders or no invaders, I *had* to reach him.

Putting my frustration aside, I tried to judge the distance to Ajax's island. I'd never been good at distances, especially on the water, but I figured it was three to four miles. Maybe closer to four.

I wasn't the best swimmer in the world, but I also wasn't the worst. I had good stamina—Tomi always told me that. I could stay in the water for hours, or until she came to the edge of the beach and yelled for me to come in.

I looked down at the waves lapping at the rocks below me like big, blue dogs. I can handle those waves, I told myself. *I don't need a boat.*

Which was good, because I sure as hell didn't have one.

Taking my time, I checked the wind, the current, the time of day. As far as I could tell, they were all in my favor. Really, all I had to do was stay afloat and let those big, friendly waves do the work.

My only concern was getting down to the water. The slope was even steeper on this side than on the side I had ascended, and there weren't any stairways or even footpaths that I could make out.

I remembered a time that Tomi and I went to a resort in the Poconos with a few other couples. The place had a big pool and a diving board that had to be twenty feet high. Everybody went off it, some more than once.

Everybody, that is, except me.

I took a lot of crap for it, too, even in the car on the way home. It didn't matter. There was no way I was going to go off that board.

Just like there was no way I was going to go cliff-diving now. "No way in the world," I said out loud.

The wind snatched away my words just as soon as I'd said them, maybe because it knew I was full of crap. How could I let a little thing like a drop of a hundred feet keep me from getting Tomi back?

I couldn't—though it wasn't just the drop I had to look forward to. There was also the possibility of some big, jagged rocks lurking just beneath the surface. And some man-eating sea life (I'd seen *Jaws* a couple of weeks earlier on one of the cable movie channels).

And even if I managed to cross the water, I'd have to get past those ships, and whatever lines the invaders had established on the island.

For that matter, I didn't know what kind of reception Ajax would give me when he saw me. For all I knew, he would blame me for his troubles and throw me off the nearest rock.

But none of that mattered. I hadn't come this far, dodging

cars and bullets and subway trains, just to chicken out now.

"I just have to find the absolute lowest point," I said, speaking out loud again because I found it comforting in the face of what I was going to do, "and also a place that lets me get a running start, which may help me clear the rocks."

I spent a few minutes exploring the ground to my right and then to my left. It didn't get me anywhere. Unfortunately, the spot where I had started was my best option.

I moved to the edge of the cliff, looked down at the expanse of royal blue water and the lines of white-capped waves crawling across it, and swore beneath my breath. Then I backed off about thirty paces and stripped away my shoes, socks, pants, and shirt. They were all that would mark my passing if I didn't make it to the far shore.

But I had a feeling I *would* make it, because I didn't think Destiny or the Fates or whoever was in charge of these things was done torturing me yet.

I took another look at Ajax's island, sizing it up like an opponent on a handball court.

And suddenly, for just a moment, I saw something else . . .

*Another place going up in flames, except it was at night and the flames were much bigger, much wilder, and I was right there in the midst of them.*

Then the image went away.

I shook my head and thought, What was *that*? A blast from my ridiculously long past? Or maybe a glimpse of my future? At the rate I was learning things about myself, anything was possible.

I turned to the island again, focused on it. Before I got any other visions, I had to get going. I took a deep breath, let it out.

Then, yelling so loud even the wind couldn't silence me, I sprinted for the place where the land ended and the air took over. At the last possible moment, I planted my left foot and dove out as far as I could. For a moment, I felt like I was flying, and could maybe fly forever.

At which point gravity took over.

Gritting my teeth, I stuck out my arms, tucked in my head, and locked my thumbs together as if in a death pact. Then the rush of air took my breath away.

I didn't see much on the way down. Just the deep blue of the water as it reached up and smashed me with the force of a speeding truck.

Somehow, I survived the impact. But my dive left me way down in the murky depths, so far down I couldn't tell which way was up.

I had read somewhere that the best thing I could do under the circumstances was watch the bubbles that had clustered around me. Whichever way they went was up. So I did my best to watch them. I watched them like crazy.

But they didn't go up. All they did was swarm around me, as confused as I was. Finally, my lungs begging for air, I lost patience with the bubble idea and started swimming for what I thought was the surface.

And swimming. And swimming some more. I was beginning to think I had struck out in exactly the wrong direction when I saw a puddle of light up ahead of me.

Hang in there, I told my lungs.

But the light wasn't as close as I had hoped. I started to lose feeling in my arms and legs. The world began going dark around the edges. The chances were getting better and better that I would black out before I cracked the surface.

Then, miraculously, I broke through.

Dragging in the biggest, most welcome breath of air I could ever have imagined, I felt myself start to drop down under the surface again. It wasn't until I came up the second time that I believed I was there to stay.

I looked around and saw that I was still dangerously close to the cliff face—so close, in fact, that a single swell could have smashed me into it. Swimming for everything I was worth, I put some distance between myself and the glistening wet rock.

When I felt I had a margin for error, I looked again at the far shore. Now that I was in the water, it seemed impossibly far away. But I knew better. Turning onto my back, I began to kick.

Slowly but surely, I left the island of the dead behind. More because of the current than anything I could take credit for, it receded into the distance. And though it hardly seemed that way at first, Ajax's island gradually crept up behind me.

That, and the long, cruel-looking boats anchored off its shore.

The swim was even harder than it had looked. By the time I got close enough to the boats to see if there was anyone inside them, I was pretty much exhausted.

As it turned out, there *were* people inside them. They looked big, strapping, with pale skin and shaved heads. To a man, they were dressed in black—just like Junior's bodyguards that day in Long Island City.

Except these guys had auras. But then, Junior's bodyguards might have had auras too. I just wasn't equipped to see anything like that at the time.

I wondered if the guys on the boats were packing.

Looking past them, I saw that the beach was empty. The invaders had pushed up into town without leaving a rear guard. Obviously, they weren't expecting any trouble from the water.

Or maybe they just figured the guys on the boats would take care of it.

I could see now by the rising columns of smoke that the fires on the island had spread. There were ten or twelve of them, and they looked serious.

Obviously, Ajax and his people had their hands full.

I wished I could have backstroked the rest of the way to the beach, just as I had backstroked most of the way already. But that would have been a good way to get spotted by the invaders, and I had to keep my presence a secret as long as possible.

So I took a deep breath, dropped down below the surface of the water, and started kicking as hard as I could. Fortunately, my lungs held out until I reached the nearest of the boats.

Placing my hand on the curved surface of the hull, I came up for air—and almost had reason to regret it. One of the invaders was sitting on the gunwale looking out in the direction of the island, and his boot was dangling just a couple of feet from my face.

Before he had a chance to look down, I set my sights on another boat, about twenty yards to my left and about fifty yards closer to the beach. Then, as quietly as I could, I drew in another breath and went under.

When I came up again, alongside another vessel, I took a quick look around. I was in the thick of the fleet now, and could be spotted not only from the boat I was hugging but even more easily from one of the other boats.

But no one had noticed me. And why should they? They would be focused on the island.

Again, I slipped under the waves. And again I came up closer to the beach by about fifty yards. But that was all the cover I would get. There was nothing between that last boat and the naked, unbroken line of beach.

I'm so screwed, I thought.

But I couldn't be. Not if I was going to be any help to Tomi.

There were about a hundred yards between me and the sand. My goal was to come up for air only once over that hundred yards. Then I would play it by ear.

I ducked under again, kicked for all I was worth, and didn't hit the surface until I thought I was going to drown. When I came up, it was only for the briefest second, I swear it. Then I dove back into the water and started kicking again.

Still, that second must have been enough to give me away, because the water around me suddenly got thick with long, wooden spears.

Got to move, I thought.

One of the spears took a fiery bite out of my left arm, just above the elbow. But I kept going, ignoring the cloud of blood trailing from my wound.

I swam for as long as I could. Only when the water got too shallow for me to keep swimming did I get up and start plowing through the surf. Of course, that made me a much easier target.

Spears rained around me, burying themselves in the water. *Chuunk! Chuunk! Chuunk!*

Miraculously, none of them found me. I hit the beach with legs that felt like they had weights strapped to them. Every breath pulled fire out of my chest.

But for the time being, at least, I had made it.

No more spears around me, either. I guessed I was out of the bald guys' range. But there would be lots of bald guys up the hill, and I'd need a new Guinness Book record for luck to get past them.

*Not necessarily,* said a voice in my head. *Take the street directly in front of you.*

*Ghost!* I thought gratefully.

I glanced back at the guys in the boats to see if any of them were coming after me. They weren't. Obviously, they didn't think a guy in his underwear posed much of a threat to their home boys.

Following the ghost's instructions, I made my way up the street just ahead of me, the sun hot on my shoulders and back, the soles of my feet slapping on the cobblestones. One of the fires was in a house up ahead, on my left. As I passed it, I saw that one of its walls had been caved in as well.

It occurred to me that there could be someone inside—someone still alive.

*There isn't*, said the ghost. *At the intersection, go right.*

At the intersection, I went right. Again, I saw one of the fires. Also some bodies.

Two men and a woman, all of them dressed in breastplates like the guys who had caught me after I escaped from the prison house. Apparently, the armor hadn't helped because it was punctured with bloody holes.

They'd been carrying bows, which were lying in the street beside them along with a slew of loose arrows. I had a strange compulsion to pick up one of the bows. In fact, I went as far as to bent down and reach for it.

Then I stopped myself. What the hell was I going to do with a bow? What was I, Robin Hood?

*Keep going*, said the ghost, sounding more than a little annoyed.

"I'm going," I breathed—strictly out of habit because it was clear to me now, after all those years, that the ghost could hear my thoughts without my saying them out loud.

By then, my wound had begun to throb, and my whole left side was full of blood. It didn't matter. One bad break and my arm would be the least of my troubles.

At the next intersection, I was told to go right. I did that. Then left, along another of the streets that ran parallel to the water. I did that too.

*All right*, said the ghost, *now it's about to get a little rougher.*

I didn't like the sound of that.

He had me stop just shy of the next intersection. I could hear why. Around the corner and up the hill, the battle was raging full blast.

*Listen carefully*, said the ghost. *If you can get past this cross street without being seen, there's a jumble of rocks and trees that stretch well up the hillside. The invaders haven't seen fit to use it yet.*

They're Junior's men, aren't they? I had to ask.

*Yes. Are you going? Or are you going to stand here and let the opportunity fade?*

I'm going.

As quickly as I could, I sprinted across the intersection. But because I was weak and couldn't resist, I shot a quick glance up the hill to see what was happening.

Immediately, I regretted it. The street was full of bodies, their blood flowing in a tortured path between the cobblestones. Most of the bodies were armored, but there were a few corpses in black as well.

Farther up the hill, there was fighting, but I didn't get a good look at it. All I saw were Junior's men making their way behind huge, wooden shields, and a barrage of arrows flying over their heads.

And auras, of course. Lots of auras on *both* sides.

But as far as I could tell, no one had taken any notice of me. Bolstered by that belief, I ran down the street and caught sight of the rock jumble. Like the others I had seen, it had a bunch of trees sticking out of it, providing plenty of cover from prying eyes.

When I reached it, I looked back to see if anyone was following me. As it happened, the street was empty, so I got in among the rocks and the trees and started climbing.

It was slow going, and it didn't help that my legs were all but useless. But, little by little I made progress, and before long

I passed the battle I had glimpsed earlier.

If the slice I could see of it was any indication, it was even bloodier than I'd thought. And the same kind of battle was going on at the next cross street down the line, and the one after that. The Isles people were holding the invaders at arm's length, but at what looked like a terrible cost.

I wished I could help them. But what could I do? They needed an army to come to their rescue, and there was just one of me.

I'd just resumed my climb when I heard something among the confusion of rocks below me. Looking back, I saw something black duck out of sight.

One of Junior's men, I thought. At the same time, I heard the ghost say: *Get out of there!*

I started climbing like crazy, casting glances over my shoulder every so often. But my picking up the pace must have tipped off my pursuer that I'd seen him, because suddenly a spear came flying my way.

Only the fact that I'd been looking for an attack enabled me to scramble off the bull's eye in time, and even then the spear point took a piece out of my thigh before it clattered away among the rocks.

But my pursuer wasn't done with me. As soon as he missed his target he started climbing faster too, and he seemed a lot fresher than I was.

And, though you wouldn't think so, he had a second spear in his hand.

# CHAPTER ELEVEN

*Crap*, I thought. I wished that I had snagged one of those bows I'd seen. Then *I'd* have had the hammer.

I turned and started to climb again, hoping I could find some bit of cover before Junior's guy took another shot at me. I couldn't. But I did find something useful.

A spear.

It still had some of my blood on it. Apparently, it hadn't clattered away as far as I'd thought.

I grabbed it and whirled—just in time to see Junior's guy stand up and take aim at me a second time. Before he could throw his spear, I threw mine.

I didn't expect it to do any good. After all, I had never thrown a spear in my life. If it made Junior's guy flinch a little and ruined his aim, I'd have been happy.

But it did more than that. It buried itself deep in the center of his chest. For a moment he stood there, glaring at me, his own spear still clutched in his hand. He even managed to take a step up the hill before he toppled to one side and lay there, motionless.

*Beginner's luck*, I thought, searching for an explanation.

I could have thrown that thing a million times and never hit my target.

*Wrong,* said the ghost.

"What do you mean?" I asked.

*You used to hit your target all the time. But we can discuss that later.*

I wanted to discuss it then and there. I was tired of everybody knowing more about me than I did.

But I wasn't going to argue. Not when another spearman might come charging up after me at any moment. Leaving Junior's guy behind, I went back to climbing the rock jumble.

Every so often, I would glance behind me. Each time, I would breathe a little easier knowing that there was no one in pursuit.

I was so intent on what was behind me that I almost didn't notice the guy standing on the rocks just above me. It was one of Ajax's people—a tall guy with blood streaming down the side of his face. He had an arrow all nocked up and pointed at me.

"No!" I yelled.

He didn't release his arrow, but he also didn't let up on the bowstring. I noticed that he was swaying a little, maybe because of whatever had made his head bleed.

"It's me," I said, "Zeno Aristos."

He didn't seem to understand what I was saying. But then, why would he? Ajax and Sasterion understood English, but that didn't mean everyone else did.

Slowly I stood up, making sure to keep my hands in plain view so nobody paying even the least bit of attention could possibly imagine that I was up to something. Then I repeated, "Zeno Aristos," and added, "I'm unarmed, see?"

For a moment I just stood there in my wet underwear, bleeding freely from my arm and my leg, my hands held up nice and high. I thought I saw understanding flicker across the guy's features.

Just before he shot me.

Stupidly, I looked down at the arrow protruding from my chest. I could tell that it had come out my back because I could feel the stiff, fiery bolt of agony all the way through me.

Great, I thought. Then, my knees giving way, I fell backward onto the rocks.

My last thought was of my shade, and how happy he would be to see me in Hell.

I was in a dark place, an impossibly hot place, huddled with other men. The air I breathed was rank with sweat.

"Who first?" I heard someone whisper.

"*You,*" whispered someone else, someone right next to me. He prodded me with his finger. "If we hear you scream, we'll know they're waiting outside, ready to run us through with their spears."

It was a joke. Still, I took up the challenge.

"Done," I said.

Ever so carefully and quietly, I slid aside a greased wooden bolt, took hold of a handle, and pulled open a trap door.

The ground was waiting beneath me, maybe ten feet away. I drew my sword and sat down on the edge of the opening. Then

I pushed myself forward and plummeted.

As soon as my feet hit the ground, I coiled behind my sword and looked around for a threat. But there was none. Only the sickly sweetness of wine and vomit in the air, and the sound of drunken singing in the distance, and a few naked men and women lying entwined on the ground. I could barely make them out by the light of the torches guttering on the soaring tower walls.

I was in a sleeping city, a city of shadows. A moment later, someone dropped to the ground beside me.

He had an eager light in his eyes and his thick, red hair was pulled back into a war braid. "The gates," he breathed, grinning like a child who couldn't keep himself from being mischievous.

He pointed, and I saw beyond his gesture the huge, iron-bound gates of the city. Their guards were sitting with their backs against those monstrosities, sleeping.

They would never know what hit them.

Suddenly, the world was flooded with light. I flinched from it, tried to escape from it.

Someone grabbed my shoulder and tried to restrain me, but I fought against the restraint. Then someone grabbed my other shoulder, and though I struggled as hard as I could, I couldn't get away.

I heard a thin, strained voice, using words that were unfamiliar to me. It was coming from right above me. I opened my eyes to see who was speaking.

As my eyes adjusted to the light, I saw an old man with

baggy eyelids, a full, white beard, and a bright green aura. He repeated whatever he had said before, though more calmly this time.

"I don't understand," I said, but it came out as little more than a croak.

The old man gestured to someone behind him. A moment later, a young woman with a long, red braid handed him a gray ceramic cup.

The hands on either side of me sat me up and the old man lifted the cup to my lips. As he tilted it, I drank. It was water, but it was sweeter than any wine I had ever tasted.

"His name is Aescalapios," someone said in a language I understood.

I followed the voice to its source. "Ajax . . . " I said, and this time I sounded a lot better.

He was hollowed-eyed, he hadn't shaved in a while, and he had a nasty-looking cut that went from his ear to his chin. It took me a moment to figure out why he looked so terrible.

"The battle . . . " I said.

He nodded. "It could have gone better." His aura flashed as he spoke, betraying his emotions.

"But . . . you turned them away . . . ?"

He held up a hand, signaling that he wished to talk about something else. "What are you doing here? Last time you almost killed my cousin trying to escape. Now you've come back of your own free will?"

"My girlfriend," I said. My head was starting to clear. "Someone told me where to find her."

"And where is that?" asked Ajax. "I hope you don't think she's *here*."

"It's called Olympos."

Judging by his expression, he had heard of it. "Who told you that you would find your girlfriend there?"

I wasn't sure I should say. Then again, I couldn't see how it would hurt.

"My shade."

He scowled. "I see. So you must have come here via the Isle of the Founders, where the gravestones are."

I nodded.

"You were were lucky the sharks didn't get you. You know the waters off our coast are full of them, right?"

"I didn't," I confessed, a chill climbing my spine as I thought about what might have been watching me beneath the surface. "Fortunately, I didn't run into any of them in the water. But I saw plenty of boats."

Ajax's mouth twisted. "There are plenty of them, all right."

"Still?"

"Yes. And the damned invaders are back inside them. If they'd pressed their advantage, they would have wiped us out. But they withdrew to their vessels."

"Why?" I asked.

"Because cats like to toy with their prey before they devour it."

I thought about how Junior had played me on the handball court back in Long Island City. And also what Dee Gangsta had said about Junior's tactics on the street.

"Can't you do something?" I asked.

Ajax made a sound of disgust. "We've done what we could. Each Isle has armed itself, organized provisions, evacuated its young and its elderly to its heights. Beyond that . . . " He shrugged.

"I wish I could help," I said.

Ajax eyed me. "Maybe you can, after you're healed."

I started to say, "That'll be a while." After all, the arrow had gone *through* me. It had to have done some damage along the way.

Then I realized that I didn't hurt very much, all things considered. I pulled aside my linen robe and looked down at the spot where I'd been skewered. All I saw there was a small scab.

I probed the area with my fingers. It was sore, but not nearly as sore as it should have been.

"How long have I been lying here?" I asked Ajax.

"I don't know," he said. "Overnight, at any rate."

"I had an arrow in me. An *arrow*."

He glanced at the old man. "Aescalapios is a fine physician."

Aescalapios said something. Ajax answered, and the old man laughed.

"He's pleased that you admire his skills," Ajax told me.

I thought about my knife wound and how quickly *that* had gone away. "Maybe I shouldn't be surprised. Drakos healed me in no time too."

"Really," said Ajax.

I nodded again. "Remember that knife wound I had the last

time I was here? After he treated it, it was gone in a matter of hours."

Ajax shook his head. "It wasn't Drakos who did that. It was Aescalapios. Your friend Drakos can accomplish many things, I'll grant you, but healing isn't one of them."

Interesting, I thought. Drakos must have wanted me to trust him, so he took credit for healing my wound. "So he lied to me. *Again.*"

"If you know him at all," said Ajax, "that shouldn't come as a shock."

"It doesn't."

*And while we're on the subject of trust . . .* "You did something to me last time I was here. I see things."

"Like what?" Ajax asked.

"People glowing. As if they had little green flames around them."

He didn't seem impressed. "Go on."

"Not everybody, just some people. You, for instance." I looked around the room. "Your pal Aescalapios." I studied the woman with the red hair, and the guys who had held me down but were now standing off to the side. "But not them."

"And you wonder why," said Ajax.

"Wouldn't you?"

"It's just a matter of discernment. You're able to tell the difference between one sort of being and another."

"But what is it I'm discerning?" I asked.

"That not everybody who looks human *is* human. The one you call Junior, for instance, or his warriors, or your friend

Drakos . . . or me. What we have in common is that some part of us, at least, does not belong to the human race."

I wrestled with that idea for a moment. It didn't fit easily into my head. And it fit even worse when I remembered what I had seen in my bathroom mirror.

"So . . . I'm not human either?" I asked. It was ridiculous. More ridiculous than anything I had run into so far. "What am I, then . . . an alien?"

Ajax looked for a moment as if he was going to answer my question. But in the end, all he said was, "You're someone who needs his rest."

I started to protest, to say that I wanted to get an answer once and for all, but Aescalapios placed something over my mouth and nose that smelled like cinnamon and, ever so gently, I drifted away.

"Get ready!" I heard someone shout in my ear.

I was rumbling across a stretch of flat ground in the shadow of a towering stone wall, a bronze-pointed spear in my hand, my chariot driven by a woman in a golden helmet. Up ahead, there was a man floating in the air.

No—not a man. Something bigger and more powerful than a man, his breastplate covered with blood and gobbets of flesh, a spear much bigger than mine held above his shoulder.

A flame burned around him—a green flame. Looming in front of me like the embodiment of violent death, he drew his spear back and sent it flying at my face.

But my driver was too quick for him. Yanking on the reins

of our horses, she dragged us hard to the left—out of harm's way. As our enemy's spear buried itself in the ground behind me, I raised my own bronze-headed shaft. And with all my strength, I drove it in the direction of the floating man.

As it buried itself in his gut, his face twisted in pain, and he roared in a thousand voices at once. Clutching at my spear, he fell to the ground.

"Good shot!" yelled my driver, whipping us around for another pass.

I was brimming over with elation. I had brought down my enemies' protector. I had filled them with fear.

But before I could finish the job, my adversaries closed around their champion, shielding him from further injury.

"It's all right," said my driver. "They're less without him. You've won the day."

A green flame danced around her as well.

"What . . . ?" I bellowed at the top of my lungs.

I heard my voice echo back at me, sounding like the ravings of a madman. Feeling cold and clammy despite the warmth of the breezes around me, I looked around.

I was sitting upright on a wooden lounge—a fancy one, with all kinds of mythical creatures carved into it—in a place with tall, white columns holding up a sculpted facade and a big, gabled roof. One of the little Parthenons I had seen from my prison, I thought.

An old man with a beard stood next to me, his hand on my shoulder. He said something to me, but the words escaped me.

As I stared at him, trying to get my bearings, I remembered his name:

"Aescalapios."

He smiled in his beard.

I heard cries from the hillside below us, followed them, and saw a battle raging in the streets. Fighting, I thought. Why? Way off in the distance, just beyond the surf, sat a fleet of red boats with black sails.

Then it all came back to me. The swim from Graveyard Island, the siege, the arrow that should have killed me. Junior's men had stopped short of taking the island last time, but apparently they were at it again.

It seemed to me that Ajax's people had retreated farther up the hillside than before. Every street was choked with makeshift ramparts made of wooden stakes, each one manned by a rank of spearmen backed by several ranks of bowmen. And yet Junior's forces, a trail of bodies behind them, were still advancing behind their big, wooden shields. As many arrows as the defenders shot at them, none of them seemed to reach their intended targets.

In fact, I couldn't find a single one of Junior's men lying dead in the street. Not a good sign.

As before, I couldn't find Junior among the invaders. Of course, he might have been concealed under one of those shields, fighting alongside his men. But that didn't seem to be his style. If he were taking part in the battle, he would have been out there in full view, daring Ajax's bowmen to take their best shots at him.

Junior or no Junior, I couldn't stay where I was. I might not have been myself yet, but I was a lot closer than before. "I need to get down there," I told Aescalapios, though I knew he wouldn't understand me.

But as soon as I got to my feet, I felt a weakness in my knees. I swayed, staggered, and would have fallen if I hadn't been able to grab a column for support. Aescalapios said something to me, his voice full of concern. Despite the language barrier, I got the gist of it.

"I can't," I told him. "Ajax and his people are fighting Junior. That makes it my fight too."

I took a deep breath, steeled myself, and let go of the column. Then I started down the wide, white set of steps that extended from the building. But at that same moment, I saw the invaders start to fall back.

They did it all at the same time, all across the island. Using their shields for cover, they retreated along streets they had already taken, stepping over defenders they had left lying there.

Just like that.

At first, the Isles people remained where they were, waiting to see what Junior's men would do next. Then, slowly, cautiously, they began to offer pursuit.

It didn't give the invaders any greater sense of urgency. Their shields held before them, catching arrow after arrow, they took their time giving ground.

Eventually, the invaders reached the beach. Slipping into the waves, they continued to use their shields as cover, even as they were swimming back to their boats. Finally, out of range of the bowmen, they climbed over the rails.

But even after the last of Junior's men were aboard, the boats didn't leave. They just sat there as they had before.

I heard a cheer go up from the defenders, but it was half-hearted at best. Then I watched them go about the grim business of retrieving their dead.

The sun was dying on the horizon by the time a couple of Ajax's people began climbing the hill toward my vantage point. They were almost there before I realized that Ajax was one of them, and Sasterion the other.

I was glad to see them. For a lot of reasons.

As they reached the white, stone steps, they had the look of whipped dogs. But then, the battle had been all one-sided, and there was no reason to believe the next encounter would be any different.

I remembered the way the Bronze Men had looked in Hell, as they made their way through that valley. The Isles men were halfway there.

Climbing the steps, Ajax looked up at me with tired eyes and said, "You look like shit."

"Actually," I said, "I'm feeling a lot better. Thanks for asking."

Ignoring me, he trudged into the columned building and dropped into a wooden chair. A moment later, Sasterion did the same. For the time being, I decided to stand.

With a wince, Ajax undid the clasps on the side of his breastplate, which was smeared with bright red blood. Then he eyed me and said, "We don't have much time to spare, but

Sasterion wished to speak with you. I told him what you told *me*, about your girlfriend and where you think she's being held. And that the information came from your shade."

Sasterion's face was a mask of dirt with streaks of sweat running through it. "Your shade is not necessarily trustworthy. After all, it has its own agenda."

Before, Sasterion hadn't seemed to care much what I thought. For some reason he cared now, or he wouldn't have lugged himself up the hill to talk with me.

"You're not the first one to tell me that," I said.

"Still," said Ajax, "you believe what it told you?"

"*Him*," I said, "and yes, I do."

I didn't mention the other things my shade told me—that Junior's men were his little science projects, which he had created by himself somehow, or that I'd have to face an angry goddess when I got to Olympos.

Hell, my hosts were skeptical already. Why make myself look even crazier?

"Did your shade tell you," asked Sasterion, "that our enemies down there in the boats are the ones who seized your girlfriend in Astoria? And that the one you call Junior is the creator of those enemies? Or did it . . . *he* . . . see fit to omit that information?"

"How do *you* know who seized her?"

"Trust me," said Sasterion, "I *know*."

"On the other hand," I said, "maybe it's *you* who have an agenda."

"Really," said Ajax. "And what would that be?"

"You had a reason for bringing me here, didn't you? For the same reason, you might want me to *stay*."

Neither of them answered right away. Apparently, I had struck a chord.

"I've been having dreams," I said. "Very realistic dreams. One was about crawling out of a wooden horse and opening the gates to a city. Another was about hitting a floating man in the guts with a spear. Back in the house of Neleos, I saw a frieze of a guy throwing a spear at a floating man, and his chariot was driven by a woman in a helmet—just like the woman driving my chariot in my dream." I turned to Ajax in particular. "You told me people who had auras—people like you—weren't human, or at least weren't *all* human. That means I'm not human either. And if I'm not human, what in God's name *am* I?"

"You're someone who, for some reason, cannot remember who he is," said Sasterion. "Which is why we put you in the House of Neleos. So your memory might be refreshed."

"After all," said Ajax, "the House of Neleos has particular meaning for you. All those friezes hanging on the walls there . . . they're scenes from your life."

My *life*? I thought he might be joking, but he wasn't laughing. He wasn't even smiling.

"In other words," I said, "*I'm* the guy in the friezes?"

"That's correct," said Sasterion.

For just a moment the world seemed to lurch sideways, and I knew with a weird certainty that he was right. The guy with the boar on his shield, the one who showed up in all Neleos's friezes . . . that was me.

*Me.*

"Crap," I said, "how old *am* I?"

"Old enough to have fought at Troy," said Sasterion. "Old enough to have known the gods."

*Again with the gods . . .*

I didn't believe it. *Couldn't* believe it. But if it were true, it would explain why Junior thought I was so special. Anybody who'd survived for thousands of years had to be a challenge.

I also understood why my shade was such a nut job. He'd been there in Hell, waiting for me to join him, since before the birth of Christ.

"Is that why I have an aura?" I asked. "Because I'm so long-lived?"

Ajax leaned forward in his chair. "What do *you* think?"

I tried to fit the information into the jigsaw puzzle. But for some reason, it didn't fit.

"There's more to it," I said. Then something occurred to me—something I would have thought of back in New Hyde Park, when Professor Anderson showed me his fifty-year-old photo, if I'd taken it more seriously. "My parents." My throat grew tight. "If I've lived as long as long as you say I have . . ."

"Your mother," said Sasterion, "was a woman named Deipyle. She was a princess in ancient Greece. Your father was a fellow named Tydeus. His family ruled a kingdom as well, on the northern shore of what is now known as the Patra Gulf, though he himself was too unruly ever to ascend to the throne."

It couldn't be. "My father was a shoemaker," I said. "His name was Isidoros. My mother's name was Demetria."

"How much do you remember of them?" asked Sasterion.

"Not very much," I had to admit. "My father worked long hours. And they both died young."

"Sisters?" said Sasterion. "Brothers?"

I shook my head from side to side. "I was an only child."

But if I had lived at the time of the Trojan War . . . how could my father have been my father? And if he wasn't who I thought he was, who *was* he?

"If you know so much about me," I said, "why not just tell me who I am—*what* I am? Why all the games?"

"Because," said Ajax, "we *can't* just tell you. We need you to remember on your own."

"Also," said Sasterion, "you'll place more faith in what you remember than in what we say."

"We could have told you," said Ajax, "that you have the ability to discern auras, because we knew that at one time you had that ability. But you would never have regained it that way."

"It had to come back to me naturally," I said, though I wasn't so sure that seeing auras was a good thing.

"Our hope," said Sasterion, "is that you will remember enough to become something more than you are. Something you were a long time ago. Because frankly, unless that happens, the invaders in those boats will eventually slaughter every man, woman, and child in the Isles."

There it was—the reason they had protected me in the Bronx, and brought me to the Isles the first time, and put me in Neleos's place where I could bask in the company of all those friezes.

So they could make me what I was, once upon a time. So I could help them against Junior.

Hell, I *wanted* to help them. But even more, I wanted to help Tomi, and if I was going to face an angry goddess it might as well be with all the power I could muster.

Only one thing bothered me—what Ithaka had said to me in Hell. Apparently, I had made him swear not to tell me about my past. Why would I do such a thing? Why would I have wanted so badly to forget who I was?

It scared me to think about it. But it wasn't going to keep me from doing whatever I could to get Tomi back.

I had barely made that promise to myself when a woman came running up the white, stone steps. Ajax got up to meet her at the top of them. They spoke in urgent tones.

"What's going on?" I asked Sasterion.

He frowned. "We have a visitor."

"Junior?" I asked, since that seemed like the logical conclusion.

"No," he said, "your friend Drakos."

Aescalapios would have had me remain in the place with the columns and the big, gabled roof, but I wasn't going to to do that. Instead, I walked down the hill as best I could behind Ajax and Sasterion, who appeared to have more to think about than whether I was going to collapse behind them.

Drakos was a couple of streets down and one street over. He had a half dozen men with him, a couple of whom I recognized from the party that had rescued me from Neleos's House. Unlike their boss, none of them had auras.

They didn't look like they were going to rescue anyone this time. In fact, they had laid their weapons on the ground and put their hands in the air, indicating to the twenty or so bowmen who had their arrows pointed at them that they weren't going to do anything stupid.

I didn't get it. Drakos had already proved that he could get the best of the Isles people. Why hadn't it worked this time? Was it just that he had been unaware of the invasion, and therefore underestimated the numbers of defenders he would be up against?

Somehow, I didn't think so. If Drakos was anything, it was well-informed.

"Are you insane?" Ajax asked as he approached Drakos, no doubt wondering the same things I was wondering.

"Not at all," said Drakos, smiling as if they were old friends. "In this instance, I'm on *your* side."

"Really," said Ajax, making his way through the ring of bowmen. "And why I would even begin to believe that?"

"Under the circumstances," said Drakos, "what have you got to lose?"

"What do *you* know of the circumstances?" asked Sasterion.

Drakos shrugged. "I know that our mutual enemy has his forces out there in those boats, primed to destroy you when he decides the moment is right. And I know you don't have the resources to stop him."

Ajax laughed—just for show, I thought. "You think we can't handle our own affairs?"

"I'm sure of it. And so are you. But with my help . . . who

knows? Maybe you'll have half a chance."

"Meaning what? You want to join us? Fight for us?"

"Why not?" asked Drakos. "He's a threat to me as well."

Ajax looked unconvinced. "So we're just supposed to trust you?"

Drakos nodded. "Implicitly."

Had their positions been reversed, would Drakos have been so trusting? I doubted it. Then again, the Isles people needed all the help they could get.

Ajax looked to Sasterion, who nodded. Then Ajax turned to Drakos again. "At the first sign of treachery—"

"You'll do your best to kill me. I'd expect nothing less."

Ajax nodded. but he didn't look happy about it. "All right, then. We'll make use of you. But—"

"First you want to know how I got here." Drakos glanced at his men. "How *we* got here."

"And?" said Ajax.

"I'll be happy to show you," said Drakos.

# Chapter Twelve

As we stood among a cascade of rocks in the shade of a big, gnarled olive tree, one of Drakos's men knelt in front of an innocent-looking shrub and felt around underneath it. A moment later he caught hold of something, gripped it with his other hand as well, and lifted.

The shrub came right up, along with a section of the grass that surrounded it, exposing a hole big enough for a man to drop into. Or climb out of. His work done, Drakos's man put the shrub down beside the hole.

"The opening widens as you go down through the rock," said Drakos, "eventually leading to a fair-sized grotto, and the water."

Ajax didn't say anything, but the muscles in his jaw rippled. He clearly wasn't happy that such a thing had existed right under his nose.

"How long has this access been available to you?" asked Sasterion, not exactly thrilled himself.

"Since before your people settled the Isles," said Drakos. "I just never felt the need to make use of it until the other day."

Sasterion turned to Ajax. "It presents possibilities. The children . . ."

"Unfortunately," said Drakos, "it's not that simple. You can't hold your breath long enough to get from the grotto to open water, much less ask a child to do so."

"Then how did *you* get here?" I asked.

Drakos shrugged. "Scuba gear. Seven sets. It's sitting down there, waiting for someone to use it. But if we're smart, it won't be for an evacuation attempt, which might only save a few lives at most. After all, the tanks hold a rather limited supply of air."

"You could have brought more," Ajax observed.

"But I didn't," said Drakos, "because we won't need them."

"You have a plan, then," said Sasterion. "But why would you be inclined to help *us*? Since when have you become our benefactor?"

"Since Junior made his move to lay waste to your Isles," said Drakos. "As I said, he's a threat to me too. And the surest way for me to ensure my demise is to sit back and watch my potential allies fall one by one. I wasn't quick-witted enough to see what was happening to the Bronze Men, but I see all too well what's happening now."

I was reminded of what a German clergyman said after World War Two—something about standing by and doing nothing when the Nazis took the communists, then the trade unionists, and then the Jews. By the time the Nazis came for *him,* there was no one left who could help.

Drakos might have read the same thing.

"You would stand with us in battle?" asked Sasterion, making it clear what they were talking about.

Drakos nodded. "You'll cry when you see me with a bow

in my hands. It's poetry."

"All right," said Ajax, maybe a little too brusquely. No doubt, he was still pissed off about Drakos's escape hole. "Let's hear your plan."

Drakos smiled at him. "A little advice, Archon—I didn't accept that tone from your ancestors. I'm certainly not going to accept it from *you*."

*Ancestors?* I thought. Apparently, I wasn't the only one whose long life had been longer than I imagined.

Sasterion held up a hand for peace. "The plan. *Please.*"

"Of course," said Drakos. "You see, our friend here—" He indicated me with a gesture. "—has a certain unrealized potential."

"Which we're helping him to realize," said Ajax. "He already sees auras again."

That seemed to surprise Drakos. "Auras . . . how interesting. But seeing auras was a talent he simply forgot he had. I'm talking about power—the kind of power *I* wield."

I didn't understand. Was he offering to make me a stockholder in Drakotech?

"We're working on it," said Ajax.

Drakos laughed. "In what way? By putting him in the House of Neleos? That may restore a few of his memories, but it won't grant him something he never had."

Sasterion looked as if he had sat on a cactus. "What are you talking about?"

"I mean he can't remember how to be a god," said Drakos, "because he never *was* a god in the first place."

A breeze blew among us, rustling the leaves of the olive tree. But neither Ajax nor Sasterion responded to Drakos's remark.

"Okay," I said, "I'd *really* like to know what's going on here."

Drakos turned to me. "No one's told you because they wanted you to remember on your own, apparently. But there was a time, long ago, when you could have been a god. All you had to do was accept the offer."

A god, I thought.

He might as well have said tadpole, or armpit, or Bunsen burner. It would have made just as much sense. Or just as little.

"How can you *become* a god?" I asked, finding it hard to believe the time had come when such a question was of practical interest to me. "Don't you have to be *born* that way?"

"Not necessarily," said Drakos. "*I* wasn't. And yet here I am."

"So . . . *you're* a god?"

"Through and through—as compared to our friends here, who are only *descended* from gods, and therefore weak imitations. That's why they're salivating at my offer to help them defend their Isles, even though they don't trust that help. It's also why they were trying to coax you into remembering who you were—because if you were a god and you *did* remember, they might have a chance against the marauders in those ships."

He glanced at Sasterion, and then at Ajax. "The bad news for them is that even though you've lived a long time, you're *not* a god. The good news is that you still *can* be."

I hated the idea of trusting Drakos, hated it like poison. And if I had turned down godhood back in the day, I must have had a reason. Hell, maybe *that* was what I didn't want to remember.

But if it meant having a chance for all of us to survive this thing—and to get Tomi back—I wouldn't turn it down a second time. "How would I go about making that happen?" I asked.

He told me what I had to do and where I had to do it. The *where* part sent a chill down my spine. It was the same place that my shade mentioned when I asked him where Tomi was.

*Olympos* . . .

"What is it?" Drakos asked.

I looked at him, not sure I wanted to say. "What do you mean?"

"You got a funny look on your face when I mentioned Olympos. Last time that happened was in my office in Manhattan. I didn't press the point then, but I will now."

I considered a lie, but decided against it. If Drakos was going to help me, he needed to know the score. "There's a goddess there," I said. "An *angry* goddess."

"How would you know that?" asked Drakos.

"My shade told me."

He smiled again. "You've been in contact with your shade. Of course. But why did it mention Olympos to you?"

I was tired of correcting the pronoun. "Because," I said, "that's where Tomi is."

Drakos took a moment to absorb the information. "Right. Now there's a coincidence. So you'll go."

It wasn't a question. "I'll go," I said.

"Aphrodite," said Drakos, as he checked the air gauge on my tank.

His voice echoed wildly in the limestone grotto, with its ceiling full of milky-white stalactites. He had illuminated the place with a couple of freestanding lights.

I looked back over my shoulder at him. "What?"

His face was dappled with wave patterns reflected off the surface of the water beside us. "You said there was an angry goddess waiting for you on Olympos. It would have to be Aphrodite. After you wounded her at Troy, her existence took a turn for the worse. The other gods seemed to take her a lot less seriously."

"I wounded a *goddess*?" I asked. Not very chivalrous of me.

"As well as a couple of gods. But Aphrodite was the one who wouldn't stop complaining about it. It drove the other gods crazy."

Of course it did, I thought. What self-respecting god would tolerate a goddess who complained all the time? Especially if he was one of the other gods I'd wounded.

"Hence, the anger," I said.

"Exactly," said Drakos.

"Fantastic."

He rocked back on his haunches, eyeballed the rest of my gear, and nodded, satisfied that I was properly equipped. "As you probably at least suspect by now, I've been lying to you about pretty much everything. Your immortality, for instance. I wasn't the one who gave you long life."

"Then who?" I asked.

"It was Athena. In your returning memories, do you ever see a woman in a helmet?"

I pictured my chariot driver. "As a matter of fact, I do."

"That's her. She's also the one who gave you the ability see those auras."

"Thanks," I said. "Now I'll have a name to go with the face."

"For all the good it'll do, since you'll never see that face again. Some time ago, she and all the other gods picked up and went away. I don't know why, but they left, and they didn't leave a forwarding address. With the exception of Aphrodite, apparently, though I'm surprised she saw fit to stick around. She was always a bit of a follower."

"Lucky me," I said.

"Indeed. By the way," he continued, "Drakos isn't my real name—I've been lying about that too. It's Menelaos."

"Menelaos," I repeated. "And why are you telling me all this, Menelaos?"

"Because there's a lot riding on your success. I'd hate to see you fail for lack of information."

"Me too."

"Remember, all you've got to do is stay with Elijah." He pointed to one of the three men he'd assigned to be my escorts. "He knows where to go, and he's a good shot with that speargun in case you run into any sharks. But in the event something happens to him, Leif and Antonio can be counted on as well."

"And what if something happens to all of them?" After all, none of them had auras.

"Then," said Drakos, "to use the vernacular, you're shit out of luck."

I nodded. "Good to know."

He held out his hand. "Knock 'em dead."

I grasped it. "You too." After all, he would have a battle on his hands.

"I'll be fine," Drakos assured me. "Too bad you won't be able to stay and watch me fight. I'm pretty good."

"I know," I said. "Poetry."

Then I put my mask on, fit the breathing apparatus into my mouth, and slipped into the water.

It was colder than I'd expected. And dark. If not for the dive lights in our hands we would have been blind.

It had been a long time since I'd gone scuba diving, and I'd never been an expert in the first place. But as Drakos had suggested, I followed Elijah, a tall, dark-skinned black man, and let him worry about getting me where I needed to go.

After what seemed like a long time, so long I thought we might be nearing the end of our air supplies, Elijah signaled for us to surface. I didn't hesitate. Breathing through a tube had been getting to me. It felt good to take in air the old-fashioned way.

As I bobbed among the waves, I looked around. We were treading water in the shadow of an island. And unless I was mistaken, I had been there before.

The Isle of the Founders, they called it. Where all the graves were. But what good was it going to do us?

Elijah gestured and led us around a headland into a little cove, where he took off his tank, his belt, and his flippers. There was a pile of loose branches piled on top of the sand,

and underneath them was a small, lightweight speedboat.

"Nice," I said.

Elijah didn't answer. He just cleared off the branches, with the help of his colleagues, and lugged the boat into the water.

"Where now?" I asked.

"You'll see," said Elijah.

We struck out for open ocean, in the direction opposite that of the Isles. The boat was fast for its size—no doubt, the fastest money could buy. Leif drove while Elijah, Antonio, and I sat in the back.

Over the drone of the motor, I asked how they had spirited a boat through Hell. "Piece by piece," said Elijah, but he didn't go into any more detail than that.

Piece by piece, I thought. And then they had to assemble it after they got out of Hell. Clearly, these guys were more than just muscle.

"Have you handled a sword lately?" Elijah asked after a while.

"A sword?" I remembered the photo Anderson had showed me. I'd been a fencer at one time, apparently. But I didn't think that was the kind of sword Elijah had in mind, and besides, that was fifty years ago. "Not lately, no. Why?"

"Because it's the only weapon you'll have at your disposal when we get to Olympos."

He flipped over a cushioned seat, revealing an equipment locker, and took out a vicious-looking sword in a dark leather scabbard. Then he slid it out of the scabbard and handed it to me, handle first.

Made of something more like steel than iron, it reflected sunlight as I turned it over in my hands. Its leaf-shaped blade, which was about two feet long, was thin but durable-looking, with a razor edge on either side. Its handle, bound in a long, leather strip to improve its grip, had a cross piece to protect the hand.

I looked up at Elijah. "Are you expecting a battle there?"

"I expect everything," he said. "It's my job."

"That's a hell of a job." A lot like the one I had when I was a cop. "But if you're anticipating a fight, why didn't you bring some of those rubber bullet guns? Or for that matter, the kind that shoot real bullets?"

"We did. But after you mentioned the goddess, Mr. Drakos told us we would have to resort to swords. He didn't say why."

"And you just happened to have swords on board?" I asked.

"In this region," said Elijah, "you have to be prepared to go low-tech. There are rules."

He wouldn't elaborate. I resolved to ask Drakos—I couldn't think of him as Menelaos—the question when I saw him again. *If* I saw him again.

I thought about the fact that none of the guys with me had an aura. Presumably, Drakos would have brought his best men with him on a mission as critical as this one. So maybe Drakos didn't have any auras in his stable after all.

Who, then? The Isles people? Maybe, but I doubted it. Drakos had barely left my apartment when I first noticed the aura guy standing outside it. And the more I thought about it, the more I saw the resemblance between that guy and Junior's marauders.

Funny thing, the day seemed to go by too quickly. Maybe it was because we were on the water, but the sun sank toward the sea as if it had weights on it. It occurred to me that I'd had the same kind of feeling back on the Isles. But I'd only been conscious there in spurts, so I hadn't thought about it at the time.

I asked Elijah if it seemed the same way to him. "The days are shorter here," he said. "It may be that this world is smaller, or that it rotates faster. I don't know."

"*This* world?" I echoed.

Until then, I had imagined the Isles were somehow in a remote part of *my* world. Or maybe some weird, little pocket of reality that most people just hadn't discovered yet. I hadn't entertained the possibility that I was on *another planet entirely*, or that the sun warming my face just then wasn't the one that shone on Astoria.

Obviously, I had a lot to learn.

It was just after sunset, with the sky still a soft rose color above the horizon, when I heard the voice. It was so clear, I thought that Elijah or one of the other two guys had spoken.

Then I realized it was inside my head.

*Ghost?* I asked silently.

*No*, came the answer. *I'm no ghost.*

For a moment, I had that disoriented feeling you get when you see your friend across the street and you wave to him, and then you get a little closer and you realize the guy you're waving to isn't your friend.

*That* feeling.

Because I realized who it was, and it wasn't the ghost. Though I had heard the voice only once before, on a handball court in Long Island City, there was no mistaking it. *Junior . . . ?*

*That's the name you've known me by. But I prefer Erichthonios.*

How come everybody had another name in his back pocket? I felt like I needed a scorecard.

*Your shade sends his regards. He says he's sorry he revealed to me what he told you. But then, you shouldn't have made it so obvious you were going to visit him in Hell.*

I couldn't begin to imagine what Junior had done to my shade to make him spill his guts. Tamping down on my anger, I thought, *What do you want?*

*You don't know what you're up against, Diomedes.*

*Who's Diomedes?* I asked in my head.

*You see what I mean?*

*All right then. Why don't you* tell *me what I'm up against?*

I figured he would say something about the armies he had at his disposal. Instead, he said, *I'm the son of Zeus.*

Considering I was already dealing with gods and demigods, I had to smile. *Who isn't?*

*You don't understand,* Junior thought. *I'm not one of Zeus's remote descendants, separated by so many generations people have lost count. I'm his* son.

I considered the claim. *No way. From what I've heard, Zeus boogied off into the sunset some time ago, along with the rest of the gods.*

*That's true. He's gone. Long gone. But before he left, he planted a seed.*

*If you were Zeus's seed, you would have died of old age a long time ago. Like the ancestors of the Isles people.*

*Only if my mother was mortal, like theirs. But my mother was a goddess. Think about that, Diomedes.*

Then the line went dead.

As I sat there in the dying light, pondering what Junior had said, I realized that Elijah was awake as well. "What is it?" he asked.

My life was pretty much in his hands, so I told him. "And he didn't sound like he was making it up."

Elijah frowned. "Telepathy has range limits. He must not be far away. Which means he knows where we're headed, or at least he has a fair idea."

"Not good," I said.

Elijah shrugged. "Get some sleep."

I tried, but I didn't have much success.

The son of Zeus and a goddess. Maybe Junior was right—to that point, I hadn't had any understanding of what I was up against. But I was starting to.

*Zeno?*

I thrashed around, trying to get free—until I realized it was only a plastic sheet I was fighting, just like the ones lying on top of Drakos's men. The tatters of a dream were still in my head, but they were fading too quickly for me to remember anything about them.

The moon rode high in the blue-black heavens. Like the sun, it looked familiar. But it could have been another moon just like it, I had no idea.

*Zeno?*

I looked at the others. None of them had spoken. As far as I could tell, they were still asleep.

*Zeno, damn it! Wake up!*

*Ghost . . . ?* I ventured.

*Who else would it be?*

Relieved, I said, *You have no idea.* And I told him about everything that had happened, including the business with my shade and with Drakos, and my little convo with Junior.

*That's bad,* he said. *Very bad.*

*What is? The part about Junior?*

*The whole thing. It stinks.*

*He called me Diomedes. And Drakos said I was almost a god. What's going on?* I thought it was time I knew. And if the ghost couldn't tell me, who could?

A pause, so long it started to worry me. *Ghost?* It would be par for the course if he disappeared again, leaving me with a lap full of questions.

*I'm here,* he said. *And it's about that time anyway. So why not?*

*Why not what?*

*Why not tell you what's going on.* Another pause. *Let me begin by saying you're not who think you are.*

I would have laughed if it didn't mean waking up my boat mates. *Boy, have I heard* that *before.*

*Your name isn't really Zeno Aristos. It's Diomedes. You're the son of a man who died nearly three thousand years ago.*

It was pretty much what the Isles people had told me. Except for the name. The only one who had used that was Junior.

*So how am I still alive?* I asked.

*You were given the gift of immortality by the goddess Athena. For reasons that have always eluded me, she liked you. So she deified you—or tried to. But you rejected the idea of becoming a god. Of course, by then you were already different from other people in that your life span was virtually endless.*

*Endless.* It was one thing to accept that you'd been around for thousands of years, and another to hear that you'd still be around when cockroaches ruled the earth.

*So why do I get hurt?* I asked. *Why do I bleed?*

*Because you're not Achilles,* said the ghost with a note of exasperation in his voice. *You weren't dipped in the river Styx as a baby. But you have a god's vitality, which keeps you from succumbing to disease or aging. Only a massive amount of damage to your person can kill you. And somehow, despite your ongoing affinity for unnecessarily perilous situations, you've managed to avoid that level of damage.*

*So why don't I remember any of this?* That was the big question, wasn't it? *The Trojan War, my friendship with Athena, her offer to make me a god . . . you'd think these things would stick in my mind.*

*It's a long story,* said the ghost.

*I've got time,* I told him. *I'm immortal, remember?*

I heard a sigh in my mind. *All right.* Another one of those pauses. *Back in the day, you were an insufferable prick.*

I thought I'd heard him wrong. *Me?*

*Yes, you. Athena was the only one who didn't seem to see it. Everyone else called you names behind your back. For one thing, you didn't treat women very well—mortal ones, at least. You loved them and left them, as the saying goes. Some guys felt at least a hint of loyalty for the women they bedded, looked after them just a little bit—particularly if they were carrying that guy's child. But not you. You couldn't have cared less what happened to—*

*All right*, I thought, maybe a bit too sharply, *I get the idea.*

*Don't get defensive. You wanted to know, right?*

*Right*, I conceded.

*Anyway, that was hardly your only personality flaw. You were also too competitive. That was fine if you were in a battle of some kind, but in times of peace it got wearisome. You'd be at a feast with everybody settling into their cups, looking forward to drinking themselves unconscious, and you would call for a contest. A wrestling match, a foot race, an archery tournament . . . and because you'd question their manhood, they would eventually feel compelled to take you up on your challenge. Which you would win, of course. Without exception. And that contributed to your third problem.*

*Which was?* I asked, though really I'd heard enough.

*A vastly overblown sense of your importance in the world. Now, it's true that you were the son of a king, and that you had a good mind and an impressive record when it came to physical prowess, but you were still a bloody mortal. You just couldn't seem to accept that you had limitations, that you could die, that you could be humbled in any way. So*, said the ghost, *it was rather ironic that Athena chose to deify you. In your mind, you'd been a god all along.*

I considered what he had said. I *was* competitive, no doubt about it. But I didn't treat women poorly. Not any more. Not since I'd met Tomi.

And as far as an overblown sense of importance . . . I didn't feel that, either. I was a cop at heart, and as a group cops weren't high on the look-at-me scale.

*At first,* said the ghost, *becoming immortal only added to your already grotesquely bloated conceit. But after a few hundred years, you began to see what others saw in you. You began to appreciate what a shit you were, and to your credit, you decided to do something about it. You decided to change.*

*Go, me,* I said.

*But self-improvement isn't easy, even for a god. Especially for a god. So you enlisted some help—mine.*

*We were friends?*

*Not at all. Barely acquaintances. But Athena knew me and she knew I had the right temperament to be of help to you. I was patient, for one thing.*

*You?* I thought. *Patient?*

*In those days, yes. I was a* paragon *of patience. And I hated you. That was the other thing.*

I didn't get it. *How did hating me qualify you to—* And then I did get it. *You didn't like me the way I was, so you were motivated to help me reform.*

*Exactly. But you weren't going to listen to me, and we both knew that. You were almost a god. You weren't going to listen to* anybody, *not even Athena if it came to that.*

*So we devised a scheme. You would drink from the Waters of Forgetfulness so you wouldn't know you who you were. Then we would imprint another identity on you, making you think you were a farmer in Thessaly, or later on a sail trimmer in Lisbon, or still later a police officer in New York City. And in those humble roles, life span by mortal life span, you would have a chance to rehabilitate yourself.*

*I permitted this?* I asked.

The ghost laughed. *It was your idea. And at first, it was a monumentally bad one. You learned nothing. Your mortal guises were every bit as reprehensible as your original self.*

*But later . . . ?* I thought, since he had qualified his statement by saying *at first*.

*Later, things began to improve a little. You showed some humility. You realized that the world didn't revolve around you, deathless though you might be. But it wasn't until this life, the one you're living now, that you showed real progress. Especially in terms of the way you treat women.*

We agreed on that, at least.

*And there you have it*, said the ghost.

I let it sink in for a moment. Then I thought, *I can't imagine being as big a bastard as you're describing.*

*That's good*, said the ghost. *It's another indication of how far you've come.*

*And what happens to the people in my life? I just abandon them when I go on to another one?*

*Something like that. Oh, you may look after them for a while, more out of curiosity than concern. But when you forget in order to assume your next identity, you forget them as well. And if they're lucky, they forget* you.

It struck me as, I don't know . . . immoral. *I just use them and discard them?*

*They're all duly rewarded for their involvement in your education, one way or the other. It's good to have an immortal as a benefactor.*

*And you don't think this is just the least bit screwed up? That I'm treating people this way in order to learn how to treat people better?*

*As I said, it was your idea.*

A fair point. *So when were you going to tell me all this?*

*It was almost time. Then the shit hit the fan and here we are, with no choice but to move up the schedule.*

I thought about Tomi. Maybe the ghost was telling the truth when he said I'd left people behind in other lives. But not in this one.

*I'm not giving her up*, I warned him.

*You've said that before. And each time, you* do *give her up—whoever it happens to be during that lifetime. Whatever you value about her, whatever you love, becomes less desirable once you know who and what you are.*

*Not this time*, I thought.

*Whatever you say.*

And he was gone.

# Chapter Thirteen

About an hour after daybreak, after we had changed the gas tank for the third time, we saw Junior's vessel and its telltale black sail. It was far away, so it wasn't much more than a speck on the horizon. But as the hours passed, and again they passed too quickly, the speck got noticeably bigger.

"How's he doing that?" I wondered out loud.

"What's that?" asked Antonio, who was sitting beside me, and had proven a little friendlier than either Leif or Elijah.

"Catching up to us. He's in a sailboat, for god sakes. And there's not even that much wind."

"He can make his *own* wind," said Antonio.

I remembered the gust that took down Arturo Baker's chopper. "Never mind."

How was I going to beat somebody like that? "Is he going to catch us before we reach Olympos?"

Antonio thought for a moment. "I don't think so. But you never know."

It was midday when we finally saw land. It wasn't just an island, either. It stretched from one side of the horizon to the other. As we got closer, I saw mountains start to take shape above it.

It looked to me like Antonio had been right. We were going to make it just before Junior's ship caught up to us.

*It won't make a difference,* said Junior, in my head again. *Even if you reach Olympos, you won't get what you want.*

*How do you know?* I asked.

He laughed in my skull. *You'll see.*

*Look,* I thought, *is all this really necessary? What are you proving by attacking the Isles?*

*The people of the Isles are human—some of them completely so, some in part. My goal is to destroy the race of men. Therefore, I have to destroy the people of the Isles.*

He was crazy. *Any particular reason you want to destroy humanity?*

**Human beings were Zeus's biggest mistake,** said Junior, *less worthy of life than the lowest insect that scrabbles in the dirt. You've lived among them, Diomedes. You've seen how they love to wallow in their own evil, drawn to it the way a fly is drawn to shit. They prey on each other, on their ancestors, on the very world that sustains them. They're devoid of piety, selflessness, courage . . . even self-respect.*

*Zeus was disgusted with them the moment he finished making them and sat back to consider what he had done. He meant to destroy them—he said so more than once. Not to banish them as he had banished his other flawed creations, the beings of the Golden Age and the Silver Age and the Bronze Age, but to wipe them from the face of reality.*

*Except he miscalculated. He thought he had all eternity to play with, and that wasn't the way it turned out. Ironically, the race of men managed to outlast him. Which is why it falls to me to complete the task of annihilating them, a task I am more than happy to carry out.*

It sounded like he'd made up his mind. But that didn't mean I wasn't going to try to change it.

*There's another way to look at the situation*, I suggested.

*What's that?* asked Junior.

*Regardless of what Zeus may have said, he never did destroy the human race. He exiled the beings of the Golden Age and the Silver Age and the Bronze Age without a second thought, without an ounce of compassion.*

Of course, I was tap dancing at this point, never having heard of the people of the Golden Age and the Silver Age. But Junior had mentioned them, so I did too.

*But for some reason,* I continued, *he hesitated when it came to mankind. Why did he do that? It's an interesting question, isn't it? Was he just too busy being Zeus to get around to it?*

*I don't know*, said Junior, a stiffness in his response.

*I don't know either, but I can guess. I think he saw some promise in men despite their shortcomings, some sign that they might be headed for greater things. It's possible, isn't it?*

No reply. Junior seemed to be weighing what I'd thought at him.

Finally he said, *That's the stupidest thing I've ever heard. If Zeus hesitated, it was out of morbid fascination. He had probably never seen any of his creations torture each other the way human beings do.*

Okay, that was another way of looking at it. *But what if I'm right, and there's something glorious taking shape in the human race? Who are we to crush it before we know for sure?*

*You*, said Junior, *are no one. But I'm the son of Zeus. And I know for sure right now.*

Hey, it was worth a shot.

*Turn back immediately*, said Junior, *and I'll spare your life. You're more than half a god. I can find a place for you. You don't need to die along with the rest of your race.*

*You know me better than that,* I thought. *I'm not going to give up in the middle of the game.*

*Even if the conclusion is inevitable?*

*Especially if the conclusion is inevitable.*

*Suit yourself,* said Junior.

And that was the last I heard of him for a while.

In the meantime, the mountains in the distance became more distinct, separating themselves from the blue of the sky. One of them was clearly higher than the others.

"Olympos," said Antonio.

I shaded my eyes to get a better look at the place where the goddess was waiting.

We reached the beach with Junior's boat still three or four football fields behind us. As we dragged our craft up on the sand, a windstorm came up on us, blinding us.

Junior's doing, I thought.

But Elijah was prepared for it. Pulling his scuba goggles down over his eyes, he handed me a pair as well. Even with them it was difficult to see, but we managed to get off the beach and into the hills that rose behind it, swords tucked into our belts.

Knowing Junior was on our trail, we kept up a good pace as we climbed. But we also knew that no pace we could keep up would prevent him from catching us if he wished to.

His men were a different story. They were strong, but not necessarily all that quick. The question was whether Junior would try to overtake us on his own, without them.

The hours on land, like those on the water, went by too quickly, as if someone was running the reel through the projector at too high a speed. I wiped the sweat from my eyes and it was high noon. I drank from one of the water bottles Elijah had given me and the sun was halfway down the sky.

Finally, we caught a glimpse of Junior and his men down below us. They hadn't closed the gap at all. If anything, they had fallen farther behind.

Junior must have seen us at the same time we saw him, because he filled my mind with the words *You don't know what you're doing. You're just going to die.*

But for the first time, I thought, he sounded a little desperate—as if he believed I might have a chance to beat him after all, and my finding Aphrodite might be the key to that beating. I found that interesting, considering the history I was supposed to have had with her.

Maybe she wouldn't be so mad at me after all.

I don't know what I had expected Olympos to look like.

Something like the Acropolis in its heyday, maybe. Majestic, white buildings gleaming in the sun, manicured walkways, pools full of crystal-clear water, statues that would have made Michelangelo gape in frustration. I mean, it was the home of the *gods*.

But even after we'd reached Olympos and started up her

flank, I didn't see *any* of that stuff. Not a sign, in fact, of a single man-made swelling. Just trees and rocks and the occasional half-hearted waterfall.

The ghost had gone silent again. I wished I knew why. But for the time being, it seemed, I wouldn't have the benefit of his advice.

About halfway up, I thought I heard a woman whisper my name: *Diomedes* . . .

I looked around, but there was no one near me. At least, not near enough to whisper to me. And it wasn't the ghost's voice I had heard, or even Junior's for that matter. So who . . . ?

It had to be the goddess.

*Diomedes*, it whispered again, touching my mind as lightly as a lover's kiss. *Come the rest of the way alone.*

Shading my eyes against the sun, I searched the slope above me. Unfortunately, I didn't see anyone. But that didn't mean she couldn't see *me*.

"Why?" I asked.

But there was no response.

"Hello?" I said.

Still nothing. Apparently, she had said all she meant to say.

"What's the matter?" asked Elijah, who had been walking beside me.

I pointed in the direction of our objective. "She spoke to me."

Squinting, he followed my gesture. "What did she say?"

"She wanted me to go up there alone."

He frowned. "Of course she did. You're an easier target without us."

I thought about it. "She's the goddess of beauty, right? And I sent her packing once already. How tough can she be?"

Elijah shrugged. "She's not known for any particular form of violence, but she's still a goddess. We need you alive if you're going to be of any help to Mr. Drakos and the Isles."

"I'm on board with staying alive," I said. "But we still need to find the thing that's going to give me all that power, and Aphrodite probably knows where it is. If I can win her over, it could save us a lot of time." I glanced back down the mountain. "And time, weird as it is around here, is still of the essence."

Elijah's eyes narrowed as he weighed our options. Finally, he said, "Okay, if you think you can do it." He gestured to the others to stop. "We'll stay here and stop Junior—or at least slow him down." Then, to me again: "Good luck."

What he was saying, essentially, was that he and the other guys were going to put their lives on the line to give me a shot at completing our mission. And I thought Junior's bodyguards back in Queens were loyal.

"See you on the way back down," I said hopefully, taking in all three of them. Then, leaving Drakos's men behind, I continued up the mountain on my own.

Was I crazy? Time would tell.

As I climbed, the wind began to pick up.

At first, I thought it might have been a wind Junior had manufactured. But after a while, I didn't think so anymore. It wasn't trying to tear me off the slope. It was just a normal wind, blowing the way normal winds do at that height.

When I looked down at the sea and Junior's ship, they seemed impossibly far below me. It was another world up there near the top of Olympos, a world far removed from the rest of the earth. I began to understand why the gods had chosen it as their own.

*Diomedes* . . .

The voice again, decidedly feminine. If I hadn't known better, I'd have thought it was trying to seduce me. But then, Aphrodite was the goddess of love. That was probably just the way she spoke.

*I'm coming*, I thought back.

There was a belt of pine trees up ahead of me. I made my way through them, grateful for the shade they offered, using their exposed roots and branches to pull myself up.

There was something very peaceful about those woods. Birds warbled. Squirrels darted from tree to tree. I could have laid down there and forgotten what faced me farther up the slope.

But I had done enough forgetting. It was time to face my past.

A few minutes later, I emerged from the embrace of the trees—and was so intent on the terrain ahead of me, I almost overlooked the little shelf of rock protruding from the side of the mountain.

Which wouldn't have been such a big deal if the rock hadn't had a female figure sitting on it, dangling her feet over its side. A female figure with an aura about her.

*Diomedes*, she thought again, though we were close enough

at that point for her to use the spoken word and be heard as easily.

*I'm here*, I replied, for lack of something better to say.

*Join me*, she said in my mind.

She didn't *sound* angry. Of course, that might have been just a ruse. And then, when I least expected it, she would nail me.

I accepted the risk and climbed as high as her rock. But I couldn't get a good look at her face. It was obscured by her long, golden brown hair, which was blowing wildly in the wind. Finally, she pulled it to one side.

"Aphrodite . . . ?" I said.

She turned to look back at me, and immediately I knew . . . *it wasn't Aphrodite*.

I had met the goddess of beauty once, under the walls of Troy. I had wounded her, and she had gone back to Olympos to complain to Zeus that a mere mortal had assaulted a god.

You'd think I would remember something like that.

But I didn't, no more than I remembered the rest of my life in ancient Greece. So I shouldn't have been able to tell whether I was looking at Aphrodite or not.

Nonetheless, I knew . . . it wasn't her.

Not because she wasn't beautiful, because she *was*—at least to me. But she didn't have the kind of looks that could define beauty for an entire civilization. In fact, the only thing unusual about her was her eyes.

They were the color of granite in sunlight, a flinty and not at all unpleasant shade of grey. That was the first thing I noticed about them. But as I stood there gazing at the woman,

I noticed something else about her eyes.

*They were blind.*

"Diomedes," she said, blind or not.

Her voice was full of emotions, among them sadness and regret. But I also heard love and longing, and a gladness that might have had something to do with me.

"I'm sorry," I said, "but I don't remember—"

She moved off the rock, covered the distance between us, and took my hands in hers. All without having the benefit of sight.

But then, she was a goddess. It wasn't that big a stretch to think she could do things like that.

"You don't remember me?" she asked, her aura jumping, her voice still a confusion of conflicting feelings.

"I don't remember much of anything," I told her.

But even as the words left my lips, I began to see things in my head. Scenes of war in which this woman was driving my chariot, her helmet and armor shining like the sun. Scenes of peace, in which she offered me wine and laughed, and caressed my brow and whispered wisdom in my ear.

She was the woman I had seen in those friezes back in the Isles. I didn't remember her when Ajax put me in Neleos's building to meditate, but I remembered her now.

And I remembered something else—that I had loved her with all my being. Not the way I loved Tomi, mind you. It was more like worship, the way a child loves a parent, because at the time I had been a mortal and she had been the daughter of Zeus.

"Athena," I said, the name half-catching in my throat.

She smiled a thin smile. "You *do* remember."

Suddenly, she threw her head back and shrieked at the top of her lungs, her aura spiking like crazy. I'd heard somewhere that the gods spoke in a thousand voices. Maybe it wasn't that many, but it was close. I had to clamp my hands over my ears, and even then I thought my brains would turn to jelly.

By the time she stopped, I was on my knees, wondering how much more I could take. When I looked up at her, her eyes were red-rimmed and she had a vacant look. I waited a good thirty seconds before I opened my mouth.

"Are you all right?" I asked. It was the stupid question of the century.

"I grieve," she said, making no effort to disguise the pain in her voice.

"For who?" I ventured.

Her aura jumped again, and a sob caught in her throat. "For myself. For my innocence."

I didn't know what to say to that, so I kept quiet.

She continued anyway, so softly that I had to strain to hear her. "I used to like to lie here alone in the sun, letting it bathe me in its warmth. It wasn't easy for me to *feel*, Diomedes—to feel *anything*—but I could feel the sun. The other gods knew not to trespass on my privacy at such times.

"One day, while I was sun-bathing, I realized there was someone standing there with me. Scooping up my robes, I covered my nakedness. Then I sat up, ready to rail at whoever had disturbed me.

"But it was only my father, Zeus. No one else.

"'My child,' he said with what sounded like fatherly pride, 'you are as beautiful as Aphrodite. More so, because there is wisdom in your eyes.'

"He had never before complimented me on my beauty. On my intelligence, yes, but never on my looks. I blushed, and thanked him.

"'Do you mind if I sit with you?' he asked.

"'Of course not,' I said.

"Then Zeus sat down beside me, and we looked out at the blue sea, lashed to whitecaps by a fierce wind. But it was cold now that I was sitting up, and he noticed.

"'Come,' he said, and put his strong, warm arm around my bare shoulders. 'No need for you to shiver when I can protect you from the wind.'

"I was grateful. And goddess though I was, there was something comforting about having my father's arm about me.

"Gently, he drew me to him and kissed me on the temple, his lips full and warm on my skin. It was unusual for Zeus to show such affection, especially for me, but I thought nothing of it. After all, he had his moods, and his current mood was obviously a good one.

"Then he kissed me again, this time on the back of my neck, from which I had drawn the hair back with a leather string. It made me uneasy that he had done so. After all, it was not the place where a father might be expected to kiss his daughter."

My heart started to beat harder. I didn't like where this was going.

"It occurred to me to say something, but I did not. Was he not Zeus, who had made us all? And did he not value my counsel above all others, even that of his brothers?

"So I remained silent," said Athena, "as silent as the snow—until he turned my face to his and kissed me on the lips. 'Father,' I tried to say, but I couldn't. His mouth was pressing too hard on mine, his powerful tongue parting my lips against my will, his very being consuming me."

She writhed as she stood there in front of me, her aura a blaze, her hands balling into white-knuckled fists.

"I struck him as hard as I could, over and over again, but I doubt he even felt the blows. I tried to scream, to call for help, but he put his paw of a hand over my mouth and stifled my cries."

Athena drew in a wretched, ragged breath, her chest heaving with the effort. It was as if she were living the misery and the horror and the shame all over again.

"Then," she said, dragging the words from the pit of her soul, "he raped me."

The wind made a moaning sound, as if it mourned along with Athena. I found myself mourning too.

Zeus was her father. They were immortal beings, the origins of whom I still didn't understand. They had as much in common with human beings as human beings had with ants.

But he was still her father.

As I stood there, wanting to hold her and comfort her but deathly afraid to get any closer, something else clicked into place. Actually, a couple of somethings. Suddenly, I was more scared than ever.

Junior had told me his mother was a goddess. He had also said his father was Zeus. If Athena had been raped by her father, and that union had borne fruit...

I bit back a curse. Junior had told me on the sea that I didn't know what I was up against. But I knew *now*.

"I hated him for that," Athena whispered. "I was the strongest of his children, the proudest of his creations. Ares was a brute by comparison, Apollo a mere ornament. I was the goddess of wisdom, Diomedes, of *wisdom*... and he used me as if I were one of his mindless mortal cows."

She lifted her chin to the heavens as if she were about to shriek again, but none of those thousand voices came out. Just a pitiful, strangled mewling.

"Why?" she pleaded. "Why did he *do* that to me?"

I had no answer.

As a cop, I had come across a million sad things. Child abuse was more common than I would ever have imagined. Incest happened every day. But that didn't make it any less horrific. And the fact that Athena was a goddess...

That made it even sadder, in a way.

"Afterward," said Athena, "Zeus seemed ashamed of himself. 'Don't look at me that way!' he roared, the way the heavens roar during a terrible storm. 'Stop it! Don't look at me!'

"But of course, in my horror, I couldn't keep from looking at him. So he brought down the lightning from the sky, and blinded me."

My god, I thought, the poor woman. To have been raped was bad enough. But to have been blinded as well . . .

"I wanted to die," Athena said, tears welling up in the corners of her eyes. "But more than that, I wanted *others* to die. Not only Zeus, but all males." She looked straight at me. "You included, Diomedes."

I could feel the venom in her words, the implied accusation. "Me?" I said helplessly, wondering what I might have done that I didn't remember. "But—"

"I *loved* you," she told me, as if she were tearing the word from her heart. "I couldn't tell you at the time, but I loved you. Why else would I have been your driver on the battlefield at Troy? Why else would I have turned a god's sword away from you, or given you the sight and the power to wound Ares and Aphrodite?" A tear ran down her face, tracing a line alongside her nose. "Why would I have made it possible for you to become a god?"

I saw it now. "So I could be with you."

Had I known it at the time? Had I accepted Athena's gift of immortality, knowing she had offered it so I could be her lover for all time, and then refused when she tried to make me a god?

I didn't think so. I might have been the prick the ghost said I was, once upon a time, but I don't think I could ever have screwed over someone like Athena. I was crazy about her, after all.

So maybe *she* was the one who had put the kabosh on the god thing. Maybe she was the one who'd had second thoughts. I wished to hell I knew what I was dealing with.

"So I hated you," said Athena. "For a long time, I hated you. In fact, right up until the moment you reached this height." Her expression softened. "But hearing your voice, feeling your presence . . . " She shook her head. "I don't hate you anymore. I can't."

I was relieved. "That's good to hear."

"And how do you feel seeing me after so long?" she asked. "Does the sight of me not rekindle old feelings?"

I swallowed, knowing I should tell Athena the truth. Sure I loved her in a way, but not the way I loved Tomi. Not the way she obviously *wanted* me to love her.

But if I told her that, she might kill me, or at least stop me from doing what I had come to do, and then maybe kill Elijah and the others. So at least in this case, honesty didn't appear to be the best policy.

I just hoped she couldn't read my thoughts.

"There are other matters clouding my mind," I said, "keeping me from considering anything else." I hoped she wouldn't be offended by the idea that something could distract me from thinking about her.

"What matters?" Athena asked.

"You know who Erichthonios is."

I watched her reaction. "Yes," she said a little coldly, "I know."

"He's created a race of warriors and used them to attack the Isles. I came here to ask for a second chance—to reclaim the power you once offered me—so I can stop him."

She looked at me searchingly, as if trying to see through

her blindness. "Why?"

"Because he's killing a lot of innocent people. And when he's done with the Isles, he'll start in on my world."

Athena tilted her head to one side. "You care so much about them, Diomedes? The *mortals*?"

"Yes," I said.

"You never cared about them before. Maybe one or two who were special to you, but never the mass of humanity."

I shrugged. "I guess I've changed."

She seemed to absorb the comment slowly, maybe wondering what else about me had changed. Maybe thinking twice about whether I was still the guy she loved.

Maybe even wondering if I could be trusted anymore.

The wind blew a little harder, sending her hair dancing around her head again. It made her look wild, feral. I was about to say something—anything—to break the silence. Fortunately, she broke it first.

"Well, then," Athena said reasonably, "if you need to stop Erichthonios, I can help you. But you have to promise me something?"

"What?"

"That you will use the power I give you to make him regret ever being alive."

I didn't need to torture him. I just wanted to stop him.

"He's your son," I reminded her.

I wasn't trying to change her mind. I just wanted to make sure she knew what she was saying. After all, the least bit of confusion might make me a dead man.

"I *know* who he is," she said, her gray eyes narrowing. "He's his *father*'s son."

I nodded. "Then we've got a deal."

There was one *other* thing—the most important thing, the reason I'd wanted to go to Olympos in the first place. But from what I could see of Athena's state of mind, it seemed like the wrong time to mention Tomi.

First the power, I thought. *Then maybe I can meet Athena on equal footing.*

It took my eyes a while to adjust to the dimness of the cave. When they did, I saw something big and chalky sitting in the middle of it—a hunk of rock the size of my stove back in Astoria.

As far as I could tell, it wasn't native to the place. Someone had shoved it in there, though I didn't know anybody who had either the motivation or the strength to do such a thing.

*Move in deeper*, Athena told me, whispering in my mind.

I moved in deeper.

*That's it. What do you see?*

I saw that the rock was flat on top—*perfectly* flat, as if someone had split an even bigger piece of rock in two and put one of the halves there in the cave.

I noticed also that there was something sitting on that flat, even surface, something small and dark. Again, I moved deeper into the cave, and saw that the dark thing was a wooden statue, crudely carved and no more than a foot and a half tall.

*The palladium*, thought Athena.

If I hadn't already been told that it was her likeness, I never would have known. It didn't look any more like her than it looked like any other woman.

*Pick it up,* she said.

I reached out and picked up the statue. It was warm to the touch, as if it had been sitting by a flame. But there wasn't any flame nearby.

*Now what?* I thought.

*Now say out loud what you told me. How you would embrace the power I offered you all those years ago, if only you had a second chance.*

I looked down at the statue. *You want me to talk to it?*

*I want what* you *want,* she returned.

I considered the palladium, if that was what it was. It had a little crack in its base, and some shallow dents, and one of its sides looked like someone had run a metal file over it. In the sunlight, I thought, I would probably notice other imperfections.

How long had it been sitting there in the cave? A thousand years? Two thousand? Three?

*All right,* I told the goddess in my head. Then I said out loud, "I wish I had the power Athena offered me long ago. I would give anything to have that power now."

I don't know what I was expecting—a flash of magical energy maybe, or a thunderclap, or at least a generous puff of white smoke. As it turned out, I didn't get any of those things. The statue just stood there and looked back at me with its blunt, silent features.

*I don't think it worked,* I thought at Athena.

*Why do you say that?*

*Because nothing happened.*

The goddess seemed to hesitate for a moment, as if she didn't understand what could have gone wrong. Then she said, *Come out of the cavern.*

With a last glance at the palladium, I did as I was told. After the dimness of the cave, the light outside was blinding. I had to shade my eyes with my hand.

"You don't feel any different?" asked Athena.

"Not even a little," I confirmed.

Her brow puckered as if she were in pain. "That tree," she said, indicating a pine next to the cave. "Hit it as hard as you can."

The tree was sturdy-looking, about as wide around as my thigh. In my wildest dreams, I would never have thought of punching it.

"Are you sure?" I asked.

"Go ahead," said Athena.

Wincing in anticipation of the pain I was about to inflict on myself, I walked over to the tree, hauled off, and socked the darn thing. But I didn't feel what I thought I would feel. In fact, I didn't feel anything at all.

The pine, on the other hand, cracked in half, one part falling across the cave entrance and the other toppling in the opposite direction.

I stared disbelievingly at what I had done. Apparently, the palladium had done its job.

I was just turning to Athena to tell her so when an image flashed in front of my eyes—that of something slender and dark sitting on a polished marble altar. Even in the guttering candle light, I could tell that the thing was the palladium.

As I reached for it, an old man entered the room through a side door. He seemed startled to see me, but not so much so that he didn't cry out and charge across the floor.

He was just an old man. I could have knocked him out and been done with him. But I didn't. I raised my sword and buried it deep in the side of his neck, almost severing his head from his body.

He fell like a sack of grain, his blood spurting from his wound. As I watched, it spread across the floor. I cursed to myself, then picked up the palladium and ran.

"Diomedes?"

I blinked . . . and saw Athena standing in front of me. "I have to go now," I said, "and find Erichthonios."

She smiled a strange smile. "Of course."

As I started down the mountain, I couldn't help thinking about the old man I'd killed thousands of years ago. The ghost was right. I really was a shit, wasn't I?

I had barely descended through the pine belt when I came across Junior and a dozen or so of his men.

"Well," said Junior, planting the butt end of his spear on the ground. "Here we are. Sorry about those three bastards you left behind. They didn't last long."

I felt my teeth grind. Calm, I thought. *You've got to stay calm.*

The palladium had given me power, all right. But Junior had power too, maybe greater than mine. And he had his men.

Up close, they looked like an army of Junior impersonators.

They didn't have his crest of red hair, maybe because they had shaved it off, but their skin was bone-white, and they had his hooked nose and his pop eyes.

It made sense in a bizarre, narcissistic kind of way. After all, Junior was the one who had created the suckers. Given his profile, it wasn't a surprise that he had made them in his own image.

Or that their strength was several times that of a human being.

*Don't worry about his men,* I heard Athena say.

*What?* I thought.

*Don't worry about his men.*

I didn't know what she meant, but I could guess. I just hoped I was guessing right.

I drew my sword. "Let's get this over with."

Junior grinned, and I heard that ringing in my ears that I had heard on the handball court in Long Island City. "In a hurry, are you?" He picked up his spear and threw it at me.

It came faster than I thought it would, faster than I would have believed possible. But I was faster too, fast enough to roll to the side and avoid it.

Having seen me move, Junior had an inkling that something was wrong. I could see it in his eyes.

Holding his hand out to one of his men, he waited for the guy to place his spear in Junior's hand. But the guy didn't budge.

Junior looked at him, his eyes full of fire. Still, the guy didn't offer Junior his spear. Ripping it out of the guy's hands, Junior glared at me.

"This is *her* doing," he said, "isn't it? All of it?"

"Do you blame her?" I asked.

Damned *right* he blamed her. She was his *mother*, for godsakes, and she had thrown a major monkey wrench into his plans.

I didn't remember my mother—my *real* one. I didn't know what she thought of me before she died. But I knew I'd be crushed if I found out she had betrayed me to one of my enemies.

"It doesn't matter," he said, failing to conceal the pain in his voice. His aura pulsed. "I'll still destroy you."

I smiled. "You know what they say on the handball courts, Junior. You talk, you walk."

He had heard enough. Raising his spear, he charged me. I braced myself, not knowing if he was going to thrust at me or just throw the thing. In the end, he decided to thrust.

At the last moment, I used my sword to beat his point aside. But that didn't end the problem for me. As strong as he was, he was still capable of caving my chest in.

I had no choice but to drop, roll backward, and take his weight on the heel of my foot. Unable to stop himself, he went flying past me.

I turned and scrambled to my feet, ready to make use of my blade if I saw an opportunity. But Junior had already recovered from his tumble, his spear in his hand, his mouth twisted around a silent curse.

Again, he charged. This time, he waited until he was at close range and sent the spear whistling at my face.

I didn't think about getting out of the way. I just *did*. Denied its target, the spear sailed down the slope and buried itself harmlessly in the ground . . .

Leaving Junior unarmed.

I moved toward him, meaning to take advantage of his disadvantage. He didn't try to escape. He just stood there, his aura dancing around him.

I wondered why—until the air around me shuddered with a pure, impossibly white light, a light that absorbed all form and color, a light that consumed the world. Only for an instant, but it was enough to blind me even with the eyes of a god in my head.

It was the same thing Junior had done in the schoolyard that day, but a thousand times worse. I struggled to find his face among all the fireworks going off in my head, knowing he would try to capitalize on what he had done, but I couldn't do it.

That was the bad news. The good news was that I could see his aura just fine.

It told me that Junior was coming for me, and that he had something in his hand. The way he was holding it suggested that it was a sword rather than a spear, maybe one that he had concealed until then.

Until I was helpless—or so he thought.

I didn't let on that I could see his aura until he was almost on top of me, until he raised his weapon for a killing downstroke. Then I brought my own blade up as hard as I could, knocking his away. It left him open, unguarded, and I didn't hesitate.

I hauled back with the fist that held my sword and, drawing on all my godlike strength, smashed Junior across the face—or at least what I thought was his face, since all I could see were the green flames seething around him.

Then I did it again. And again. Until he lay on the ground, his aura little more than a flicker.

By that time, my sight had begun to come back a little. I could see that Junior was lying on his belly, one arm tucked underneath him, and that he wouldn't be getting up any time soon.

I could easily have finished the job. I could have thrust my sword between his shoulder blades and put an end to him. But instead, I thrust it into my belt.

Junior didn't say thank you, not that I expected him to. In fact, he didn't say anything at all. I took in a deep breath, let it out, and thought, I'm done.

It was hard to believe, after everything that had happened. But I'd beaten Junior. I'd satisfied Athena's thirst for revenge. The only thing left was to find Tomi and go home . . .

Wherever home might be, now that I had made myself persona non grata in Iraklion, New Jersey and probably the rest of the tri-state area.

Suddenly, a thought appeared in my head. It rang like a church bell, pushing out everything else. The thought was: *Kill him.*

# CHAPTER FOURTEEN

I looked up and saw Athena standing just below the pine belt. Even from a distance I could see the cruel twist of her mouth and the way her hands had clenched into fists.

*What?* I thought back at her.

*Kill him.*

I held my hands up to her, one empty, one holding my sword. *What's the point? Look at him.*

*The point,* Athena thought at me, *is what I say it is. Or do you defy me now—me, who offered you the mantle of immortality in the first place?*

*It's not defiance. It's just—*

*You didn't suffer the weight of Zeus on your back!* she shot back at me, her mind white hot with pain and rage. *You didn't feel him violating you, crushing you, treating you as one beast treats another. You didn't give birth to that . . . that aberration . . . knowing it would always be a reminder of your humiliation.*

*Now he's the one who's been humiliated,* I reminded her, hoping she would see reason.

*No,* she insisted, her thoughts edged with venom, *it is not enough. He must be expunged from the lands of the living.*

Athena had been my protector, my shield, the one who gave me glory and long life and now the power of a god. And she was hurting. She needed me to do one thing for her, one small thing to set her free from her nightmare.

Yet I couldn't do it.

*Please*, I begged her, *reconsider* . . .

For a long time, she remained silent. I had gotten through to her, I thought after a while. But then, Athena had once been worshipped for her wisdom. Despite everything she had gone through, she must still have been capable of rational thought.

"Thank you," I breathed.

Then I heard a scraping sound behind me, and I looked back over my shoulder—just in time to see one of Junior's men charging at me with his spear.

I barely got my sword up in time to ward off his attack. In my mind I struck back twice as hard, sending the bald guy flying end over end. But in reality, the force of his assault was enough to send *me* flying end over end.

Scrambling to my feet, I looked up at Athena. She returned my scrutiny coldly, without expression—and I understood. Somehow, she had taken back the godlike strength she had given me.

Just as I had asked her to before, thousands of years earlier. Except this time I hadn't asked. This time she had just *done* it.

I had barely come to the realization when Junior's man pressed his attack. I sidestepped his thrust, if only by a hair, then slashed him in the ribs as he went by.

He groaned, clutched at his side, and ran himself into the ground not far from Junior. I hoped that Athena had used up her anger in sending the guy against me.

She hadn't.

A second spearman was already coming at me from another direction. Whirling to face him, I managed to knock his point offline. Then I buried my sword in the hollow of his shoulder.

As he staggered backward, grimacing, I pulled the blade free—just in time for me to face a third guy. This one had a sword, and a big one. Seeing he was coming in high, I ducked—and let him cut the empty air above my head. Then I swept his legs out from under him and lunged forward, smashing him in the temple with my hilt.

Unfortunately, my next adversary was already on the way. *Athena*, I thought, *don't do this* . . .

It didn't change anything. The guy kept on coming. Too tired to try to avoid him, I threw my sword up. My arm went half-numb absorbing the impact, but it saved me. His next blow was even harder. Somehow I deflected that one too.

It wasn't until he drew his weapon back a third time that I got my timing down. Before he could strike again, I got inside his guard and slashed him across the belly.

He dropped his sword and doubled over, his face a mask of pain. But even before his knees hit the ground I was ready for the next guy, because I *knew* there would be a next guy.

Except it wasn't one of Junior's men that I saw. *It was Tomi*.

She was walking down the slope behind Athena, her dark hair moving easily in the wind, as beautiful as I had ever seen her. *She was alive*. Alive and, as far as I could tell, completely unharmed.

My heart jumped in my chest, smashing against my ribs like a hammer. I had never been so happy in my life.

Until I noticed the aura of bright green light around her.

*No*, I thought, my throat tightening. *It can't be.*

And yet there it was.

Tomi had been my rock in a sea of shifting truths, the only part of my life I could depend on. And now I saw that even *she* wasn't what I'd thought she was.

I would rather one of Junior's men had cut me in half.

"Isn't she the one you came here for?" asked Athena, speaking out loud again. "Not for me, but for *her?*" She laughed. "I have known about your lover's ancestry for some time. But for you . . . it comes as a surprise, does it not? A shock, you might say."

Tomi stopped next to the goddess and stood there. But she wasn't in control of herself. I could tell from the pinch of skin between her brows that always meant she was frustrated about something.

"Her job," Athena continued, "was to keep an eye on you. After all, the people of the Isles were leery of Menelaos. They needed someone to balance him out, if it came to that, and you—as far as they knew—were the only other surviving god."

I looked around. Junior's men were biding their time until Athena finished speaking. I was grateful for the respite.

"Then Erichthonios took her, to see what you would do. To get an idea of what he was up against if he tried to do to humanity what he had done to the Bronze Men. And what did he see? Nothing that would make him think twice about invading your world when he decided the time was right.

"But I couldn't let that happen. I needed to thwart his plans because they had once been Zeus's plans. So I assumed control of Erichthonios's creations—enough of them to carry out my scheme, but not so many that my son would miss them.

"Then I used them to wrest your lover from Erichthonios's control, and to bring her here. Because I knew that if I brought her, I would bring *you* as well. And if I brought you, I would bring Erichthonios. And everything would be in place for me to realize my revenge.

"Now you have to finish your labor, Diomedes. You have to kill Erichthonios for me. I would do it myself, but it's wrong for a parent to commit a crime against his . . . against her son."

"So you were playing me for a fool," I said. *Just like Junior. And Drakos. And Tomi.* "You don't care for me. You just needed me to get rid of your son."

"That was the plan," said Athena, "and so far, it has worked to perfection. I was not known as the goddess of strategy for nothing. You, of all men, should know that."

I shook my head. "I'm not going to kill him. Not while he's just lying there."

Athena's smile faded, became a thin, hard line. "I was right to hate you, Diomedes."

Then, unexpectedly, her smile returned. "It's all right. Don't trouble yourself. If you won't kill Erichthonios, I'll have one of his men do it. But not before I see *you* die first."

Then the bald guys went after me again. Not toe to toe the way they had before, but as if they were baiting me, as if

I were a wounded animal and they were having some sport at my expense—one after the other, rapid-fire, attacking and retreating, attacking and retreating.

I fought back as best I could, but I took some shots. Some hard ones, too. it wasn't long before I was bleeding in a dozen places, and my sword was so heavy I could hardly lift it.

I didn't know how much more I could take.

Why fight, anyway? I thought. The result was inevitable. But I *had* to fight. Regardless of how my education had changed me over the centuries, I couldn't give in.

It wasn't in my nature.

Just up the mountainside, the blind goddess looked down at me as if she could see. Sooner or later, she would get her way. One of her puppets would get in a disabling blow and it would be all downhill from there.

After all, I was only human again.

*Hang in there, Diomedes.*

Another voice in my head. But it wasn't Athena's.

*Ghost?* I thought.

*Yes. And no, Athena can't hear me.*

*That's wonderful*, I thought, defending myself from another assailant as he tried to impale me on his spear. *But . . . hang in there? I don't think I can.*

*Try*, he told me.

It was easy for him to say.

My adversaries, meanwhile, were picking up the pace. Athena must be getting impatient. I thought. They were coming at me in twos and threes, swinging at me with all their strength, trying to wear down my last bit of resistance. And it was working. I was no longer warding off their blows so much as slightly redirecting them.

Finally, I couldn't hold onto my sword anymore. One of Junior's men sent it flying out of my grasp. Then he pulled his blade back and aimed it at my head.

If I'd had any notion that Athena was just trying to teach me a lesson, it was dispelled. The blade missed my neck by a hairsbreadth, and only because I threw myself out of harm's way.

*Just a little more*, said the ghost.

Finding a last reserve of strength, I plowed into the nearest of my enemies, knocking him off his feet. Obviously, he hadn't expected me to do that. None of them had. Raising my fist, I brought it down in the middle of his face.

Blood gushed from his nose. But before I could hit him again, someone grabbed my wrist and twisted. Feeling my bones grind, I cried out in pain.

Swords raised all around me.

This is it, I thought.

I glanced in Athena's direction, curious to see how she was enjoying the spectacle.

As it turned out, she wasn't. At least, she didn't look like it. She was sweating, pale, exerting herself almost as much as I was. But then, she was pulling the strings of so many puppets at once, it had to be a strain on even her.

Then I saw something else. I saw Tomi coming up behind Athena, a sword in her hands.

In her struggle to direct so many minds, Athena must have lost track of Tomi. Tomi was *free*.

But why pick up a sword? I thought. The goddess would probably have let Tomi live. After all, she no longer needed her as bait to lure me to Olympos.

And yet there Tomi was, risking her life.

Not for me, of course. I knew that now. Whatever she did, it was for the Isles.

*Diomedes!* said the ghost.

I wrenched my wrist free and rolled off the bull's eye, squirting between a couple of legs. There was an uproar, and the circle moved after me. I was still in the game.

But not for long. Someone kicked me in the ribs, taking my breath away. Someone else ground my face into the slope, holding me down while the others got ready to dig in with their spears.

But I was facing in the right direction, and as I watched, Tomi took a hard, well-placed hack at Athena's slender, pink neck.

For a long, terrible moment, the goddess seemed to remain intact, her expression still one of intense concentration. Then her head toppled onto the ground, trailing strings of blood and gore, and her body folded a moment later.

I cringed, because I was still being held down by Junior's men, and I knew they still had their weapons pointed at me. But they never used them. Without a word, they left me there and moved away down the mountain.

I had no idea where they were going until I realized that Junior was nowhere to be seen. He wasn't lying on the ground where I had left him anymore. He was gone.

And I didn't have the strength to go after him. At least, not yet.

"Zeno?"

I looked up and saw Tomi kneeling next to me. "Are you all right?" she asked, her eyes wet with tears.

I didn't answer her. I just got up and limped over to where Athena's head lay in the short mountain grass. Her blind, lifeless eyes stared up at me, still full of a kind of wisdom, I supposed.

She'd been my friend once, I thought. *It always feels bad to lose a friend.* I glanced at Tomi, who was still kneeling where I had left her. *And worse when you've lost* two *friends.*

"What's going on?" she asked me.

"You're from the Isles," I said. "I know all about you."

Her mouth opened, but she didn't say anything. Pretty much as I had expected. But then, what do you say to a man you've tricked into loving you?

I looked around for my sword. I didn't feel any need to bury Junior's men, but it didn't seem right to just leave Athena lying there. Settling for one of the bald guys' swords instead, I picked it up and started back to where the goddess had fallen.

Suddenly, I was tackled from behind.

Not again, I thought.

With a twist of my hips, I did a quick one-eighty in my attacker's grip. At the same time I pulled my fist back, meaning to bury it in his face. But it wasn't a Junior lookalike looking back at me.

It wasn't even a *he*. It was Tomi.

I absorbed the facts of the situation, but—like so many other times in the past couple of weeks—I couldn't quite wrap my head around them.

"Did you just tackle me?" I asked.

She didn't speak in response—she *growled*, as she climbed up on top of me. "Damned right I tackled you. And I will beat the living *shit* out of you before I'll let you get up and walk out on me."

"Walk out on you *who*?" I asked, sadness tightening my throat. "You the woman I used to love? Or you the spy for Ajax and Sasterion?"

"*Both*," she told me. "I'm not going to deny what I did, or why I did it. But somewhere in the middle of that mess I started to love you, you idiot. I didn't want to, I didn't expect to, but I *did*. And I love you now, and I'm never going to stop loving you. And I know you love me, so don't even *try* to put me out of your life because that's not going to work and you know it!"

I closed my eyes and let the back of my head come to rest on the ground. A week earlier, I had known who I was and who I was in love with. So much had changed. So much . . .

"Don't pretend you're dead," said Tomi. "I can hear you breathing."

I smiled. I mean, it was funny.

"What are you laughing at?" she demanded.

"You," I said. "And the ghost."

He was going hard in my ear. *I'm serious, Diomedes. Don't be an ass. She's telling the truth. She loves you.*

How do you know? I thought. *You didn't seem to know what*

was on her mind before, when she wasn't who she was supposed to be.

That's because she loved you before as well. I can't read people's minds, but I'm always on target when it comes to reading their hearts.

"Who's the ghost?" Tomi asked.

"I don't know," I said. "But whoever he is, he's on your side."

She got that little pinch of skin between her brows. Her beautiful, dark brows, the ones I kissed sometimes after we made love.

I pulled her face down and kissed them now, and said, "Listen, the next time you're a spy from another world, would you just freakin' tell me? I don't think I can go through this again."

She sighed. "Sure. As long as you get off your ass and get yourself a job."

*All very nice*, said the ghost, *but you've got a lot of work ahead of you. You should have killed Junior when you had the chance.*

*The old Diomedes would have*, I thought. *But I'm not the old Diomedes, remember?*

*Leave it to you*, he said, *to be conceited about being humble.*

I laughed again.

"The ghost?" said Tomi.

"Yup."

"I guess," she said, "there are a few things *you* haven't told *me*."

There were, I thought. And I would.

But first, I had a goddess to bury.

# ABOUT THE AUTHOR

Michael Jan Friedman is the author of nearly 70 books of fiction and non-fiction, about half of them set somewhere in the wilds of the *Star Trek* universe. His first book, *The Hammer and The Horn*, was published by Questar, an imprint of Warner Books, in 1985. In the next couple of years, he wrote *The Seekers and The Sword* and *The Fortress and The Fire*, completing what has come to be known as The Vidarsaga Trilogy, as well as the freestanding novel *The Glove of Maiden's Hair*.

In 1992 Friedman penned *Reunion*, the first *Star Trek: The Next Generation* hardcover, which introduced the crew of the *Stargazer*, Captain Jean-Luc Picard's first command. Over the years, the popularity of *Reunion* spawned a number of *Stargazer* stories in both prose and comic book formats, including a six-novel original series.

Friedman has also written for the *Aliens, Predator, Wolf Man, Lois and Clark, DC Super Hero, Marvel Super Hero,* and *Wishbone* licensed book universes. Eleven of his book titles, including the autobiography *Hollywood Hulk Hogan* and *Ghost Hunting* (written with SciFi's Ghost Hunters), have appeared on the prestigious *New York Times* primary bestseller list, and his novel adaptation of the *Batman & Robin* movie was for a time the #1 bestselling book in Poland (really).

Friedman has worked at one time or another in network and cable television, radio, business magazines, and the comic book industry, in the process producing scripts for nearly 180 comic stories. Among his comic book credits are the *Darkstars* ongoing series from DC Comics, which he created with artist Larry Stroman, and the *Outlaws* limited series, which he created with artist Luke McDonnell, as well as tales of Superman, Batman, Green Lantern, Flash, Fantastic Four, and the Silver Surfer. He also co-wrote the story for the acclaimed second-season *Star Trek: Voyager* episode "Resistance," which guest-starred Joel Grey.

Friedman lives with his wife and two sons on Long Island, where in his rapidly dwindling free time he enjoys running, kayaking, and playing (what else?) single-wall handball.

# Want to read more books by Crazy 8?

# Check out this sneak peek of our next offering:

## The Battleplain of Marsay

*i.*

*Mandraques do nothing in half measures.*

That had always been the unofficial motto of the five clans. Aside from their mutual contempt, it might well have been the only thing that united them. It was a motto that applied to all things, all dealings, all clanwars. And it very much applied to the battlefield, which was running green with Mandraque blood.

The field was flat and lifeless, with the bodies of hundreds of Mandraques scattered in various places and assorted pieces. Nothing was moving except the flies, and the air was thick with the stench of bodies, decay and waste. There had been choruses of groaning, cries for help, moans of "My leg!" and "Help me, damn you!" and "I'll kill you all for this!" Eventually they had tapered off. Only the corpses remained.

One Mandraque in particular had not gone down easily. His sword was clenched tightly in his clawed hand. His armor was in tatters, and through the holes one could see the blue/green scales that was the typical skin covering for the species. He had been massively muscled. Like most Mandraques, his scaled head was round, his eyes little more than slits, his parallel nostrils cruel lines in the middle of his face. His mouth, in death, was drawn back in a sneer, which actually mirrored the way it had normally appeared in life.

Insects were gathering upon his forehead, working their way into his nostril slits, as he stared lifelessly at the sky above. It was a gorgeous day if one was willing to discount the smoke that hung in the air from the various fires . . . fires that had resulted from the flaming arrows filling the air like so many shooting stars. Those arrows had been largely responsible for the second aroma, that of cooked meat hanging heavy in the still air.

A slender hand, fingernails thick with dirt, skin abraded on the back, reached over and brushed the flies away from his forehead. The hand's possessor slowly hauled herself forward on her hands and knees. She had only just come around, shaking off the darkness that had claimed her. She could not have been more different from the dead Mandraque prostrate upon the ground. Her skin was smooth and tanned, and copious amounts of thick black hair hung in her face. Her eyes peered through the strands, and reflected in them was a soul with the frailty of a crippled sparrow. The various stenches assaulted her as her full senses began to come around, and she coughed in violent spasms, her breasts heaving as she did so.

She was bloodied from having been thrown around during the fighting. Her mind was a blur . . . images tumbling one over the other . . . blood flying, teeth tearing and ripping, terrifying and unrecognizable roars of defiance and death, death all around her . . .

"Greatness?" she said softly. Her hand hesitated over him, because she was never supposed to touch him without his permission. Nevertheless, this time she took the risk and rested her fingers tentatively upon him. Her fingers were tinted green with blood.

No response.

A bit more boldly, she shook the Mandraque as she whispered his title into his earhole. "Greatness?" she repeated. "Greatness... what do you wish me to do now?"

Still no answer.

Caution dissolved within her. She grabbed the dead Mandraque with both hands and shook him violently. "Greatness! *What do you wish me to do! Tell me! Greatness . . . !*"

Her cries were so loud that she didn't hear the footsteps behind her, crunching across the ash and rubble-strewn land. She continued to shout at the dead Mandraque, pounding upon his chest with a combination of mounting fury and terror, and would have continued to do so until she'd collapsed in exhaustion had she not been startled by a loud clearing of a throat.

She turned, jumping back, startled. She rubbed some stray soot from her eyes and wiped dirt from her face, leaving smears from the back of her hand. She squinted at the new arrival and had no idea what to make of him.

He was neither as tall nor as wide as the Greatness had been. His visage was fearsome and feral, but surprisingly it was mingled with a gentleness such as she had never seen in all her life. She didn't truly know how old she actually was. She had once asked, and the Greatness had told her she was between fifteen and twenty cycles around the sun. He couldn't be more specific beyond that.

The newcomer's skin was similar to her own, but an even darker hue. He had a mop of curly brown hair that hung in ringlets around his triangular face. He looked at her, tilting his head from side to side in curiosity, and the curls bounced around as he did so. Save for a large, thick band of leather that wrapped around him from waist to shoulder, he was naked from the waist up, displaying a flat stomach and taut chest. It was a warm day, so his relative lack of apparel didn't surprise her terribly. She herself was not wearing much: Scraps of cloth to accentuate the curves of her body, gauzy and filmy and out of place in the blood-soaked environs.

What did surprise her was that, from the waist down, he was covered with thick brown fur. His legs bent at an odd angle to the knees, and tapered down into cloven feet.

"I don't think he's in much of a position to respond," he said. His voice was rough, but there was amusement in it. He glanced around the scene with obvious interest. "He certainly gave an accounting of himself in his final moments."

"Final . . . moments?" she said slowly.

"Well . . . yes. Look," and he pointed at the devastation in the area immediately around the Greatness.

She studied where he was indicating, truly seeing it for the first time. There were other Mandraque bodies strewn about, their weapons broken and scattered. Even the least damaged of them were ripped up or gutted. Most of them were missing pieces of their bodies: arms, legs, tails and such. There were still trickles of blood from some of the severed limbs. She saw that there was a Mandraque with his teeth sunk into the Greatness's leg.

She looked back up at the newcomer. "Final moments?" she said again.

He stared at her, clearly disbelieving. "Yes. He's . . . dead. You *do* understand that, don't you?" He took a step toward her. "You're a human, aren't you? A human female. I've never seen one of you living before. Does your kind have names? What's your name?"

"Final . . . moments?"

Blowing out air through tight lips in annoyance, he said, "Are you . . . mentally deficient in some way? I don't mean to be insulting. It's just, well . . . if you are I can probably save myself some time. I'm Karsen, by the way. Karsen Foux." He paused for a moment, frowning, looking as if he was trying to recall something. Then he smiled, having mentally retrieved it, and he extended a hand with the palm sideways. "This is how your sort greets, does it not?"

As he approached her she stepped back reflexively. Her arms crisscrossed her breasts protectively, and she twisted herself around to keep clear of him despite his lack of outward aggression. "He is the Greatness! His . . . his kind does not have final moments!"

"He is flesh and blood, my sweet," said Karsen. "I assure you, he has final moments, just like the rest of us." He looked around at the corpses. "Quite a fight this was, I'll grant you. Brutal, too. A number of them cut down by blades, but others . . . look at this. Their throats torn out. Necks broken. I'll give your Greatness credit, he was certainly versatile in the way he killed his enemies. Now what's your name?"

She began shaking her head ferociously. She was starting to look less like a human rational being and more like a trapped beast. Her eyes were hot and glowering. "Keep away from him," she said.

"I don't have to actually," he told her. "He's fair game, under the Treaty. So why not let me do my job, and you can go and do yours . . . whatever that might be."

He approached her with slow, measured strides. She wanted to remain where she was; she wanted to find some way to stop him. She kept looking down at the Greatness for hints or a measure of guidance, and nothing was forthcoming. Instead her mind was gradually pointing her down a road that she had no desire to travel.

She now realized the Greatness's hide was cold beneath her fingers. No life pulsed within his frame.

She was alone.

She had never been alone. Not since she had first come to the Greatness's court, so far back that she could not recall a time when she hadn't been there.

Panic began to seize her. She started trembling, shaking her head as if she could deny what was occurring. Karsen looked concerned as he drew closer. "Are you . . . all right?"

She turned and bolted.

Immediately she nearly tripped over a fallen arm, righted herself and ran from the scene, hoping that she could expunge the hideous sights she had seen from her memory, knowing that she never could.

Soot was settling upon the ground, and her delicate feet were leaving a trail of prints behind her. She risked a glance over her shoulder. There was no sign of the creature calling itself "Karsen."

She let out a sigh of relief that she wasn't being followed, and then shrieked as she nearly plowed straight into Karsen, now inexplicably in her path. As it was she lost her balance, staggered and fell. Karsen stood over her, looking down impassively.

"In answer to what you're probably thinking . . . no, you didn't run in a circle or circumnavigate the globe," Karsen assured her. He advanced on her, his patience ebbing away. "Now if you'd just allow me to—"

The instant he came within range, she drove a foot straight up and into the area of his loins. The impact had the same effect on Karsen as it did on males of her own race. He doubled over, his face becoming pale, and he clutched at his groin, cradling something thankfully unseen deep within the fur.

She did not wait to see if the attack had any further results. Instead she ran.

She ran over the battle-scarred land. She ran past the fallen Mandraques, past the tents that were still smoldering, past the makeshift fortresses and the trenches that had been dug but only presented minimal protection. She ran and ran, her heart pounding as if intending to flee the protection of her bosom. She could barely breathe, her throat sore and rasping from the smoky, stale air. She was sobbing, but her eyes were dry of tears. She had no idea what she was running toward. All she knew was to follow her impulse to get as far from the scene of the Greatness's death . . .

*The Greatness's death!*

It was the first time she had actually said those repellent words to herself, and she still couldn't believe them. The Greatness couldn't die. He was . . . he was the Greatness! He . . .

She tripped.

She didn't simply trip. Her foot hit something, the exact nature of which she never knew. Perhaps it had been a stray rock or random piece of a body. Either way, it sent her sprawling, hurtling through the air flat with her arms outstretched as if she were flying. She did not remain airborne. Instead she crashed to the ground, tearing her skin even further, slamming her jaw down with such force that it jarred her brain. She skidded several more feet before grinding to a stop. The world was swirling around her. She was sure from the tightening of her stomach muscles that she was going to vomit. She did not, although it might have made her feel better if she'd done so.

She closed her eyes to block out the spinning. Then she heard footsteps in front of her. It seemed impossible. She had dealt him a fearsome blow, had run as fast as she could. How could he conceivably have caught up with her?

She tried to pull herself up, to keep going in the vain hope that he hadn't spotted her somehow, when suddenly rough hands were yanking her to her feet. She gasped and was twisted around to face two Mandraques. She recognized them immediately, more from their signs of rank and various ribbons of lineage than their faces.

They looked battered and bloodied, both relieved to be alive and also a bit chagrined. One was taller than the other, and the shorter one said, "Ranzell . . . I think I recognize this one. What's her name . . . ?"

The one addressed as Ranzell snagged her free hand and shook her, snapping the arm as if cracking a whip. He carried no sword, but Jepp saw an impressively large war hammer strapped to his back. Its handle was half as long as Ranzell himself, and the rough-hewn stone head was flecked with Mandraque blood. Ranzell's associate was busy tossing aside his own, broken sword, and was hefting a sword picked up from a corpse, swinging it this way and that to gauge the weight. Ranzell flinched slightly, scowling in an annoyed way that indicated the sword had come a bit too close to him for comfort. "What's your name, girl? One of your betters has asked you."

Her mouth moved with no sound emerging at first. The two Mandraques didn't seem sympathetic. Tokep, the shorter one, grinned in a way that only made him look sinister. "I recall now. Her name is Jepp. She's the Greatness's pleasure toy, aren't you, Jepp?"

She managed a nod. They didn't seem particularly friendly, but that was certainly about normal for the entirety of their race. "Yes . . . I am . . . I am the Greatness's. I have always belonged to the Greatness."

"Good t'hear," said Ranzell. "And now you're ours."

"No," she told him, trying to pull away. "I am the Greatness's . . ."

"We passed the Greatness. He's dead. You belong to—"

"To me."

They turned and there was Karsen. He was a few feet away, and he must have moved like a demon to get there, but he didn't seem especially tired out.

"What's a Laocoon doing away out here?" said Tokep. His body was tense in a manner that suggested he was going to attack if he didn't get an answer he liked.

"Finding things," said Karsen. "In this case, I found her first. *First*, my friends. And the laws of salvage, as laid out by the Treaty, say she's mine."

Tokep processed the information, and then he visibly relaxed. The two Mandraques looked at one another and shared a laugh. "It's a Bottom Feeder," said Tokep with a snort. "A godsdamned Bottom Feeder."

"I've always preferred the term 'reclamation expert,'" Karsen said.

Ranzell was nodding in recognition. "We've even encountered each other before, haven't we? Yes . . . it was after the Battle of the Shifting Plains. You were there scrounging, just like all your ilk. You ran away at the first sign of trouble, as I recall."

"My ilk prefers discretion to foolish altercation."

"You mean cowardice to bravery."

"Just so."

Jepp wasn't entirely sure how any of this was going to play out, but she knew she'd prefer to be elsewhere when it did. Still lying on the ground, she started to edge away, hoping that no one would notice. The hope lasted for as long as it took Ranzell's thick round tail to snap around viciously, extending to its full length and slamming down in front of her, cutting off her retreat. "Stay where you are, pleasure girl," warned Ranzell. "This won't take long. We just have to send the Bottom Feeder on his way . . . "

"But I found her first!" Karsen said, sounding not a little whiny. His tone of voice was distressing to Jepp. It certainly didn't sound like that of someone she could count on.

Tokep didn't seem any more impressed by Karsen than Jepp had been. *"Balls!"* snarled Tokep. "Why'd we find her alone, then?"

"She ran off. I just now caught up with her." He spoke with uncertainty, as if fishing for explanations.

"Too bad," said Ranzell. "Not that it would have made much difference. Even if she'd been with you, we'd still have taken her off your hands."

"Don't you have any respect for the Firedraque Treaty?"

Ranzell spat on the ground nearby. The liquid was thick and viscous and sizzled slightly when it struck the dirt. "That for the Firedraques and for their damned treaty. And that for you as well."

"That's not very respectful," said Karsen. "Now I'm sure you don't want me to register a formal complaint . . . "

Ranzell turned to the Mandraque standing next to him. "Tokep. Make this idiot stop talking. Knock him out or rip off his head. It makes little difference to me."

Karsen stepped back, fear flickering in his eyes. "Well, I . . . I have to say it makes something of a difference to *me*. I . . . I really don't want to fight."

"Then go away," said Ranzell.

"*No!*" Tokep abruptly said. "I don't want to let him off that easily. I've lost a brace of kinsmen this day, almost got killed myself, and now I've had to stand here and listen to a Bottom Feeder spout off? Enough! I'm looking for someone to hurt and this fool is it."

"No, look!" and Karsen was trembling. He forced a smile, backing up. "I'll . . . just be on my way, all right? She's not worth it. You're not worth it," he said to Jepp. "No offense."

The girl looked from Karsen to the grinning Mandraques, and back to Karsen. "You're . . . you're not going to leave me with them . . ."

"Yes, he is," growled Ranzell.

"Yes, I am," Karsen said.

"But . . . you need to save me!"

Karsen sighed heavily. "The truth of the matter, girl, is that I am exactly what they say. It's a great fool who doesn't know the reality of himself, and I am many things, but a great fool is not one of them." He bowed to the Mandraques, his hands clasped palm to palm. "War be with you."

And then, just like that, he was gone, propelled from the scene by his powerful legs, moving with startling silence.

"Please, don't!" Jepp cried out, having no clue as to whether her voice was even reaching him. "You have to save me! You have to be Great for me! I know you have the potential . . . !"

Part of her was stunned at her own aggressiveness. It was not within the purview of one such as her to tell others what to do. In fact, she could not remember ever having done it before. Then again, she had always been under the command of, and subject to the whims of, the Greatness. So it had simply never come up.

"He was just trying to salvage you so he can trade you for goods and services," Ranzell said. "If he wasn't planning to have you service him in addition. His type is the lowest of the low, girl. You're better off with us. Trust me."

Jepp studied him tentatively, and then withdrew from him. She saw vast amounts of cruelty within him, far more than in even the Greatness. Tokep didn't seem any different. They frightened her. She wanted nothing but to distance herself from them as soon as possible.

They were disinclined to cooperate. Tokep advanced, swinging his newfound jagged sword in Jepp's direction. "Where do you think you're going, girl?"

She had no idea why she cried out. But she did, and what she said was, "*Karsen!*"

"You idiot human!" said Ranzell. "He's gone! He won't help you!"

Except he wasn't. And he did.

For Karsen was suddenly in the middle of the clearing. Confusion flickered upon Karsen's face for a moment, but then the certainty of his actions clarified for him what he was about to undertake. He was crouched low, his legs coiled, one hand touching the ground. His face was twisted in what seemed grim amusement.

Tokep needed no further urging. He switched targets and moved. He swung the sword swung viciously toward the Laocoon, and Karsen easily vaulted over not only the sword, but over Tokep himself . . . and landed on Ranzell's shoulders. Ranzell grabbed at him, but Karsen's powerful legs pushed off, like a swimmer moving through air rather than water. He vaulted away from Ranzell and landed directly behind him.

Ranzell yelped and grabbed at his back, his frantic fingers

confirming what the loss of weight had already told him: Karsen had ripped the war hammer off his back. He spun just as Karsen twisted at the waist, whipping around the war hammer. Ranzell ducked under it. Tokep turned around to find out what all the yelling was about. The hammerhead slammed against Tokep's head. The Mandraque's skull practically exploded from the impact, bits of blue matter and green blood spattering everywhere, including Jepp's leg. She let out a disgusted shriek and brushed it away.

Karsen faced Ranzell, and Jepp saw the war hammer was covered with much fresher blood than it had been before.

Ranzell grabbed up Tokep's fallen sword and the Mandraque charged, bellowing in a voice so deafening that Jepp clapped her hands to her ears. This time Karsen did not leap out of the way, probably because the Mandraque was expecting it. Instead he swung the hammer to meet the arc of the sword. The two weapons came together with a resounding clang, and the sword's blade snapped in three pieces. Ranzell stared dumbly at the hilt with a bit of steel protruding from it that wasn't more than an inch.

Karsen didn't stop moving. He spun in place and brought the hammer down, around and up. It caught Ranzell squarely in the chest and Jepp heard something crack within Ranzell. The Mandraque fell backwards, his arms flailing, a deep wheezing in his chest.

Karsen took a step back and coldly regarded his handiwork. He didn't appear to have exerted any effort. He nodded once, and then dropped the war hammer. Ranzell watched him approach and actually forced a smile.

"You're . . . skilled," he said. "And merciful. That is a—"

At which point Karsen began to kick him with his hard-edged, cloven hooves. He kicked him in the face, the chest, everywhere he could reach. The Mandraque's scaled hide provided some protection, but huge welts were rising everywhere Karsen's hooves came into contact. Even after Ranzell lapsed into unconsciousness, Karsen continued to beat him for a time, either to make sure he was really unconscious, or else because he didn't feel like stopping.

Finally he tired of his activities. He crouched and fumbled at the straps upon Ranzell's chest for a few moments before pulling the straps free that served as the hammer's harness. Then he buckled them onto himself, picked up the hammer, and sheathed it on his back. He turned and scowled fiercely at Jepp, and she shrank back. Then, like the passing of a summer squall, the ferocity was gone. He looked around at what he had wrought, and there was regret and even chagrin upon his face.

Then he turned and started to walk away.

Jepp lay there, watching him, and then slowly got to her feet. He kept on walking, stepping over the strewn bodies, paying her no mind at all.

She should have taken the opportunity to flee, to get as far away from him as possible. She surprised herself again with the sound of her own voice saying, "Am . . . am I supposed to come with you now? I . . . I thought you . . ."

He stopped. He did not turn to look at her. Instead he sounded rather tired as he said, "Do what you want."

He kept going.

She hesitated for a time that seemed far longer than it was, and then she fell in behind him.

*ii.*

It wasn't easy for her to keep up with him. His stride was far longer, and he seemed to move with a sort of bounce of his legs. There were so many things she wanted to ask him, but it was taking all her effort and breath just to maintain the pace, so she remained silent.

At one point, Karsen picked up an equipment bag lying next to one of the corpses and slung it over his shoulder. After that, every so often, he would stop without warning and study one of the bodies, removing trinkets or particularly well tended weapons. He was limited in the number of swords he could transport, but a goodly number of daggers found their way into the bag.

At one point he was hunched over a pair of warriors who had cleaved each other's skulls, taking some ornate wristbands off them. Then he looked up in surprise as Jepp reached down and into the armor chest plating of one of them. She fished around, the tip of her tongue visible as she concentrated, and then she extracted a small leather bag. She handed it to Karsen, who tugged open the restraints and upended the contents onto his open palm. An assortment of precious stones spilled out.

"Mandraques usually have small hidden compartments inside their chest plating in which they store their valuables," said Jepp.

Karsen stared at her. Then a small smile played across his lips.

"*Karsen!*"

A high loud voice rang across the field. Jepp blinked in surprise.

It was a female of the same species as Karsen. Like him, she was nude from the waist up. Her breasts were small and hard, and the lines in her face indicated that she was considerably older than Karsen.

She was also much larger. Her shoulders were wide, her arms

thick and muscled, and her face was blocky with a pitiless expression. Her hair was tinged with gray. Several large sacks were slung over her shoulders, each sack stuffed to bursting. Jepp didn't think she would have been able to manage even one of the bags. This female was toting at least five with what appeared to be little effort.

"Karsen!" she said again. "What the hell are you doing with that?"

"It's a human." Karsen glanced at her up and down to double check. "A female, I'm fairly sure."

"I know it's a human female! What are *you* doing *with* it?"

He smiled and said with what appeared to be great hope and eagerness, "She followed me home, Mother. Can I keep her?"

You thought you knew about King Arthur and his knights? Guess again!

Learn here, for the first time, the down-and-dirty royal secrets that plagued Camelot as told by someone who was actually there, and adapted by acclaimed *New York Times* bestseller Peter David. Full of sensationalism, startling secrets and astounding revelations, *The Camelot Papers* is to the realm of Arthur what the Pentagon Papers is to the military: something that all those concerned would rather you didn't see. What are you waiting for?

DuckBob Spinowitz has a problem. It isn't the fact that he has the head of a duck—the abduction was years ago and he's learned to live with it. But now those same aliens are back, and they claim they need his help! Can a man whose only talents are bird calls and bad jokes be expected to save the universe?

*No Small Bills* is the hilarious new science fiction novel from award-winning, bestselling author Aaron Rosenberg. See why the NOOK Blog called it "an absurdly brilliant romp"—buy a copy and start laughing your tail feathers off today!

# CRAZY 8 PRESS

**Peter David**
**Michael Jan Friedman**
**Robert Greenberger**
**Glenn Hauman**
**Aaron Rosenberg**
**Howard Weinstein**

Go to crazy8press.com
to check out more CRAZY books
from our collection of crazy-talented authors!

Made in the USA
Charleston, SC
29 January 2012